The Cove

JULIE DIDCOCK-WILLIAMS

Table of Contents

DARKNESS

Ceredigion Mental Asylum, West Wales
June 1983 10am

Yes, I'm Freyja.

It really is you.

When they told me you were coming I didn't believe it, I thought they were having me on.

Come and sit down next to me. There's a good view of the sea from here. It's like back home, except the sea isn't so wild.

Let me hold your hands and look into your eyes. I'm sorry. I'm shaking seeing you after such a long time.

I didn't think I'd ever have the chance to see you again and now you're here. I can hardly believe it's you. You're not such a peedie one any longer.

I don't mean to cry like this, you'll have to excuse me. It's a shock, is all.

I must look a fright.

I don't?

You're too kind. I know I must, dressed in these clothes. Look at me. Nothing fits. We're not allowed our own clothes. You have to wear what they put out.

You're right, it's rotten.

I had my hair long once, like yours. They cut it off when I arrived at my first place, so they could put those sticky pads here and here on the sides of my head. I find it's easier now to keep it this length. It's not so bad.

They used the pads to burn my brain. It's what they did. Supposed to make us better, that and the drugs they jabbed into us. How that was supposed to help I don't know.

Everything that's done is done and in the past, and there's no changing it, however much they tried to shock it out of me.

They'll bring us our morning coffee soon and biscuits too if there are any. It's her we need to ask. Ellie. She's the nicest nurse of them all.

What's that you've got?

I haven't had a new record to listen to since...

He's on the front cover, oh my.

He looks so handsome and smart in his white tie and tails. I never saw him dressed like that. I always wanted to. He's still got that hair of his surrounding his face like a halo.

So this is really it.

He wrote this for me - *Symphony No5 in E flat major*. E flat major, his favourite key. Maybe we can listen to it now. What do you think?

He's called it *Freyja by the sea*. That's nice.

He conducted it too, look – '*The BBC Symphony Orchestra conducted by Magnus Olafson*' – he always did prefer to conduct his own symphonies. It was so he could ensure that the orchestra made the sound he heard in his head, exactly as he wanted it, that's what he told me, but he told me a lot of things. Maybe that one was true.

I feel quite proud of him.

You think I'm silly.

Let me have a minute, won't you?

You're right. There's no rush. We have all day, longer if you like.

You must think I'm a dreadful old fool to be so upset by a record, but it was part of everything that made us who we were. His music was the twine that bound us together.

Here's Ellie with our coffee. Look at this, Ellie. See, I was right. He *did* write me a symphony and here it is. Let's put it on the player so we can listen.

That was really good. Takes me back to when we were together walking the cliff tops on Tor Ness Head, the Atlantic rolling in and crashing against the rocks, the seabirds squawking and screeching in the air above us. You can hear it in the music.

You want to know what happened?

That's a long story.

Seems a shame to break the mood by telling you. You're sure you want to hear about it?

It all began and ended along the cliffs at Tor Ness Head, where we all lived on the Orkney island of Falun. It's a small island, right on the limits of Orkney, on the north-west side, where the Atlantic meets the North Sea.

Sorry, I forget you know. No one here's heard of it.

What I'm going to tell you, it's not a nice story, but you know that already. Maybe it isn't a nice story because I'm not a very nice person. I wasn't the person people wanted me to be, I know that, but who is? But now you've finally come you might as well see me for who I really am, even if it means this'll be the first and last time you'll visit me.

You say that now, that it won't change anything, and you're not going anywhere now you've found me again. Maybe not, but I'm afraid of what you'll think and rightly so as you'll see. They didn't bang me up in here for no reason.

At the end of my story, which is our story, you'll make your judgement of me. And then we'll see if you ever want to come back.

Tryggr, Falun, Orkney Islands
Summer 1955

Within many families there is an event that changes everything; something so catastrophic that everyone is thrown in different directions and it can be hard, impossible even, for them to find their way back together again. It may be that you have to go back a long way, many generations even, to find that kind of event, but it will be there. Some of the people I knew when I was growing up said that their family's moment was when the Vikings arrived and changed the landscape and us Orcadians forever. The arrival of the Vikings in the longboats may have altered our family beyond recognition, but I don't know anything about that. It may have blighted us forever. Certainly, their landing on the rocky shores of our small island altered our family name. MacAulay comes from the Norse name Olafson. It doesn't sound like it does, I'll admit that, but that's what Father told me, that's the myth he trots out on occasions such as Hogmanay, when he feels nostalgia for our past and weariness about the future. But don't worry, I'm not going to give you a history of the MacAulay family from the Viking invasion till now. I'm not that mad, despite what you've probably been told about me. But in our family, the event that changed everything, that does centre around me. There's no getting away from that.

I'll start with my birth in 1946 because it was unusual and in part it made me who I am. I arrived in this world fully dressed. My tiny pale head, with its mass of red hair, was encased in a strange, papery hat, a caul. Father was fair excited about it and danced like a crazy man, Mother said. He, like all his forefathers before him, was a sailor. He had a trawler business with William MacKenzie, the father of my friend Joe. Sailors believed that any child born in a caul could never drown. I was considered lucky, special and because of it, I was allowed out to sea earlier than was usual. I came to love the wildness of the ocean and the tang of saltiness on my skin and in my hair. Later, I came to see my luck in a different light, as something that set me apart from everyone else. When you live on an island, in an isolated house up on the cliffs, being different can be a hard part to play. I'm not blaming everything that happened on that, but it didn't help. Whatever, my luck, such as it was, didn't hold, but we'll come to that. Mother kept the caul, the midwife pressed something to it, paper or cloth, so that the caul stuck fast and we could keep it as an heirloom, but I don't ever want to see it again.

After my fortuitous birth, my life and my family's life, proceeded uneventfully. Jeanie, who was older than me by a few years, relished the freedom my lucky charm bestowed on us and, in turn, I adored her more than anyone else in the world and couldn't bear to be away from her. Even though I'd been born in a caul and considered lucky, my parents didn't feel themselves touched by that luck. In their eyes, the arrival of my screaming self was a distressing addition to an otherwise perfect unit.

Jeanie was a shining light in our family. She had an aura that touched everyone. It wasn't only me that said that. I loved her and it wasn't a surprise to me that Joe MacKenzie was in love with her too, even though she barely noticed his existence. Initially this annoyed me. Well, it would, wouldn't it? What child wouldn't be annoyed to discover that their friend only came around to play so he could spend time with her sister? But I forgave him for it and between us it became a bond – that we both adored Jeanie. Joe denied it at first, of course he did, but it didn't take me long to work out that when we were together we'd chat quite easily about everything and he'd allow me to sit between his legs, wrapping his arms around me to keep me warm, and when he sat on the rocks waiting for the fish to bite, he'd spend the time in between excavating bogies from his nostrils, which he'd inspect fully before flicking in my direction. This was one of his, and my favourite games even though I'll admit now it was quite revolting. I would be ready for him though; I always saved my greatest ones behind my ear ready to attack him. When Jeanie came to the coves with us, Joe would be stiff and speak in a higher voice than usual. He'd never dream of hugging me or flicking bogies when Jeanie was around. That's how I knew. The butcher acted in the same way around Mary Leverhulme from the Post Office just before they got married.

I remember the very day that Joe fell in love with Jeanie. It didn't take much, not when you consider what a big thing falling in love is. It was April and Father, Mother, Jeanie and I were out cutting the peats. We had our own peat bank further inland, towards the Tor that loomed in the centre of our island, an area brown and scarred from years of cutting. Joe came with us. Father cut the peat out of the ground and it was our job to lay out the fads to dry. We were lucky the weather was on our side and although it was blowing a guster, the rain held off. It was hard work. Mother sang as we worked, a tune that echoed the song of the golden plover which she claimed sang *a hearty summer, it is coming*. That peat cutting season was the last time I heard her sing like that. It was also the last happy time we had as a family. The last time the feeling of space and freedom out on the peat bank, with the huge horizon dotted with all the other islands hulking in the mists, made me feel bigger and stronger, like I could do anything. I joined in singing along with Mother, jabbing Joe and Jeanie in the ribs until they gave in and sang with us, our voices bouncing against the tors and echoing back at us.

'Don't you love it, Father?' I said.

'Ay,' he said. 'That I do. We MacAulays have been cutting here forever. We're made of this stuff.'

That made my throat block up, like it does when you're about to cry, when the feelings of joy inside you want to burst out, but you're too worried about what everyone'll think if you let them, so you squash them in, pushing them back down hard, hidden. But that sense of safety in the past is all very well when there is a future to stride towards. Once that's gone, the past is only there to haunt you, to remind you of what you once had that is now lost.

After a couple of hours, Joe and I had had enough and we were hot and thirsty. Father had one last can of water which he handed around for us to share, but Joe, the idiot, knocked it over and there wasn't much left once we'd righted it and Joe hadn't even had any. He was about to cry, which would have embarrassed him no end, especially in front of Jeanie. I clasped and unclasped my hands. Wrung them together so the knuckles bleached, then hung them limp and useless by my sides. I thought, should I go to him? Stand back? I shouldn't look at him, that'd make him cry. Maybe if I did look at him, then he'd stop. What should I do?

Then Jeanie stepped forwards and said he could have hers. She wasn't thirsty, she said, although she must have been as parched as us. Joe and I drank it down and didn't leave much for her. She had a few of her precious boiled sweets in the pocket of her tunic. She gave those to us too. I don't think she kept any back for herself.

Joe talked about her non-stop after that. Told everyone he knew I had the best sister in the world and wasn't I lucky to have a girl like Jeanie in the family. And although I knew he was right, at that moment, when I had failed and she had succeeded, having someone like Jeanie around, someone who everyone loved and admired, was as sure a way as any to me being the person everyone expected to be the opposite. I lived up to my own expectations of myself, of course.

It wasn't Joe falling in love with my beloved Jeanie that changed everything, though it could have been. I could be telling the story of Joe and Jeanie's courtship and marriage and the two of them leaving Falun for good and abandoning the rest of us. Now I wish that had been the case. No, that isn't the story I'm telling you. That summer of 1955 was to be the last summer when Jeanie would come home from school every night of the week and walk with me along the long track that led from the main brae to our farmhouse. From August, Jeanie would be going to the Mainland, to boarding school, there being no senior school on our island. I found it unimaginable that she would sleep away from me and the room we shared. I couldn't begin to think about being separated from Jeanie. I didn't know how to be if she wasn't there.

The summer before she left, we had the best time ever. The sun shone every day, or at least it seemed to; the weather on Orkney is well known to be one of the vilest there is. You can tell by the number of words and phrases we have to describe the wind.

Anyhow, we spent our days combing the beaches for things we could sell, anything metal we could get a good price for. You'd be surprised how much washed up on our beaches: pots, kettles, aluminium buoys, floats and wire. Henry MacRae, the only builder on the island, also had a side-line in scrap which he would collect and take to Kirkwall. We'd wait till we had a good hoard before making the trek into Skellinwall, as the more we had the better the price. Bottles were good finds too as we could earn the return price: sixpence on a big bottle and threepence on a small one. In the 'r' months we'd look for spoots and welks. The welks were easier to collect as all we had to do was pick them off the rocks and put them in a sack until we had a bushel. I'm not sure how much that is in weight, but then it was a sack full. We needed at least that to be able to sell it. We'd get ten shillings a bushel, most of which we handed over to our parents, but we were allowed a few pennies to spend on sweets. If we were lucky, we'd catch a crab in one of the creels Father had given us, which we'd leave in various prime spots around the rocky coast at the bottom of Tor Ness Cliffs. Joe often came with us to the coves and he was particularly good at catching crabs and we'd eat them, cooking them in sea water over a fire on the beach.

Father and Mother were fair excited for Jeanie going to big school. She was a clever girl and had always come top of the year, mostly top of the whole school even when she wasn't one of the older ones. Everyone expected her to do well at senior school and maybe even go on with her education after that, which was unusual. We had high hopes. That's what everyone said about Jeanie: *we have high hopes for that girl*. I used to wonder what 'high hopes' were and if people had them why they didn't hand them over, rather than keeping them hidden. I imagined them to be red glass like balls of boiled sugar, that tasted of strawberry or raspberry and I longed for people to have high hopes for me too.

I remember the day of our first separation, when Jeanie and Mother went to Kirkwall to pick up her new school uniform. A trip to Kirkwall was something that happened rarely for me and I became manic with the excitement of it all, screeching around the house until Mother yelled at me to go out and wear the excitement off as all my fussing would stop the hens from laying. I knew I was on the brink of giving her one of the headaches my presence always brought on, but I was excited and didn't have the sense to know when to hold back, so I remained in the kitchen, making myself a cup of tea, clinking the spoon against the mug in time with a tune inside my head.

'I don't know why you're making such a fuss, Freyja. Mrs McLeod has asked if you could help sort her wool. Better you stay here. You've no manners for travel and you'll only be in the way over there.'

Out of the kitchen window, I could see the tips of the Atlantic waves turning white in the westerly that had started to blow in and I could feel the fizzing violence in those crests creeping inside me. How could she even think that Jeanie would go to Kirkwall without me? There was no way Jeanie would do something like that. The fear that she might made me shake so violently that I threw my mug on to the tiled floor, smashing it into so many pieces I didn't yet know the number to count to.

'I want to go too,' I yelled. I had never yelled at Mother before and I think I was as shocked as she was.

'You'll go straight to your room. Now. You cheeky peedie whalp.'

That was the first time she called me a little devil, but it wouldn't be the last. It was who I became in the days of darkness that followed.

For the rest of that day, I was confined to my room and didn't get to leave, even to help Mrs McLeod who was the only other person I would have liked to have spent the day with. Jeanie went to Kirkwall: I couldn't believe she'd gone ahead and left without me. When they came back, bags bulging with Jeanie's new clothes, she hung them up with more care than I'd ever seen her use before. Jeanie came and sat on the end of my bed and stroked my hair.

'I don't want you to go. I don't want to be left behind. Stay until I'm older and we can go together,' I said.

'Don't cry, Freyja. Before you know it, it will be the holidays and I'll be back. It'll be like I've never gone.'

I wanted to believe her, but I didn't. I couldn't imagine a life without Jeanie. To me we were two halves of the same thing and even that one day she'd spent in Kirkwall without me had shredded my insides, leaving them raw and bleeding.

In the week following Jeanie's trip to Kirkwall, the house had a strange, strained air to it and even Joe lolloped around like a lost puppy until, unable to bear his misery a moment longer, Mother would send him packing. Mother and Father were excessively polite to one another when usually they teased each other incessantly. Actually, I suppose it was Father who did the teasing on the whole; he was always the more fun of the two of them and liked to play practical jokes on her or challenge her to a game of cards, telling her that if she lost she'd have to give him a piggyback around Tor Ness Head, right up to the point where there was a grand view of the lighthouse, and back home again. Mother never lost, though there was always the possibility. That's where the fun lay. Mother was too proud not to carry out the penalty, and she'd also have been too proud to have allowed us to see him let her win so they must have found some balance. That balance teetered on the edge after it was decided that Jeanie would go to boarding school. Great thunderheads gathered on the horizon, inching forwards day by day and there was nothing I could do to stop them clotting above our heads and bringing darkness to our world.

It wasn't long after that initial day that Jeanie and I spent apart, a day that had left me broken and hollow and gripped with so much fear I didn't know what to do with it all, that I sat at our bedroom window, the one that looked out over the track and towards the island's interior, and I watched as Jeanie walked out of the house wearing the red gingham dress I coveted more than any of her others. She paused at the corner of the track and turned her head, looking up at me over her shoulder, her long blonde hair catching the light as it bounced on her shoulders, and she smiled and waved before disappearing around the bend. That was the last time I saw Jeanie.

She walked out of our lives on fourth of August 1955 and she never came back.

My devotion to Jeanie must have been suffocating for her, and although I didn't realise at the time, in the months leading up to her walking out of our lives, she was always trying to say goodbye, always trying to leave me behind.

I remember one day at the beginning of the summer, probably around June, just before Midsummer, when we liked to make the most of the seemingly never-ending light. Jeanie and I were having a wonderful day together, just the two of us. It was always better when it was just me and her, but those days had become rarer and more often than not, I was alone at Tryggr with only the chickens for company; Jeanie was off learning to be independent, that's what Mother called it, and the harder I gripped hold of her, the more she seemed to pull away.

Earlier in the day, Jeanie plaited a red ribbon into my hair. It was her ribbon. Mother bought it for her on a rare trip to Edinburgh – she bought me a dull navy one - and Jeanie was very attached to it. The colour clashed horribly with my hair, but I didn't care. Mother hadn't bought it for me after all, but for Jeanie to wear with her red gingham dress. I wore the ribbon proudly and kept running my fingers along the length of my plait so I could feel the smoothness of the ribbon contrasting sharply with the roughness of my thick springy hair. Jeanie and I were sitting in the garden, behind the chicken coop, out of the worst of the wind, covering a cushion with patchwork using the leftover scraps from a rag rug we'd made a few weeks before. We'd sewn a pile of small hexagons, crinkly with the newspaper centres we used as templates.

'I wonder how many girls will be in my dormitory and whether they'll like me,' Jeanie said.

She didn't look at me as she said it but carried on folding the fabric around the paper and tacking it into place. I knew she wanted to talk about her forthcoming adventure and she knew there was no way I would discuss it with her. For to discuss it, to talk about it openly, made it tangible and exciting for her, and real and devastating for me.

Jeanie gathered a pile of hexagons, pulled the paper out and started to pin them to the cushion we intended to cover, arranging them in a pattern that pleased her.

'Will you tell me about the selkies again, Jeanie? It's almost Midsummer. I want to hear the story again,' I said.

I took a handful of my own hexagons and mingled them amongst hers and for a while we shuffled them around in silence until a pattern started to emerge.

'Maybe I'll take this cushion with me, Freyja. To put on my dormitory bed. What do you think? It will remind me of this moment, of us sewing together. This is what I'll miss.'

We sat silently for a long time, securing the pieces into place, until the cushion started to come together. Above us, the clouds had started to roll in once again, sending the air ruggy and grey and we shuddered as the warmth evaporated. We took it in turns to sew on the hexagons, passing the cushion between us in the steady rhythmic way that people who know each other well can easily achieve.

'I think we should go and watch for selkies by the lighthouse once we've finished this,' I said.

I handed the cushion back to Jeanie so that she could finish the final seam along the side. It was the hardest part and her more experienced fingers found it easier than mine.

'I won't be gone for long. Only the term times. They'll fly by, won't they? There it's done. What do you think?' she said holding up the cushion.

'They won't love you as much as I do. I don't know why you want to go so much.'

But Jeanie didn't get to answer as two of her school friends, Billy Jansson and Melanie Houghton, both from farming families in the interior of the island, came yelling into the garden, pushing their bicycles ahead of them.

'Jeanie, do you want to come with us? We're going to Tor Ness Cove,' Melanie said, adding, 'Hello, Freyja.'

I raised my head and gave Melanie the briefest of smiles, unable to hide my irritation that they'd come and ruined the afternoon. Watching for selkies wouldn't happen if Billy and Melanie were with us. There'd be no point – the selkies never appeared for a crowd. Jeanie stood up, dropping the cushion on to the rug. Forgetting our work in the presence of her friends, she went inside with them to fetch them a drink after their bicycle ride. I picked up the cushion. It was lovely. I traced the intertwining pattern we'd created. Anyone else would have seen a random patchwork, giving the cushion a homely friendly feel. I, however, could see each of our own contributions clearly, each piece dependent on the other. I looked at Jeanie's careful stitching of the final seam. She'd used small delicate stitches that could hardly be seen. Jeanie always took care over things like that. She liked things to be perfect, ordered, but she'd failed to fasten off, distracted by the arrival of Billy and Melanie. I took the unpicker from our sewing box and levered its sharp point under the last stitch, easing it out of place, careful not to break the thread. I wanted it to look as though it had unravelled in my hands as I'd admired it. I didn't have long - I could hear their excited, high pitched voices coming back out of the house. I managed to undo about a quarter of the length of the seam. It would be enough. Jeanie wouldn't go off with her friends and leave it unfinished. She wasn't like that. She'd stay with me now for the rest of the afternoon to fix it. Billy wouldn't be patient enough to wait. He had ants in his pants, that's what Mother always said. She knew his sort, apparently, the sort who jumped in and did what they shouldn't because they hadn't thought it through and one day it would end in tears.

'That Melanie should watch out, hanging around with a boy like that. No good'll come of it, you mark my words,' Mother said time and time again until we all rolled our eyes at her.

As soon as I saw them come around the back of the house, I jumped up and ran to show Jeanie, pulling the seams apart, forcing the tears out of my eyes.

Then I saw it, that look in her eye, the goodbye already brewing, waiting to fly out and devastate me.

'Don't worry, Freyja. It won't take me a minute to fix that later. I'm off to Tor Ness Cove now. I'll see you later. Why don't you see if you can fix it yourself? You can show me when I come back.'

Jeanie linked arms with Billy and Melanie, and they ran off together in a line, screeching and laughing along the track without even a backward glance. After Jeanie had gone, I threw the cushion to one side, my interest evaporating without Jeanie there to finish it with me. I was lost without her and wandered idly around the garden unsure of what to focus on. August flashed before me; an emptiness looming on the horizon, ready to swallow me.

'What are you up to, peedie one?' Father's voice boomed behind me making me jump. I hadn't heard him return from fishing. He laughed when he realised he'd caught me unawares for once and scooped me up on to his large shoulders and raced me around the garden to the dry stone wall at the end and back.

'Can you see any seals?' he shouted up at me.

From my height advantage, I could see all the way to the very point of Tor Ness Head and out on to the skerries where the red and white striped lighthouse stood fat and proud, erupting out of the water alerting ships to the savage rocks that tumbled away from the cliffs and hid under the waves for a long way out; an edge of menace that had grounded many ships in the past. The rocks on which it stood were a favourite spot for the seals who liked to bask in the reflected light that bounced off the white and watch us playing on the sandy beach.

'None today,' I said.

'They'll be out at sea, swimming with the selkies,' he said. 'Let's go and see what your Mother has made us for lunch, shall we?'

'Race the clouds,' I shouted, holding my hands high in the air and gripping his neck as hard as I could with my thighs.

Father looked up, pointed at one particularly speedy cloud and ran as fast as he could to keep up with it. I screamed, 'Run, run,' as loudly as I could, listening to my voice vibrating as Father's motion bounced me up and down. My hair blew behind me like a rocket's flame and I reached up, up, flying.

That was one of our favourite games, when we were all happy, before Jeanie left me and everything changed.

In the kitchen, Mother had laid out fat slices of ham and triangles of cheese. Beside these she'd placed a bowl of pickled onions. She never served them out of a jar, always decanted them into a bowl. She said it was so I didn't gobble the whole lot in one go, but Father told me it was because she was refined and liked to keep up with her family's airs and graces, even though he wasn't sure they deserved to have them. He'd winked at her as he said this, to let us all know that he was joking, but Mother never found jokes like that funny, jokes about her family and she stiffened and pulled her mouth into a tight line, giving Father such a look that we stopped talking and put our heads down. He'd crossed a line and he knew it. After a while, Father stopped making such jokes. I liked them though, liked the idea that she was putting on airs and graces even in Tryggr, our rough and tumble farmhouse out on the wildest point of Falun. It made me feel that I belonged to something larger than just the four of us.

'After lunch, Freyja, you can help your Father mend the nets, now you're good with a needle,' Mother said.

I thought of the cushion Jeanie and I had sewn, still lying where I'd dropped it out on the lawn. I knew I wouldn't try and sew it myself and eventually Jeanie would do it for me, for us. She wouldn't want to take something half-finished to boarding school with her. The thought of her leaving brought to mind that look I'd seen in her eyes earlier. The look I never wanted to see again, the one that said *I'm leaving you.* I'd have to find a better way next time to keep her with me. One that would stop her going.

A few days later, mine and Jeanie's favourite night of the year had finally arrived: Midsummer's Eve party night. It was the only night of the year we were allowed to stay up late and I was determined that this year we'd see the selkies. Watching for the mystical creatures was one of our favourite games. If we actually saw them, Jeanie would never leave. She'd be so enchanted she'd realise Falun was where she should stay.

By the time we made it down the steep steps to Tor Ness Cove, the party had already started and the beach was crowded with people from the whole island, young and old alike. Jeanie and I carried our lit lanterns and placed them at the foot of the cliffs alongside everyone else's. It had become a tradition on our island to place a line of lanterns at the foot of the cliffs on Midsummer Eve's night to scare away the dreaded finmen from our waters. Jeanie and I placed ours with a practised reverence. We were a fishing family after all and the finmen were our enemies, stealing fishermen's hooks and sinkers if we accidentally strayed into their waters. I was pleased to see that the huge bonfire we'd all helped to build over the previous months had yet to be lit. It was a moment I enjoyed immensely – the first rush of sound, that all-consuming roar as the flames caught the fuel and leapt into life. Father left us and raced to the water's edge to join the group of his fellow fishermen, including William MacKenzie and Joe, who already had beer tankards in their hands, even Joe, who grinned at his luck, winking at me. They were singing the old shanties and soon I joined in, singing them softly to myself, skipping to the beat and kicking up the sand behind me. Father towered above most of the men around him and stood out even more with his shocking red hair and beard, hair colour that I had inherited. Jeanie had Mother's white blonde hair, which hadn't ever dulled or darkened as she'd aged.

Melanie saw us as she lifted her head from Billy's shoulder. They'd been hugging each other in a way I'd not seen before. She ran towards Jeanie, grabbing her hand and dragging her off to be with their group from school. I held on to Jeanie's hand as long as I could – *stay with me Jeanie, watch for selkies* - but as Melanie pulled her, our fingers loosened and fell apart. As they walked away, I saw Jeanie's head drop and Melanie put her arm around her shoulders leading her to the edge of the Cove where a stack had broken away from the cliffs and beyond it the skerries, topped with the lighthouse, tumbled into the sea.

'Hello, Freyja.'

Annie McLeod stood beside me, a towering Canadian woman of around thirty with an accent softened by the years she'd lived on Falun. She handed me a bottle of strawberry cremola, which I accepted greedily. It wasn't often that I was allowed drinks like that and strawberry cremola was my very favourite. Mrs McLeod was widely viewed as Falun's wild eccentric. An artist, she lived alone, at Lochinsay, in a too large house on a wild promontory south of Tryggr. Part of the house's garden had become separated from the island and stood on a huge stack that appeared to be floating out to sea and could only be reached via a metal footbridge. Although it took at least forty-five minutes to walk there from Tryggr, along a treacherous path, I visited her often. She'd been recently widowed. Her husband, Ben, a photographer and fellow artist, a native of Falun, had died suddenly. I'd overheard Mother saying how sad it was that they'd bought such a large house in the anticipation of having a huge brood of bairns and now she was left alone to rattle around in that sad place. I didn't find the house sad, however, and loved to visit. For some reason, Mrs McLeod liked me more than Jeanie and that was such an unusual experience, adults always preferred Jeanie, I embraced it totally. I knew she preferred me to come alone, without Jeanie. I didn't imagine that, or make it up as people said when I stupidly boasted about it, she'd actually said it to me, that she preferred me to Jeanie. She claimed that she saw a wildness in me that she recognised from her own youth.

'That's hard for you to imagine now, isn't it, Freyja?' she said.

I told her it was which made her laugh; she liked me to be honest with her.

'People mature, Freyja, but if that wild streak is there, it only becomes hidden under layers of respectability, it never goes away. We get better at concealing it. That's what you need to do sometimes, my dear. But here, with me, you can be yourself. You remember that.'

I found her fun and bracingly honest. She didn't seem to care what other people thought about her. Mother cared too much in my opinion and as I looked at them standing next to each other, Mother smart, but dull in her classic tweeds, and Annie, despite her widowhood, dressed in a garish orange long skirt and blue blouse with a striped orange and purple turban wrapped around her head, I knew who I'd rather be like.

'Thank you, Mrs McLeod,' I said, taking a gulp of the strawberry drink.

I always addressed her formally. Even though she'd asked me to call her Annie, Mother wouldn't allow it. We chinked bottles together and walked with Mother towards the group gathering around the bonfire. The fishermen had paused their singing and Father, as the head of the local fishing collective, held the flaming torch aloft, praising the island and praying for good fortune from both land and sea in the coming year, as he lowered the flame to the wood pile. The flames grabbed at the chance of life and the bonfire roared. Annie was the first person outside my family that I loved. It didn't matter to me that she was old, or that the villagers thought her strange for locking herself away on a remote part of the island and keeping herself to herself. What mattered to me was the way she didn't take any nonsense, didn't mind what people said about her.

'Know your own mind, Freyja,' she said, when I complained that some of the farm boys had teased me for one thing or another. 'Know the truth about yourself and you'll be fine.'

She had no truck with the idea that goodness and virtue led to being an interesting person either. She wanted me to grab hold of life and make the most of it. She considered Jeanie one of the dullest people she'd met. Even though I disagreed vehemently, and said so, I revelled in the wickedness of her opinion. It was the only time I got cross with Annie. She was pleased with my flash of anger though. She said it showed strength on my part that I could stand up for what I believed to be right, against someone who was my friend.

'It's harder to stand up to those who are close to you than those you are indifferent to.'

She never spoke ill of Jeanie again after that and I savoured that feeling, that I'd defended Jeanie, for a long time. I looked around desperately for Jeanie, raising myself on tiptoes to look over everyone's heads. She couldn't miss the lighting of the bonfire, but she was nowhere to be seen. I wanted to run and find her, to share the moment with her as everyone clapped and cheered, but then I noticed that Mrs McLeod didn't join in with the applause and I knew I couldn't leave her. I dithered for a moment. I'd find Jeanie in a minute.

'Are you all right, Mrs McLeod?' I said.

She knelt down on the white sand so her head was level with mine. 'I'm completely fine, Freyja. Thank you for asking.'

I could see that her eyes were shiny and damp and I knew this meant grown-ups weren't as fine as they pretended to be. Adults were strange. They'd tell you off and give you a right hiding for telling lies and yet they never told the truth themselves, not to us children at any rate. Maybe they did to each other when they huddled in corners speaking in whispers.

'Are you thinking about your dead husband?' I said.

I stumbled as Mother clipped me around the ear.

'Goodness, Freyja! What are you thinking, saying things like that? I'm sorry, Annie. This one doesn't think before she speaks,' Mother said.

'It's alright, Morag. As it happens, she's right. Ben loved the lighting of the fire, the sight of it burning like that. He would have loved to have been here tonight. He would have captured its essence.'

I felt bad upsetting her like that. I should have kept quiet and gone to find Jeanie. She would have got things the right way around, unlike me. Mrs McLeod must have noticed my discomfort, as she rested her hand on my shoulder and tapped it gently. 'You're right, Freyja. It's better not to pretend, better to tell people how you're feeling, isn't it? Come on, let's look and see whether any good shells have washed up overnight.'

I hesitated for a fraction of a second. I should find Jeanie first, but Mrs McLeod took my hand and we walked up and down the water's edge, listening to the singing and laughter going on around us. I saw Joe with two of the farm boys, Callum and Donald, by the fire. They were singing with their arms around one another and doing a line dance, kicking their legs out in time with the music. Boys were odd. One minute they're aloof and the next they're hugging each other like girls. We found some good shells, some with ready-made holes in them so Mrs McLeod could thread them on strings of leather and make necklaces and I could look like a mermaid. It was this side of Mrs McLeod that I loved; she always saw the possibilities in things around her. I wondered if it came from being foreign. Maybe not being from here made even a simple shell exotic and exciting to her, but maybe it was her ever-vigilant artist's eye that made her see the beauty in life and to be always trying to capture it. It was her special gift and I wished that I possessed it too. We chatted as we wandered up and down the shoreline. She told me about the shells she'd found as a child. They'd travelled a lot as a family and she had a collection of many fine specimens, she said. I'd seen some of the larger shells at Lochinsay. She and Ben had made a feature of them in one of the rooms looking out at the sea.

'Your outside-in room,' I said, knowing exactly which room she meant. It was my favourite room. The grey walls faded away into the landscape beyond the window so the outside could creep in and inhabit it.

'That's exactly it, Freyja. You are clever,' she said. She paused suddenly, looking along the beach. 'Is that Jeanette?'

I pinched my thigh. How could I have been carried away thinking about shells and rooms that I'd forgotten about Jeanie? We were at the far eastern corner of the Cove and Jeanie, if it was her, was still under the shadow of the lighthouse at the water's edge.

'It looks like she's crying, poor love.'

I shaded my eyes with my hands as I peered along the length of the beach. 'How can you tell?' I said.

'By the way she's bowed her head and rounded her shoulders. Ah, her friend's walking towards her. She'll be fine now, I expect. Must be hard for her, leaving her friends behind when they're all staying together. I remember that feeling from my younger days.'

I made a noise as though I was agreeing with her, but I was actually thinking it wouldn't be as hard for Jeanie as it would be for me, left behind on my own here on Falun. We walked back along the shoreline to the centre of the beach where most of the crowd had congregated. I looked to see if it was Jeanie crying by the water's edge, where a group of her friends had gathered, but I couldn't pick her out. They were pointing out to sea and as I followed their gazes, I saw black heads bobbing in the water. Occasionally an arm or flipper rose out above the waves and in the slanted white light of the midsummer sun it looked as though they were beckoning for us to join them.

The selkies had come. I had to find Jeanie. I knew she'd be as excited as me. We had to see them together. If we did, she'd never leave. I broke free from Mrs McLeod and ran towards the group crowded by the shoreline, yelling, 'Jeanie, where are you? They're here, the selkies are here!' But I wasn't tall enough to see over everyone, and I couldn't find Jeanie. I yelled her name again and again, but the noise of the sea and the crowd on the beach drowned out my cries. By the time I reached the water's edge, I found myself alone and the black heads of the creatures had gone. I'd missed my chance again.

Tryggr, Falun, Orkney Islands
4 August 1955

I ran upstairs to our bedroom to see if Jeanie wanted to go to Tor Ness Cove, our very favourite place in the world, where we'd spent most of the week enjoying our last days together. Our bedroom was empty, and Jeanie's bed still unmade, something that would make Mother angry if she'd seen it, but that day she had *a lot on* and wanted us out of her way and quiet. She obviously hadn't checked we'd finished our chores. I looked out of our bedroom window, the one that looked out over the track and towards the island's interior. The track was empty. I was about to turn away, when I saw a flash of red between the gap in the hedgerow, where the track curves around what was once the old well – Jeanie's red gingham dress. There she was. I banged on the glass to attract her attention. *Look back, look up, Jeanie.*

I ran back downstairs and pulled on my boots. I tried to quell the feeling of anxiety that she'd left already and I had failed to stop her in time. I pushed the panic back down into the deepest part of me, holding it in with a great big breath. She must be going into town on an errand for Mother. I had to find her. If I was quick enough now, I'd catch up with her. I wanted to spend every moment possible in her company for, however long we spent together, it was never going to be enough. Boots on, I ran as fast as I could, hair streaming out behind me, chest burning with the volume of air needed to power my legs. I ran, keeping first the seamark and then the lighthouse in my eyesight, solid and real things I could rely on, things that were always there, lighting a path through the panic.

She wasn't on the track. She wasn't in Skellinwall. I kept on running, turning back towards the lighthouse. At the top of the cliffs at Tor Ness Head, I looked down at the white sand of St Ninian's Cove, where we sometimes played. It was empty, the sand washed clean by the earlier high tide. Even our game of hopscotch, which I'd dug deep into the highest part of the beach a couple of days earlier no longer remained. The beach lay bleak and barren. I screamed Jeanie's name from the top of the cliffs, but the wind snatched my words and threw them out over the ocean where there was no way she'd hear them. I carried on nevertheless, screaming and screaming her name over and over until eventually my voice died and I could say her name no more.

It may have been many hours later, or no time at all, that Father found me lying, exhausted and shivering, amongst the delicate flowers of the sea pinks. The weather had changed and the sea churned and hissed beneath us, crashing so hard into the cliffs the island's very existence was threatened. Above us, the sky had become as solid and dark as pewter and flashes of light pierced the clouds out to sea. It wouldn't be long before the full force of the storm hit us. Father picked me up and carried me koala bear style. He held my chest against his so I could feel his heart pounding next to mine. I clung around his neck, my legs around his waist, and like that we walked back home in silence.

Mother had drawn all the curtains against the coming storm and had lit lamps and candles and the house had an airless density I didn't like. I was surprised to find the house was full of people: Mrs McLeod, Mr and Mrs MacKenzie, the doctor, PC Thunstrom, the local bobby, and some others. I'd given them a scare running off like that, Mrs McLeod said. She took me from Father's arms and held me tight, whispering it's all right, it's all right, over and over again. She placed me on the sofa and wrapped me in a blanket, tucking it in tight and I began to warm up.

Mother sat in the armchair clutching Jeanie's panda, the one with the squeak in its stomach that was hard to press, and everyone moved around her in a strange dance with Mother at the very core. I asked her if she was all right, but she didn't respond and instead spoke in a strange, babbling way as though speaking a foreign language. I shrank away from her. She looked different, scary in a way I couldn't comprehend. Mrs McLeod finished tucking me in, then moved to kneel on the floor next to Mother, smoothing her hair back from her forehead, giving it a shiny flattened look that emphasised her eyes, which bulged red and shining. That look remained on Mother's face long after that night, as though she'd turned to stone like one of the seamarks on our landscape, always stationary, always watching.

Father joined the men huddling in the corner, rubbing his face. The doctor said something to him, turned to look at me, then back at Father. Father paused, then shook his head. Mrs McLeod disappeared into the kitchen, then brought me a mug of warm milk with whisky in it. After that, my head had a whooziness about it that left me unable to stand up.

'Why are all these people here?' I asked her in a whisper.

She was about to answer me, when Mother chose that moment to let out an almighty wail, like an animal dying, and Mrs McLeod rushed to comfort her leaving me alone.

I watched the comings and goings in the room with a mixture of fascination and dread. No one paid much attention to me and after a while I think they forgot I was there. Because of the whisky I'd drunk in the milk, everything around me became strange and chaotic, as if I was looking at the room through shards of broken mirror glass, each one reflecting only part of what was around me, the images flying around, broken and cracked, in different directions. People wandered in and out soaking wet, torches in their hands, heads shaking at one another, speaking in hushed voices. The men huddled together when they weren't coming in and out with torches and lanterns, ears cocked to the shipping forecast on Father's wind-up wireless. The women kept themselves separate and busy in the kitchen making endless cups of tea and passing around plates of sandwiches and biscuits. Every now and then, Father would move away from speaking with one of our friends or neighbours and would take a moment to kneel in front of Mother, take her hand in his and mutter something I couldn't decipher before once again moving away. Mother's position didn't alter – she sat in the armchair, hands in her lap, staring at the door as if waiting for someone to walk through it. Her grey expression remained fixed and after a while I couldn't bear to look at her any longer. She'd become a lifeless doll, one of those horrid ones with a china face that had always terrified me.

Later, after the house had grown quieter and the worst of the storm was over, I woke up. I hadn't realised I'd fallen asleep until Mrs McLeod came to speak to me. Her words left me screaming a scream so violent and devilish it tore into every crevice in the room, rattling the very brickwork of the house.

No one reacted until Mother finally stood and yelled. 'Shut up, Freyja! Shut up!' with her hands over her ears.

Once the screaming was over, a stillness took hold of me that was more terrifying than what had been there before and my whole body shook and I couldn't control it, couldn't stop it. Father scooped me up, blanket and all, and rushed me out of the room and upstairs. As he carried me past Jeanie's bed to my own, I saw that her bed had been made after all and my heart lifted. She'd come back! But our bedroom was empty.

I rounded on Father. 'Where is she?' I said, struggling to release myself from his grasp so I could look for her. I wanted to tell her that I was sorry I'd ruined the cushion we'd made; sorry that I hadn't been grateful for the time she'd spent doing it with me. Sorry for everything. Sorry.

He looked at me, full of nerves and something else too, with a sideways glance that didn't meet my eye.

'She's gone on a long journey, Freyja, a new adventure. I'm sorry, she's gone.'

Ceredigion Mental Asylum, West Wales
June 1983 10.30am

I am all right. Really, I am. Try not to worry. It's the drugs that make me shake, is all. I'll finish my coffee and then I'll be able to carry on.

It arrived on a Tuesday. On Tuesdays, we have Group Therapy when we do craft. At the moment we're learning appliqué. That's what they call it when you stick pictures on things and cover them with varnish.

Yes, that's right. You know what I mean.

I'm decorating a wooden box I made when we did woodwork in another one of the group sessions. Appliqué's not as hard as making the box itself and it looks nice.

We talk things through as we work. It's easier to say what's on your mind when you're concentrating on something else and you don't have to look everyone in the eye. Anyway, we'd been sticking and varnishing for an hour or so, chatting away, when Ellie came in with our coffees. I saw immediately that she had a funny, excited look on her face and then I saw the envelope on the tray. We hardly ever get letters here, I never do, so there was a lot of excitement about whose it was. Everyone was hoping it was for them. Ellie strung it out and gave us our coffees first, then to my surprise she handed the letter to me. What a shock.

Once I'd opened it and read the letter inside, I said, 'I can't believe it', over and over.

Well believe it, Freyja, Ellie said. *It's true.*

'See I'm not mad. I was right all along, wasn't I?' I said.

No one disagreed with me. They all kept quiet. I hugged your letter to my chest the whole day long and walked around in a daze. I've slept with it under my pillow counting down the days until today.

Once I'd read your letter and what you said had sunk in, that you were coming, the shadow that's existed on the very edge of my vision all these years, that I knew was there, but couldn't bring into focus, suddenly came out and stood in front of me.

And now you're here.

26

Tryggr, Falun, Orkney Islands
16 August 1955

When I came downstairs in the morning, Jeanie wasn't there. Father sat in his usual place, where he could look out of the window and watch the weather rolling in from the West. The shipping forecast was on as usual, except he wasn't listening. The station had been knocked off its frequency and the voice speaking broke constantly, interspersed with static. I looked at Mother. She too sat in her usual spot with her back to the range. Jeanie always sat facing Mother. Mother held her knife and fork in her hands, hovering them over her plate of eggs, but made no attempt to eat. I couldn't understand what was wrong with them both. Neither of them noticed me enter. Jeanie's chair was vacant and her toast lay cold and rubbery on the plate, the butter soaked in. She wouldn't eat it like that. Not with the butter melted. She liked the butter cold, on top. I walked towards the wireless and switched it off. Neither of them moved or commented. As I passed by Mother, I saw that she had the patchwork cushion Jeanie and I had sewn, and she was using it to support her back. The side seams I'd destroyed remained unfinished and the fabric had begun to fray. That cushion would never be mended, not now. My hand reached towards it, ready to grab it back and press it close into my chest. It was mine, not hers, but I resisted the impulse, fearful of Mother's reaction. The anger, however, bubbled inside me and I forced myself to push it down, further and further so it couldn't come out.

I looked at my place, the chair facing the door. Jeanie always joked that I needed to see the means of escape. No breakfast there. What had I done wrong? Why did Jeanie, who wasn't here, have breakfast, and I who was, didn't? I shuffled over to the range and scooped a rubbery lump of scrambled eggs out of the pan and it fell in a clump on to my plate. I banged it down on to the table, hard. *Look at me. Notice me.* Mother jumped and dropped her fork, but she didn't look at me.

'Will you please...' she said but didn't finish. I stared at her pale, tired face, but her eyes remained looking down.

'Where's Jeanie?' I said. She was never late for breakfast.

I took a mouthful of eggs. They were burned as well as cold and they left a sour, rancid taste in my mouth. If Jeanie wasn't going to eat that toast, then I would. It was the last of the loaf, so it was that or nothing. I reached over the table and swiped it from her plate, shoving it in my mouth before they could stop me having it.

'Freyja,' Father said, through his hands, which he rubbed up and down against his beard, making a hideous scratching sound.

Mother stood up and our cushion fell to the floor. She made a terrible noise from deep within her chest, then ran out of the room, dropping the knife.

'What did I say?'

I didn't understand. The kitchen table had always been the place where we held family discussions and we were encouraged to ask about whatever was bothering us. I only wanted to know where Jeanie was. Why she was missing breakfast. The fear that she'd already gone to boarding school, gone without saying goodbye, gripped me hard and the cold clammy toast stuck to the roof of my mouth.

Father had always encouraged me to speak my mind, said it was essential that I learned to have my own opinions. I know not a lot of people, men especially, thought that about girls, but Father was different, or at least I thought he was. Now I wasn't so sure. I wanted to tell them I'd seen her, out on the track, walking away, so she must be somewhere; we had to just look, but I knew Father wanted me to shut up and be quiet and I didn't know what to do, what was expected of me. I put my head down and tried to finish my breakfast, but I couldn't eat it. The silence between us grew until neither of us could stand it. We cleared up and parted company. As I left the kitchen, I picked up the cushion, paused, and then placed it back on Mother's chair. She could have it if she wanted it that much. None of us spoke to each other for the rest of the day and when darkness fell only the three of us went to bed.

After Jeanie left, things changed. Time became something I could no longer measure with any certainty now that the punctuation marks Jeanie made in my life had gone. Every minute was the same as the last and the same as the one that came after it. Mealtimes were silent and oppressive when we sat together, which wasn't often, like that eerie cessation in time that occurs just before a storm cracks the air in half. Mother laid cold food out on the table or left something simmering on top of the range, and Father and I helped ourselves whenever we were hungry. Mostly, I ate alone. Although my questions about Jeanie's prolonged absence and the date of her likely return burned constantly in my mind, in the silent world I existed in at home they remained unanswered, and instead they curdled the contents of my stomach so I felt a constant and painful nausea. You see Jeanie was the twine that held us all in place and the day she disappeared, the three of us began a slow creep away from each other, collapsing in on ourselves and wrapping around us thoughts of what Jeanie would do, how she would behave or think, until our worlds became too small to see, like they weren't really there. And although no one ever acknowledged it, there was always an undercurrent of expectation that one day Jeanie would come back.

Jeanie disappeared on Friday and by the following Monday she still hadn't once shown up for breakfast and no one said a word. Mother washed and ironed the bed linen as she always did on Mondays, and she did Jeanie's too, even though she hadn't slept in them for the whole week. I wouldn't have bothered. It would serve her right if she came back to stale sheets after going off. I asked Mother why she'd cleaned them, complaining when she asked me to help her peg them out, but she stared right through me like I wasn't there and I had to jig about in front of her to try and find her line of vision, and even then she didn't answer.

If they weren't going to answer my questions I'd go out and look for her myself, see if she'd left any evidence on the track that time I'd seen her. It must have been her that time after all. I finished helping Mother with the sheets and then ran through the house and out the front door in such a hurry I forgot my coat and had to double back to retrieve it. Back in the hallway, I saw that Jeanie had been hiding there the whole time.

'There you are! Where've you been, Jeanie? Why are you

standing there, hiding in the coats?'

But Jeanie kept quiet and didn't respond. I rubbed my wet eyes hard and poked Jeanie in the ribs. She vanished. All that remained of her was her winter coat hanging on its peg over her boots, shiny and clean, recently polished. I ran out on to the track. It was cold and empty, but I carried on running until I couldn't run anymore.

Mother only ever had a few photographs of each of us on display in frames around the house and they were formal: our Christenings, outside the Kirk, our first Christmas, photographs that showed us as a smart family. It was important to her that we looked respectable. Our house was neat, clean and practical, rather than homely and decorative as Mrs McLeod's, and to some extent, even the MacKenzie's houses were. After Jeanie left, everything changed. Mother insisted on putting nearly every photograph we had of her in a frame and she placed these in prominent positions around the house: ones of her laughing on the beach and standing next to huge sandcastles we'd built; sitting on a bench in Skellinwall, ice cream dripping over her hand; the two of us holding hands in Princes Street in Edinburgh, unsure about the big city and the noise. When I thought of her, it was these images that floated up in front of me. Relaxed happy photographs that captured who she'd been at those moments. Outside of those pictures I could no longer visualise her. I asked Mother about it, whether she had other memories of Jeanie and how she'd looked that she could tell me about. She scolded me and told me not to be stupid with such anger that a ball of her spit lodged in my long fringe and I could see it hanging over my eye. I wanted to brush it away, but I was scared to move and disgusted enough not to want it on my hands, so I stood there looking at her, wondering what to do next.

'Go to your room and tidy up,' she said eventually and turned away from me, her back heaving up and down, the way Father's did when he was trying to loosen his muscles after a long night's fishing.

Mother never wore colours again after Jeanie left, just black, that reflected the mood in the house. Wherever I looked, I could see Jeanie's face staring back at me. It wasn't a comfort. I found it alarming if anything, like Jeanie was watching my every move to see where I would slip up and I learned to navigate our house with my eyes downwards so I wouldn't see the photographs.

Jeanie and I loved our bedroom. It looked out over our garden and towards the lighthouse and the sea at the back, and the track and the interior, where the tors rose and fell in frozen waves, at the front. I preferred the view out of the back window as the West was where most of our weather came from and I liked to watch it rushing towards me, especially on the wildest days. I found it exhilarating and freeing, especially after Jeanie left, as it gave me some release from the tension that always simmered underneath my skin.

We filled our room with as many possessions as we could, each competing to out-do the other in making our side of the room more exciting. It was the one place where we had control and could make it a reflection of who we were. Jeanie's side was, of course, neat and tidy. On her shelf, she had piles of books, odd little knick-knack statues I couldn't abide and her wooden dancing doll laid neatly in a cardboard box. My side was on the surface more chaotic, but was actually very ordered. I had shells, stones, fossils which were my absolute favourite, and various skulls and bones which I'd boiled clean and labelled. I kept my toys in a box under my bed. They were thrown together, tangled amongst my puppet's strings.

Between our two beds was a chest of drawers which we shared. Jeanie had the top two drawers and I the lower two. On the top, were two blue glass dishes that Mother had bought in Inverness some years before in a second-hand shop. They captured the light and shone like a rare clear summer sky. They were for us to keep our hair ribbons in. These ribbons were very precious to us and we spent many hours rolling them into tight swirls like tiny snails. Jeanie loved her red one more than any of the others – the one she had plaited into my hair that day we made the cushion. One day, when she wasn't looking, I snatched it away and hid it in my cardigan pocket. Jeanie was upset for days over its loss. I told her it must have fallen through the cracks in the floorboards and she spent many hours with a torch looking for it. Mother was angry with her, the only time I remember her being so, as it had been the most expensive one she'd bought, and it had been hard to find a colour like that. I knew Jeanie thought she'd let her down with her carelessness and the mystery of its disappearance worried her for days. She never once thought I might have taken it though; it never crossed her mind that I would do something like that to her, something so hurtful.

Once she disappeared, I held on to that ribbon and kept it in my pocket so that I could run my fingers along its silky length. The feel of it against my fingertips was soothing whenever the loss threatened to overwhelm me. One day, a couple of weeks after Jeanie had disappeared, I was in the kitchen waiting for Mother to cut me some bread, absently running the ribbon through my fingers. I hadn't realised I was doing it until Mother stopped what she was doing, leaving the knife halfway through the loaf, and staring at me with wild eyes.

'Where did you get that, Freyja?' she said.

Her voice was very quiet and even, and I didn't realise immediately what it was she was referring to. I think it would have been fine, I would have made something up, said I'd found it dropped somewhere and that would have been the end of it, if Father hadn't at that moment walked into the house. He saw it immediately, the flash of red so obvious against the drabness of Mother and I, and he strode up to me and snatched it out of my hand. The motion burned my skin as he whipped it away. He held it in his raised fist. I thought, I know what's coming and without thinking I flinched, only slightly, but he saw it and that was it. His anger flew out of him in an unforgiving torrent, so vast and unexpected neither of us knew how to step out of its way and none of us, him included, could bear to be in its presence.

I fled as fast as I could out of the kitchen, out of the house, across the garden and the dry stone wall, skinning my knees in my desperation to escape the terrible roaring I could still hear coming from the house. Since Jeanie had gone, Father had changed. He mostly retreated into a silence where he couldn't be reached, but sometimes I sensed anger simmering beneath the surface which scared me. I ran and ran, in the direction I always went, towards the lighthouse and into the mist that blew in from the sea in great swirling sheets that covered my skin in a damp, cold saltiness. At the seamark, I hesitated for a moment, gripped with pain from the stitch in my stomach, before taking the path towards Tor Ness Cove and away from St Ninian's Cove. At the top of the steps I looked down to see if anyone was on the beach.

I saw her. Jeanie. She was standing on the tide line, the waves crashing on to the sand behind her, sending up sheets of spray that must have been soaking her. I screamed her name, wondering how she'd got there and more importantly why she didn't respond to me or move. I stumbled down the steps, slipping on the damp stone. At the bottom, I kicked off my shoes and ran barefoot along the sand towards Jeanie, but the closer I got to where she was, the further away she moved. I ran faster and faster, kicking up the sand behind me so it stuck to my clothes and in my hair. When I reached the rocks at the far end of the Cove, where the headland jutted out and cut the beach off, I realised I'd missed her. I looked back along the beach, but all I could see was the lighthouse watching me.

Jeanie wasn't there. She'd never been there. The emptiness in me twisted itself hard so that everything that should have been inside me suddenly wanted to be expelled. I turned towards the sea and vomited.

After many hours, I made my way back home slowly, fearful of facing the consequences of my theft, but the house was quiet when I walked in. Mother had retired to her room to pray and Father sat slumped in the armchair that faced the door. He would no longer allow the sitting room door to be closed. He wanted to be able to see into the hallway and the front door. He'd be there all night I knew, watching and waiting. He hadn't gone to bed since Jeanie left, as though he thought if he sat there long enough, Jeanie would come home. It was this silence that scared me the most. He no longer cared to hear my opinions, or even worried whether I had any. His silent anger consumed him.

Although our community had rallied around us in the weeks and months after Jeanie's disappearance, bringing pies and stews and huddling in corners with Mother speaking in hushed voices that lowered even further when they saw that I was listening, as time passed they came less and less, except Mrs McLeod who never stopped coming, who never faltered in her support. Mother called her *her rock*, said it was funny wasn't it that it took a crisis to discover who your friends were; that people she'd known her whole life could hardly face her and it was the relative stranger who showed her true friendship. It was because she understood, that's what Mother said. She knew what it felt like to be broken hearted. And in the days I spent at her house in Lochinsay, when Mother couldn't bear to have me at home, she was the only one who spoke to me about how I felt; about how utterly bereft and alone I was at night, lying in the room I'd once shared with Jeanie; about how her empty bed loomed next to me bigger in the darkness than in the day and how it filled and emptied with the pulse of brightness from the lighthouse beam; about how I'd hide away from its weird heartbeat of life with my head under my pillow and I'd hold on tight to that red ribbon that I'd found later, dropped on the kitchen floor, praying that she'd come back to us and suspecting the whole time that, of course, she never would.

One afternoon, Joe appeared on his bicycle to ask if I wanted to come out and play. I hadn't seen much of Joe as he preferred to spend more and more of his time with the farm boys, particularly Callum. I'd heard Mother and Mrs MacKenzie speak about how they'd become *as thick as thieves*, spending night after night camping together in the interior and being *proper boys* for once. It was this being a proper boy I sensed pleased Mrs MacKenzie the most, as if Joe spending time hanging around Jeanie and I was less desirable.

So, when Joe finally appeared willing to spend time with me I jumped at the chance to escape the oppression in the house. Father was sitting in his armchair staring at the door, so if Jeanie did come back when I was out, she'd see him and she wouldn't think we'd all gone out and not bothered to wait for her.

Outside in the shed I dithered for a moment over whether to use my bicycle, which had grown too small for me, or whether to use Jeanie's. Mother and Father had promised me a new one that summer, but in the excitement of planning Jeanie's big adventure, and the devastation following her disappearance, they'd forgotten. I grabbed Jeanie's. She could shout at me all she liked when she came back. It would serve her right to see that I'd made the most of what she'd disregarded and left behind.

We pushed the bicycles to the footpath that ran along the side of the garden and then jumped on.

'Race you to the seamark,' Joe said, giving himself a head start.

Typical boy. He always had to cheat to win. It was the same with Callum and Donald. They didn't realise that a victory through cheating was no victory at all. That's what Father had repeated to us throughout our lives. I pedalled as fast as I could and soon my legs were burning with the effort. Joe was bigger than me, but he was a sprinter and soon his stamina failed him and I, who was better over longer distances, continued at a steady pace until I sensed him start to slow down. I picked up my speed and beat him, much to his annoyance.

'Which way? Tor Ness or St Ninian's?' Joe said, arms pointing in opposite directions, bicycle balanced between his legs.

The effort involved in racing Joe must have had something to do with it, but all the blood in my veins fell suddenly to my feet, and the clear view I had had of the lighthouse shattered into bright, broken prisms of red and white light as I fell down on to the grass. I must have been out for moments only, as when I opened my eyes Joe was still standing in the same position.

'What are you doing?' he said.

'Nothing. Let's go this way,' I said heading towards Tor Ness Cove.

I couldn't look back to see if he was following me. As I'd fallen to the ground an image had flashed at me that had been too bright to look at and instead of running towards it, I wanted to put as much distance as possible between me and what I'd seen.

On the beach the tide was out and on the skerries great fat seals lay resting. Joe headed out on to the rocks to pull up a couple of his lobster creels in the hope that we could eat one. We were lucky as there was one great big fat one which he carried carefully back on to the beach. Joe kept the pot and a knife in a sack hidden at the back of one of the caves where the tide couldn't reach it. I was still shaking a little from my earlier episode and I made Joe do the fetching and carrying of seawater and bits of driftwood we'd need for the fire. Soon he had a good fire going and once the water was boiling, he threw the lobster in. As I hated that tiny hissing scream as the poor creature boiled to death, I looked away out to sea.

On the horizon fat billowing clouds ballooned upwards. We wouldn't be able to sit there for long. Just past the lighthouse, but within the confines of the bay, two heads poked out of the water. One ducked under as I spied it, scared of being caught so close to the shore. The selkies had come again. Cold fear gripped my stomach. As Joe chattered on about the whelks he'd collected in the bay around the main town harbour, I remembered Jeanie standing by the tide line at the Midsummer's Eve party. She'd cried into the sea, hadn't she? That's what Mrs McLeod had thought and if anyone could sense how a person was feeling it was her. Mrs McLeod could always tell the moment I arrived whether or not to offer me a chocolate biscuit immediately, or whether I had the ability to wait. If she thought Jeanie had been crying into the sea, she'd have been right.

'Joe, shush a minute. Remember Midsummer's Eve, the party? Remember Jeanie cried into the sea?' He looked at me blankly. 'Come on, Joe. You remember. Melanie Houghton was there with her and Billy Jansson. They were all crowding around her? It was the night Billy kissed Melanie in front of everyone. Come on, Joe, remember.'

'Uh-huh.'

My mind cleared suddenly and I could see it all: what it was that had been bothering me since she left. I'd got it wrong, but now it was so startlingly clear it was as though the lighthouse beam had penetrated my skull. I knew where she'd gone when she'd headed off along the track.

'Do you remember Jeanie's stories about the selkies?'

Joe nodded and shifted his weight closer to me. He was as obsessed with the selkies as I was.

'She said that Midsummer's Eve is the most magical night of the year. It's when the selkies are able to leave the sea, shed their skins and become human and walk on the land with us and dance on the beaches. Once the male selkies have shed their skins and stand like men on the beach, Jeanie said they are incredibly handsome and women fall in love with them at first sight and can't resist them.'

'Yes. And on that night if a woman cries seven tears into the sea, the selkie will hear her distress and come to help her,' Joe said standing up.

'A selkie man must have been out that night, the night of the party. Jeanie was sad, she was crying, I remember Mrs McLeod pointing that out. The selkie man must have come to help her. He waited until he found her alone and then he would have taken his chance and approached her. That's where she's gone, Joe. She's gone to be a selkie.'

As we talked through the story, I could see what had happened to Jeanie as though it was happening in front of me right there. I could see the selkie man rising up out of the sea, catching her tears in his hand. She wouldn't have been able to resist the call of the selkie; no one can resist that call. She wouldn't have been able to go with him that night, not with us watching her, but he'd held on to those tears and waited. The day she'd gone out alone, walking along the track, he'd have been waiting. He'd have called *Jeanie, Jeanie, come with me* and she wouldn't have been able to resist. She would have gone to the beach and stepped into the water, holding on to his hand as he led her in. The waves must have lapped at her waist and as the water flowed around her it would have changed her skin into the skin of a seal so that she no longer felt the cold water biting at her skin. When she went under, her hair would have transformed into the soft fur of a seal. Kicking her new flippers, they would have dived into the sea and swam out to the underwater kingdom.

I couldn't breathe. My chest felt tight as though Joe had me in one of his grips where I had to fight to escape or surrender. I couldn't stay there on the beach with him. All I could think was, why wasn't it me? Why hadn't I cried that night instead of Jeanie? The selkie wouldn't have been able to take me, not with my caul to surround my head. I cursed my 'luck' and wished with everything I had that I could have passed it on to Jeanie. There was something I could do, though, and to do that I needed to get back to Tryggr. I stood up, leaving Joe and our lobster and bolted towards the steps.

'Freyja! What is it? Wait, come back,' Joe yelled, but I ignored him.

I grabbed Jeanie's bicycle and raced back home as fast as I could. A couple of times my feet slipped from the pedals and they continued to spin around crashing into my shins, causing me to cry out in pain. I rubbed the tears away with my sleeve and pushed myself onwards towards Tryggr.

I dropped the bicycle outside the shed and raced into the kitchen where Mother was chopping vegetables. If she heard me enter, she didn't look up. Some of the potatoes had fallen on to the floor and I skidded on one.

'Mother,' I said, still panting from the exertion.

She looked up briefly, but her gaze was vacant and I wasn't certain she saw me.

'Mother,' I said again, more forcefully.

Her hand stopped chopping for a moment. Some of the potato pieces still had the skin on and others had been peeled. The water in the saucepan was cloudy where she hadn't washed off the mud and starch. Nevertheless, she put the pot on the range to cook.

'Hmmm,' she said.

'I know where Jeanie went. I've worked it out. She's with the selkies. We can take the boat and go and look for her. Can't we, Mother? We can go and find her and bring her back.'

'Yes, dear. That's right. Pass me that pan will you,' she said.

I passed her the pan and tugged on her sleeve.

'Mother? You'll ask Father. About going out and looking for her?'

If I could persuade Father to go out in the boat, we'd find her. We could pull her from the selkie's grip, the two of us together, I was sure of that. Father was a big, strong man. He'd be able to do it.

Mother put carrots in the pan. Some were chopped, some were whole with the tops still on, but they all went in together. I couldn't keep still with the excitement of my discovery, but as I watched her listen calmly to my revelations, I realised what her lack of interest meant. She'd known this all along. It wasn't news to her. It was hopeless. There was nothing we could do and Jeanie was never coming back.

One week later, Mrs McLeod and I arrived in the island's main town, Skellinwall. Mrs McLeod had promised me a boat trip if I helped her with her shopping. Mr MacKenzie had built her a new boat so she could tour the bays around Falun and go to the other outlying islands. The boat sat fat and heavy in the water and was similar to the ones I'd watched him build when we were young and we, Joe, Jeanie and I, would sit on the steps of the boat shed watching him work until he tired of our presence and shooed us away. The boat was similar to the Norse birlinns that obsessed Mr MacKenzie. He would tell us every detail about those original boats as he worked, something we were desperate to hear. Mrs McLeod's boat was different, but if you'd asked me to point out how I wouldn't have been able to.

I suspected that Mrs McLeod was taking me to Skellinwall to get me out of the house and the boat being ready at the same time was an excuse. Mother hadn't been herself since Jeanie disappeared and when Mrs McLeod had come to visit the day before with a few others, friends of Mother's and Father's, the women had spent a couple of hours cleaning up the house whilst Mother sat red-eyed and listless in a chair holding Jeanie's panda. She hadn't even looked embarrassed that other women were dealing with our mess. She would have done once, before

Jeanie left. Then, our house was always tidy, always sparkling. I felt ashamed of Mother, and us, allowing outsiders to see the state we were in and I vowed that I'd do the cleaning after that. I wouldn't have everyone thinking we were dirty and lazy.

In the town, Mrs McLeod asked me to wait for her on a black iron bench by the quayside. As I sat there, I scuffed my sandals into the dirt that had accumulated around the feet of the bench. The water slapped against the stone steps that led down into the dark water, hissing and sucking. Each small wave tried to lick the next step up, reaching towards the land to escape the boundary we had imposed on it. The bruised sky above us cast the sea into a fathomless inky darkness. If I fell in there, would I sink and sink and never come up, or would my magic caul protect me? Behind me the wind pushed at my back, tying my long hair in a knot in front of my face so I couldn't see. I rose out of the seat as the wind curled around me and encouraged me towards the swirling blackness. My feet shuffled towards the edge of the quay and my toes, which for a while now had spread forwards over the front of my sandals, reached for the lip of the stone and curled over the edge. The wind at my back urged me on and on. And in the shadowy depths, I saw a flash of brightness, light hitting the scales of a fin that turned in the currents. The flicking tail of the selkie propelled him towards me. I saw his smile, and I realised that everything Jeanie had told me about them was true: he was handsome, beautiful even. His hands reached up through the water and his arms opened wide. *Jump to me, jump to me*, he said. *Come with Jeanie and me, come to us.*

Mrs McLeod caught me from behind just as I was about to hurl myself into the selkie's wicked arms. I pulled against her grip, screaming, let me go, let me go! This is my chance to be with Jeanie. I reached my arms outwards. *Come back, come back and let me ride on your back.* But he swam away from me and I doubled over in Mrs McLeod's arms, my hair hanging down in front of my face, hiding my shame from the fishermen preparing their nets on the quayside.

Mrs McLeod sat on the stone steps, cradling me in her arms for a long while, stroking my hair and muttering softly. She said the weather wasn't right to go out in the boat after all. She'd thought the conditions had looked promising, but it turned out that the shipping forecast had been wrong and we'd be better off doing something else. I protested and said that the weather looked as good as it could get, that the conditions were as perfect as they were likely to ever be at that time of year, but I was grateful to her for reading through my protestations and angry tantrum and realising that there was no way I was getting in that boat, not when the selkies were out there waiting to steal me away too.

Mrs McLeod asked if instead of the boat trip, I'd like to go back to her house for the afternoon, as she had something she'd like to give me. On the bus, Mrs McLeod encouraged me to speak about Jeanie. Relieved, I spoke continually, unable to bear the silence I felt would have been between us otherwise. Mrs McLeod was the only one who spoke to me directly about her absence. She understood how I felt; her husband dying and leaving her suddenly like that when she expected to have years and years more with him. It wasn't the same, but we had in common that sense of loss boring through us both, pinning us to the ground so at times neither of us could take one more step forward.

When other people spoke about Jeanie, they always elevated her to a position of greater virtue and beauty than any child had ever occupied. The stronger the myths about Jeanie's perfection became, the more lacking I was in comparison. Mrs McLeod didn't do that. Her version of Jeanie was different, more like mine, and I preferred it. The bus took us close to Lochinsay and we walked the final mile or so from the road along the narrow track that led to her house. It was a lonely, isolated position; her house sat on the sheer cliffs that dropped in huge black stacks straight down into the sea. There were no coves or beaches at Lochinsay, only a thin line of shingle when the tide receded and the waters around the headland were treacherous, swirling and dark with fierce rip tides that would grab you without warning and drag you under in seconds.

At the house, Mrs McLeod left me alone for a moment,

disappearing upstairs, and I wandered into her studio. It was a huge room, a new addition to the otherwise old house, and it had a roof with large skylights and windows all around. As a result, it was one of the brightest rooms I'd ever been in. It smelled strongly of the oil paints she used. Wooden palette boards were scattered everywhere, covered with mounds of dried on paint that Mrs McLeod was able to bring to life with a little effort. I loved her studio: it was comforting and familiar and in it I was able to relax more fully than anywhere else. Leaning against the walls were canvasses at various stages of completion. In her pictures, she caught the landscapes around us so clearly I recognised the places immediately, and yet she'd seen something in them, something new I hadn't spotted before. Once I'd seen our island in the way she had, I couldn't believe it had been there like that all the time, sitting there outside my vision and I hadn't noticed.

'Here we are, Freyja. I've found it.' Mrs McLeod held out a brown leather case on a long strap.

'What is it?'

'Open it and see.'

Mrs McLeod looked excited, pleased with herself. She'd obviously given the leather a quick shine as there were parts under the metal fasteners holding the strap where she'd failed to remove all of the dust.

'It was Ben's. I think he'd have wanted you to have it, rather than it sitting upstairs gathering dust.'

The case was held shut by a metal fastener. I turned the peg and lifted the lid. The camera was heavy and big in my small hands. I took the cover from the lens and looked through the viewfinder out of the window and towards the cliffs. I'd never looked through a camera lens before and it was strange and unnerving to find the world both so clearly in focus and yet so limited at the same time, concentrated as it was into one small point.

'Here are a couple of films too,' Mrs McLeod said, handing over two cylindrical containers.

She took out one of the films. The smell struck me immediately – the chemical tang wasn't something I'd encountered before and I loved it. Mrs McLeod opened the back of the camera and handed me the film, explaining step-by-step how to load it. She never showed me how to do things; she always made me do it following her careful instructions.

'Come outside and you can take your first photograph,' she said.

We went out into her windy garden. Her clothes were drying on the washing line, cracking and dancing as the wind whipped them into life.

'What shall I photograph?' I said, suddenly scared that I would waste the precious film on something stupid, that I wouldn't get it right.

'Take whatever you like. Whatever interests you. That way you'll learn how you see the world. When you've finished the film, we'll have it developed and see what you've got.'

'What if I get it wrong?' I said.

Mrs McLeod knelt down next to me and held the camera in front of her. 'There's no wrong, Freyja. Take what you see. Looking through a viewfinder distances you from whatever it is you're pointing the camera at. It stops you being scared and allows you to see. Take it home with you and take as many photographs as the film allows. Don't think, just look. You might surprise yourself with what you'll find.' She paused, then added, 'It'll help, I promise.'

I couldn't imagine what it was she thought it would help with, so I shrugged and nodded and that appeared to satisfy her. Before I left, Mrs McLeod cut me a slice of cake to take home. I headed out towards the Sky Path, a treacherous footpath that led along the cliff tops linking Lochinsay with Tor Ness Head. There was a sheer drop into the sea along one side and a sloping bank on the other. I'd named it the Sky Path as it was like walking along a tightrope through the air. Mrs McLeod made me promise to keep looking, to keep taking photographs. I promised although I had no idea what it was she wanted me to see.

Out on the Sky Path, the wind whipped against me and down at the bottom of the cliffs the sea boomed and hissed as it swirled in whirlpools around the stacks. I took the camera out of its case and wrapped the strap around my wrist, terrified that I would drop it and it would crash on to the black rocks below. I turned to face the direction I'd come from and fixed Mrs McLeod's house at Lochinsay in the centre of the viewfinder, adjusting the lens so the focus was clear and sharp, then I pressed the button and the shutter clicked as it captured the image. I tried to push from my mind any worries I had about not seeing anything worthy of capturing and after I'd taken a few photographs, I began to relax and enjoy looking for things to take: flowers, the glacial blue of the sea where it churned and writhed around the rocks, a fishing boat on its way back home, the seagulls following behind, catching the guts thrown into the sea from the back. The storm that had darkened the sky earlier that morning had not materialised and the low sun had started to pierce small breaks in the clouds, sending lines of light skimming across the tops of the waves. I felt lighter and freer than I had for months, since Jeanie had left, and I was glad Mrs McLeod had trusted me with her dead husband's camera.

As I rounded the bend, the lighthouse came into view and I lifted the camera to my eye once again. I tried to make the lighthouse the central image in the shot, with the cliffs above the bays on either side: Tor Ness Cove to the right and St Ninian's Cove to the left, curving into each bottom corner of the frame. I turned and turned the lens trying to find the focus, but my hand shook and the lighthouse danced in the left hand side of the picture and refused to move into the centre. My skin turned cold and clammy and a slick of perspiration coated my palms and forehead. My chest tightened and spots of light danced in my eyes.

And I was back to a time when Jeanie was with me, to a time where my memories still existed and I could see the way the light caught her hair as she walked towards that selkie, how she'd turned back to look at me, smiling and waving; to a time before everything faded to nothingness and all I could see was a darkness as deep and dangerous as the geos that plundered our landscape, sucking the land in on itself, leaving great holes of air where something solid had once been; to a time when I'd had the opportunity to tell Jeanie everything and anything; to a time I'd taken for granted and now had passed.

My feet slipped from the path and the next moment I found myself falling, slipping, tumbling down the steep bank, the camera flying through the air and smacking me in the cheek as I came to a stop. I sat up immediately and checked the camera, fearful that I'd broken it, but it was fine. I knew I should test it, take another photograph to be entirely sure, but nothing could make me pick it up at that moment and look through the viewfinder. Mrs McLeod had been wrong. It didn't put you at a distance, it didn't make you less scared. Instead, it brought everything closer into focus, made it more vivid. I pushed the camera back into the case, snapped the fastener shut and I ran back home as fast as I could.

I crashed through the kitchen door, swinging against it so hard it bounced back on to me as I ran through. Mother was sitting in her usual spot, staring at a full mug of coffee. She looked up, startled by my sudden entrance.

'Freyja? What is it? You look like you've seen a ghost.'

I didn't stop to answer her. I couldn't say anything. There were no words to express the horror I'd felt out on the Sky Path. I pounded up the stairs and into my bedroom, opened my bottom drawer and pushed the camera underneath my clothes, right at the very back where I couldn't see it, slamming the drawer shut so the whole chest shuddered and the two blue glass dishes clinked together, cracking one of them. I threw myself on to my bed and pulled my pillow over my head, until eventually I fell into an uneasy sleep, dominated by the flashing eye of the lighthouse and its beam that only revealed parts of the landscape at a time.

Ceredigion Mental Asylum, West Wales
June 1983 11.30am

I need to rest for a minute.

Can you smell that?

It's our lunch cooking. You are staying for lunch, aren't you? I would like you to stay if you can.

I can't guarantee you'll enjoy it. I'm used to it, but even I know the food's not very good. That smell reminds me of the day I arrived at my first asylum.

Don't be shocked. Everyone here knows what kind of place we're in. There's no good to be had hiding from the truth. If I've learned one thing, it's that.

My first place was in Scotland. It wasn't as nice a place as here. I don't mind Wales. The weather is familiar, comforting. Here I can look out at the Irish Sea and at times I can almost convince myself I'm back on Falun and this is Tryggr and everything that happened to me is just a dream. At the other place, all I could see were thick woods closing in around me, guarding the exits. Not at first though. At first, I could see nothing but walls.

When I arrived at that place, I was bound up in a special suit, a straitjacket. They didn't put me in it at first, they waited until after we'd made the sea crossing from Falun. I came on the coastguard's boat with the doctor and the policeman. No one else. I don't know if Mother wasn't allowed to come with me or whether she chose not to come. I think it must have been that she wasn't allowed.

A doctor and a nurse met us at the port and they forced me into the suit, said it was for my own protection what with all the fuss I was making screaming about not wanting to get off the boat, not wanting to leave the coastguard behind, not wanting to leave what I felt was my last link with Falun. They bundled me into an ambulance, not the emergency kind with lights and sirens, it was more like a small bus with AMBULANCE printed on the sides. I didn't understand. I didn't realise I was ill.

We travelled a long while through the dark. No one said anything to me and after a while I stopped hitting my head against the windows, stopped asking where we were going, where they were taking me, and why, why, why, when I never got a response. Eventually, we drove off the main road along a driveway that went on for a long time through the pine forests. At the end of it was a huge building. It didn't look welcoming. It was called Kincraig Castle. There was a sign on the gate saying so. It wasn't a grand sign, in fact the 's' had come off and it was only later that I realised the place I'd arrived at wasn't a dairy farm. Calling it a 'Castle' makes it sound grand and pleasant, but it wasn't. They pulled me out of the ambulance and handed me over to another nurse waiting at the entrance. She said, *You've to come with me.*

Once we were inside, she dragged me along a corridor. My head ached from where I'd banged it repeatedly against the ambulance windows. The corridor stretched endlessly ahead; it had door after door along both sides and a tiled floor that wasn't clean. A nauseating food smell wafted towards me and I retched many times, but I wasn't sick.

Hold it in, Freyja, I said to myself, don't shame yourself in front of these people.

Eventually, we arrived at a door that had a small round window at head height, just big enough to see into the room. The nurse slammed a metal cover over it, then opened the door and I saw straight away that there were no windows to the outside. I couldn't go into a room like that, so I panicked and stopped, but she pushed me in. She shoved me in my back. I dug my heels into the floor to stop myself, but it did no good as they slid on the tiles.

Once in, I couldn't breathe. It was so hot and stuffy, the air burned into my lungs. Fight her, fight her, don't go in there, I thought. I couldn't use my hands, so I bit her wherever I could find an inch of exposed skin, sinking my teeth into her soft, fleshy arm. I drew blood. Her spectacles fell on to the floor when I rammed my whole body into hers, pushing her against the wall so I could carry on biting harder and harder, sinking my teeth further in, as far as I could, right down to the bone. That's when the screaming started, hers and mine. I stamped on her spectacles so she wouldn't be able to see. I stamped on them over and over until the lenses turned into a pile of dust.

Yes, I know I don't look strong enough for that kind of behaviour.

Somehow, the nurse managed to slam her hand hard against a red alarm button on the wall. There was blood everywhere – red sticky handprints on the blue walls, smears and spots all over the floor and my suit. I could smell it on my face and taste its saltiness in my mouth. I spat and spat trying to get rid of it. People came running into the room, with them was the head doctor. He started yelling at me the minute he walked in. Said I was a stupid, evil girl taking an outburst like that and I had to be punished. Before I knew what was happening, he jabbed me full of paraldehyde which knocked me out for days. When I came around, I stank of it. It seeped out of my pores. I couldn't stand to be in my own body it smelled so bad.

I know it sounds shocking, what I did to that nurse, but you'd have fought too. Imagine if you'd been taken from your home. Imagine if you'd been dragged away from everything you loved in the middle of the night and left with strangers and you didn't know why and no one would tell you what you wanted to know. You'd fight against it. You couldn't go into a room with no windows, with stale, dead air filling your lungs, not knowing if you'd ever leave it again. You'd kick and scream like I did. I knew I'd done wrong things. Many wrong things, but how could anyone be ripped away from their life and not fight?

My therapist here says my reaction was normal.

I was jabbed full of paraldehyde many times during my time at Kincraig Castle. All that stopped when I moved here. They couldn't handle me in that other place. So, after a while, I think it was a few years at least, I was shipped off in the night and brought here. I think it would have been different if I hadn't been so alone. I didn't know what was going on, what was happening to me. No one told me anything. Same thing my whole life. I was always kept in the dark about the truth of things. If someone, Mother, Father even, had come with me that first night, or even after that, I might have behaved, I might have settled in and coped and in the end managed to leave and go back home, but it didn't happen like that. So here I am.

You're the first visitor I've had for eighteen years.

Tryggr, Falun, Orkney Islands
September 1955

By the autumn, I began to realise what Jeanie's disappearance meant for me. You probably think it strange that I hadn't considered that before, but when she went, I lost my anchor and I didn't think very much about anything. Other than the obvious consequence that I missed her terribly, what I hadn't anticipated was that Mother wouldn't allow me out of her sight. In the immediate aftermath of her disappearance, Mother didn't much care for my presence, but it didn't take long for that to change and she constantly wanted to know where I was. Even in the house. If I hadn't seen her for a while, she'd suddenly start shouting for me, or running up the stairs two at a time, I could tell from the thuds she made. Once she'd seen that I was in my bedroom she'd calm down. On the rare occasions that I managed to escape, other than to go to school, Mother would insist on knowing every detail of my plans: who I'd be with, how I was getting there, details that had never bothered her before, until eventually there were only two places she'd allow me to go to alone: Mrs McLeod's house and Joe's. Mrs McLeod told me it was because she loved me, but that was nonsense. It was a terrible burden, one that weighed down on me making me feel that I had to be someone I wasn't, someone more like Jeanie. How could that be love? As a result, I became secretive and cunning and made more and more elaborate stories to cover my whereabouts. Often, I didn't go very far; it was the secrecy of my adventure that thrilled me, the fact that I'd managed to find some space and time of my own.

Going to school was fine. I'd walk to the end of the track and along the brae to the village school. It was only a couple of miles and whereas once I'd complained about the walk, now I relished it, even on the wildest of days when the wind tore at my hair and I arrived at school soaked. It was good to be out and free.

One night, however, I overheard Mother and Father talking. I'd crept down the stairs, long after bedtime, something I'd taken to doing, mostly because I hated staring at Jeanie's empty bed on the nights when the moon shone full and bright into our room. I was sitting on the bench by the front door, under Jeanie's coat so I could inhale her smell and imagine she was back. The door to the sitting room was ajar enough for me to hear the wireless murmuring in the background and Mother and Father's quiet voices.

'I've been thinking, Wallace, about Freyja's education,' Mother said.

'Hmmm.' Father was reading the newspaper; I could hear the rustling of paper as he turned the pages.

'I'm thinking she's a bright girl and perhaps will go on with her education as we'd planned for Jeanie and maybe the island school isn't suitable for her any longer.'

She paused. I left my hiding place and crept closer to the open door, peered through the crack between the door and the frame, and saw father fold the newspaper and place it carefully on the arm of his chair.

'You want to send her away to board *now*? Is she not too young?' He leaned forward resting his elbows on his knees, and with his palms together he bounced his mouth against his fingertips.

Mother shot out of her chair and her knitting fell to the floor in a clatter. 'No!'

Her reaction made me jump, but Father barely reacted. Instead he remained in the same posture. Mother recovered her composure and sat back down.

'What I mean is, I'll teach her here at home. We can find someone to help, if we need to. She'll be able to focus more without the others distracting her. She can stay with me.'

She didn't say it, she didn't have to: Freyja can stay with me, where I can watch her and stop her escaping like Jeanie did. My body felt heavy, solid, like it does in those dreams when you need to run, to escape and you can't move no matter the danger you're in. I managed to make it back upstairs and into bed, but I didn't sleep. Every day I existed, I reminded Mother of what she was missing: Jeanie. The chain that extended from me to her, and to some extent to Father too, the chain that kept me locked on our island, grew shorter and shorter.

It wasn't long after I left school to be home-educated, that Mrs McLeod came to Tryggr and asked Mother and Father if I could go across to a neighbouring island, Skopinsay, with her and Joe for the day.

'I'm very keen to try out my new boat over a longer distance, Morag, and Skopinsay is perfect. Joe's coming too. I could use Freyja's navigational skills and it would be good for her to get out,' Mrs McLeod said. 'She needs to be a child still, Morag. Let her go.'

I could see that Mother was reluctant to agree and so was I. The selkies would be waiting for me. They'd reach their scaly hands out of the water and grab me, pull me under, flipping their tails, propelling us further and further beneath the waves. Although I'd hardly been anywhere since stopping school and I'd been driven mad sitting at home with only Mother to talk to, the fear of the selkie man skimming beneath the surface of the sea held me back from begging Mother to let me go.

'It would be a real help to me to have another pair of seafaring hands on board, Morag.'

That finally swayed Mother. She could justify it as helping Mrs McLeod. She had been so good in the aftermath of Jeanie's leaving that I suspect Mother felt she owed her, but I couldn't go out in the boat. It could so easily overturn; we could hit a wave starboard on and be tossed into the treacherous waters.

'We could take photographs by the lighthouse instead,' I said, desperate for Mrs McLeod to change her plans. I looked from her to Mother and back again. Say *yes*. Say *yes, that's a good idea, Freyja. Let's do that*. I'd rather face my fear of looking through the lens again, than face the selkies.

'You'll be perfectly safe with me and *The Ragnhild*. She's a sturdy boat, built for these waters. What can happen? You're a sailor, Freyja, my dear. Your caul will protect you. Won't it, Morag?' Mrs McLeod winked at Mother.

I'd been going out on fishing boats with Father and Mr MacKenzie since before I could remember. It was the one thing I'd shared with Father that Jeanie never had. With him, I learned to read the patterns and temperament of the water. I'd seen all its many faces, good and bad. I knew when a patch of oily stillness meant danger, keep away. When a feathering on the surface illuminated the rocks lying beneath. Once the skin of the sea took on a pitted appearance, like the skin of an orange, I knew I was in the waters of the surrounding islands and had left Falun's. I could sense a change in the tide, a shift in the wind before Father even. I knew when to press on and when to turn back. I was the safest sailor on Falun, that's what everyone said. That was before. Before the selkies rose out of the sea and took my Jeanie.

'That's settled then, Freyja,' Mrs McLeod said. 'I'll pick you up after breakfast tomorrow at high tide. Don't forget to bring your camera. You can photograph Falun from different angles. You might see something you don't expect.

After Mrs McLeod left, I went and sat with the chickens for a while and counted the times they pecked in the dirt by the peat shed.

That night I couldn't asleep. All I could think of was the empty stretch of water between us and Skopinsay. I tried to make myself imagine crossing it and reaching the huge stacks on the Southern side of Skopinsay, the side that faced us on Tor Ness Head, that had years before broken away from the main cliff face. On a clear day, I could see them from our bedroom window. The stacks had been colonised by a huge flock of solan geese. I slid out of bed and put an extra film into my bag from the spares Mrs McLeod had given me. I'd take photographs of the birds. If I concentrated on that, on taking the best photographs I could, I'd keep the selkies away.

When Mrs McLeod arrived the next morning, I was already sitting waiting on the doorstep with my tin box containing my canister of water and a large currant cake Mother had baked the previous night. Mother had warned me not to keep her waiting.

In Skellinwall, we walked down the brae, over the little bridge that spanned the burn which ran almost the entire length of the island, and down the steep street to the quayside where Mrs McLeod had moored her boat *The Ragnhild*. Joe was waiting for us on the bench, sitting next to Callum and laughing at some private joke, so he didn't notice us immediately. Once we joined them, Callum slunk off, giving Joe an odd backwards glance I couldn't make out.

The wind was sharp that day, with a strong seaweed tang to it and the water had small rushes of foamy white water cresting the top of each wave even in the harbour, but I didn't care. Once at the quayside, my old excitement at the prospect of being out on the water began to overtake my fears. Mrs McLeod was right. I was a sailor, a good sailor. Nothing would go wrong. I would be leaving our island for the day and the worst the Orkney weather could throw at us would not dampen my spirits. As we boarded the boat, Mrs McLeod passed Joe and I plastic bags to wrap up everything that could potentially ruin if it got wet. Then came the equipment checks. I listed all the items we needed to have on board and it was Joe's job to check we had them. Joe and I had been through this routine together many times. Mrs McLeod said she wanted to watch and learn.

Radio. Check.

Charts. Check.

Compass. Check.

Binoculars. Check.

Lifejackets, harnesses, lifelines. Check.

We were ready. I raised the anchor, taking care to wash off the black mud from the harbour's seabed before stowing it away. Then I took my position next to the tiller. I would steer us out of the harbour and on to Skopinsay. Joe hoisted the sail, the wind caught it and we were off.

As we left Falun's waters, I threaded through the hidden rocks which lay in wait for the unsuspecting seaman, on the outskirts of the headland where the Norse seamark stood guard.

'Well done, Freyja. That was magnificent steering,' Mrs McLeod said.

As we headed out into the open sea, I felt the surface of the water lift with the swelling of The Sound. The sea took us in its longer, bigger rhythms, carrying us up and away towards Skopinsay. The wind caught the sail, billowing the white fabric out into a magnificent arc and we raced across the water. Mrs McLeod screamed with delight as we cut through the waves.

'Look!' I shouted.

Above us, we saw the first solan goose cruising as it looked for the flash of silver that would give away the location of its prey. Its white body and black-tipped wings folded in on themselves as it fell from the sky, piercing the skin of the sea, spearing the fish beneath. I re-checked the compass and the charts. We were on track.

Ahead of us, the towering stacks of Skopinsay thrust out towards us. The rocks were alive with the birds roosting there. As we neared Skopinsay, I steered *The Ragnhild* across the smaller waves; the boat moved like a barrel over the white crests before skating down the back of the waves into the trough behind them. I released my grip on the tiller as we entered the bay, allowing *The Ragnhild* to find her own way, dropped the anchor allowing it to run through the fairlead and into the sand. Joe unstepped the mast and folded the sail into its bag. We had arrived. Joe and I disembarked first into the small surf and helped Mrs McLeod to the beach. There was no harbour or quayside as no one lived on the island. Once we were on the beach, Mrs McLeod decided we should have some tea from her flask and maybe a bit of Mother's cake to keep us going. We ate the whole thing. With our stomachs full, Mrs McLeod sent Joe and I off to explore while she relaxed. I guessed she wanted some time alone.

It was a steep climb up from the beach to the top of the cliffs and at times we were on all fours, clambering up and holding on to clumps of dried sea grasses that sprouted from the rock face like the widow Nugent's old lady chin tufts. At the top of the cliff, we ran like wild things across the rabbit-soiled grass until we came to a great hunk of nothing carved out of the ground: a geo.

We lay on our stomachs and looked over the edge into the ferocious torrent of fresh water that poured out of the island, mingling with the churning blue sea that rushed into the dark fissure. The waves thundered into the small space, sending jets of spray into the air dampening our faces. I pulled myself closer to the edge, so my head hung over, reaching into the darkness of the abyss swirling beneath me. All I could hear was the roar of the sea and the pounding of blood in my ears. My eyeballs bulged with the pressure of looking down, but I didn't look up, didn't pull back, even when the lights started to flash in my vision and my throat thickened so I could no longer swallow. I allowed my head to fall further and further forwards so my shoulders balanced on the rim of the emptiness and I could easily tip over into the darkness that flickered and grabbed at me. In the distance I heard my name. Jeanie? I peered even further into the damp gloom, trying to see where the voice had come from, using my hands to pull me deeper and deeper in.

'Stop messing around, Freyja!' Joe's hand grabbed my jumper in the middle of my back and yanked me out of the darkness. 'What are you doing?'

It wasn't a question, more a declaration of his irritation that I was wasting our precious time when he wanted to see the birds on the stacks. As he pulled me upright, I saw something running across the sand of the beach beneath us, an image that flashed and burned out: it was most likely a shadow dancing in the light. I paused for a moment, trying to see if it would come back and show its face again, but the beach remained desolate and empty. Sensing Joe's agitation, I pulled myself together.

'Come on,' I yelled.

I raced ahead of Joe, relishing the freedom to run and run until my chest felt as though it would collapse with the effort. At the top of the cliff, next to the largest of the stacks, the noise and acrid stench of the screeching birds filled the air. Joe finally caught up with me. We again lay on our stomachs and peered over the edge. It wasn't as sheer as it had appeared when we were out on the sea and there was a natural pathway that led down to the small rocky cove at the bottom. I set off down the cliff face before Joe could say he wouldn't go. Joe was afraid of heights and would have resisted if I hadn't already started. Off to the left of the path, there was a ledge and from there would be a good view around the stack to Falun and Tor Ness Head. That would be the spot from which to take my photographs. I was so intent on my mission that I failed to see the darkening thunderheads looming in the near distance.

When I was a little way down, I looked back to see if Joe had started to follow. He was on his backside, shuffling along the path like a fool.

'Don't be such an idiot,' I yelled. 'You're more likely to slip coming down like that. Stand up and walk.'

Joe shook his head and continued his shuffle down the cliff. I reached the small ledge that jutted out of the black rocks in a white horizontal stripe. I could feel the air cooling and the light fading.

Joe continued his slow shuffle along the cliff edge until finally, as the first smatters of raindrops landed on the hot rocks, sending up a dusty wild scent, he reached me. Across The Sound, Falun lay bathed in a deep orange slab of sunlight. I took the camera out of the case and started to focus on the lighthouse and the two bays either side that swept away from it.

'Why d'you take scenery all the time?' Joe moaned next to me. He kicked a pebble down the cliff and watched it bounce against the rocks on the way down. 'It's so boring.'

'Stand there,' I said, pointing to the left along the ridge. 'I'll have you in it too.'

Joe hesitated.

'Go on, we haven't got long. Look at the sky. Right now, the light is perfect.'

Above us the clouds had thickened into dense black mushrooms. Joe shuffled along the lip of the edge, slipping a little on the damp rocks.

'To the left more,' I said, waving my hand for him to move. 'I can't get what I want if you don't move.'

Through the lens, the lighthouse flashed in and out of focus. To the right of it, the white sand of St Ninian's Cove slashed the darkness.

'Further along,' I said to Joe.

I couldn't focus the camera on him and the lighthouse and the bays. At that moment the thunder clapped above us. Joe must have stepped further to the left with the fright of it, as suddenly he was waving his arms wildly reaching for something to grab hold of, but all he found was air. At the same moment, I clicked the shutter.

Joe's screams ended with a dry thump as he landed on the

rocks beneath. I thought, I can't look, I can't look. What if he's dead? What if I've killed him? I opened my mouth to shout his name, but no words came out. Look Freyja. Look down, but I couldn't.

A high piercing scream stretched the air. He's alive. I tipped my head over the edge, eyes tight shut. One, two, three, open. Just do it, Freyja, and it'll be done.

Joe's bent body lay on a ledge beneath me, about ten feet down. He's lost a leg, I thought, until I realised it was bent up behind his back and he was lying on it. He looked as though he was lying on one of those beams we had in the school gymnasium, one of those ones you balance on. He didn't look good. His face was wet and blue and screwed up tight in a bunch. I'm not sure how long I stood there staring at him. He was dying and it was all my fault. I could hear his screams bouncing off the cliffs, but they didn't register and instead of galvanising me into action they pinned me in a cage. I realised he would die if I left him there.

I ran back up the scratchy path, across the grass, past the gaping blackness of the geo and back to the bay where *The Ragnhild* floated peacefully in the water and Mrs McLeod sat on the picnic rug under an umbrella, knees hugged to her chest, looking out across the water. I shouted to gain her attention, but the wind whipped away my words, casting them aside. I half ran, half slid down the cliff face back to the beach, my hands cut and bleeding from the sharp rocks and razor grasses.

'My goodness, Freyja! What on earth?' Mrs McLeod said as she turned around, stood and ran towards me.

'Joe. It's Joe,' I said, panting so hard I couldn't get the words out, pointing back in the direction I'd run from. 'Radio. We need the radio.'

Mrs McLeod grabbed my hand and pulled me towards *The Ragnhild*, dragging me through the surf and into the boat. She sat me down on the gunwale and pulled the radio out of its protective case.

'Tell me what and where, Freyja,' she said as the coastguard's crackly voice came on the line, pushing through the static.

It was Tom Bellingham on duty, I could tell by his thick Lewis accent. He'd come from the Hebrides to Falun late in life. He was the calmest man I'd ever met and his soft, deep voice breaking through the static pushed aside my anxiety. I took a deep breath and related the facts as I knew them. If Mrs McLeod was shocked at my recklessness, she didn't let it show.

Back on the beach, Mrs McLeod poured me some hot tea from the Thermos and gave me a chicken paste sandwich on thick slices of her white bread. She knew Joe and I loved them. 'How can I eat?' I yelled at her, throwing the sandwich on to the ground. 'We need to go to Joe now.'

Mrs McLeod took hold of me. 'We need to show the coastguard where he is. We have to wait here until they come.'

I tried to pull away from her, to run to Joe and help him, but Mrs McLeod kept hold of me, forcing me to wait. Even though I railed against her like a mad thing, she didn't react. She stayed calm and eventually I took a hold of myself and we waited. I still couldn't eat the sandwich though. That stuck in my throat and not even the tea would wash it away. The coastguard and the doctor came quickly, especially considering that the wind had picked up and turned into a right skolder, whipping the tide into a frenzy. I had to run with them back up the cliff face and across the grass to the spot where Joe lay still and silent on the ledge. He'd died. We were too late. I vomited and it splashed everywhere, but no one commented.

He wasn't dead, but he was delirious and shaking with the wet and cold, screaming, 'What about rugby?' over and over. As they lifted him on to the stretcher, it was obvious that his leg was badly broken and he screamed like a whalp when they straightened it so he could lie down. I knew the answer to his question. Rugby wouldn't happen for him. Not now. He'd been fair excited about his trip to the mainland with the school team. Callum and Donald were going too. The first time they'd all been chosen to go. He'd been so proud of himself and I'd ruined it for him. Once they'd pulled him up to the top of the cliff and the doctor had stuck a needle in his arm for the pain, and placed a mask over his mouth to help him breathe, I tried to take his hand, to talk to him and tell him I was sorry, sorry I'd made him shift so far to the side, to say anything that would make it right between us, but he turned his head away from me and refused to look back.

Joe had to go with the coastguard to the hospital on the mainland, so on the way back Mrs McLeod and I had to manage *The Ragnhild* alone. Mrs McLeod took over the sail which she managed easily. She'd watched Joe carefully and knew exactly what she needed to do. It was a hard journey back, the peaks and troughs on the water were larger and harder to manage, but we did it together. Keeping us on course and safe gave me something to focus on, other than the agony on Joe's face and the way he'd refused to look at me.

Mrs McLeod said she'd explain everything to Mother and Father so I wouldn't have to, but when we arrived back at Tryggr, Mother's face was at the window and I saw that she already knew. It happened that Betty Tidy from the haberdashers had met her in the village and she'd heard it from Mrs Nugent, who'd overheard someone say that Tom Bellingham had said. News travelled fast on Falun. Father was waiting in the kitchen, sat at the table. I expected to get a good hiding and I could hardly lift my face to look at them both, but they didn't shout at me, didn't seem to blame me in any way. Instead, they gave me a hug which lasted for longer than I was used to. The kind of hug I imagined Jeanie would have had. We ate together that night. Mrs McLeod joined us, but even with her there, no one spoke much. We were all worried about Joe. Whether his leg would mend, whether he'd be able to play rugby again, how differently it could have turned out, what if...? I worried whether Joe would ever forgive me. And whether I could forgive myself.

For a few days, maybe even a week, after the incident on Skopinsay, the gloom that surrounded Mother and Father lifted a little and they became more like themselves. We played cards together in the evenings after our meal and sometimes I came close to winning. Their brighter outlook rubbed off on me and I came to fear less and less going up to my bedroom and seeing Jeanie's empty bed.

One afternoon, Mother and I returned from the village shop to find that Mrs McLeod had developed my photographs and left them in the kitchen for me. I rushed upstairs to look at them, eager to see the results of my work. Some were awful, blurred or crooked or of nothing of any note, but others competent enough – they were in focus and were of something describable. For a first effort I was pleased. I hadn't finished looking through them, when Mother appeared at the door asking if she could see them. I handed her the pile and she studied them with care, taking time over each one, and smiling at both my successes and my failures. Then suddenly, she paused, taking too long studying one particular photograph. She stood up, scattering the others on to the floorboards, red-faced and puffed up, waving the photograph in front of my face and yelling, 'What's this?'

But she wouldn't let me see it.

Mother paced up and down our bedroom, looking at the photograph, then waving it back at me. 'I can't understand you. Why would you do this?'

Finally, I saw it. The last photograph I'd taken: Joe, his arms windmilling as he fell from the cliff.

'You're a wild and selfish creature, Freyja MacAulay. A right whalp with no thought for others. How could you have been so stupid? After everything that's happened?'

Mother threw the photograph on to the floor and stormed off crying and muttering about how stupid and selfish I was. Her bedroom door slammed shut and I didn't see her again until the evening.

The photograph was useless, so it hadn't even been worth the damage taking it had caused. Even so, I put it up on my bedroom wall with all the others as there was something about it that fascinated me. Although Joe, the lighthouse and Tor Ness Cove were all jagged and blurred, running across the right-hand side of the frame the cool white strip of sand at St Ninian's Cove cut the picture horizontally in half as clearly and precisely as a blade of glass.

Ceredigion Mental Asylum, West Wales
June 1983 12.30pm

After I had the shocks, I stopped being interested in photography. Someone must have told them I liked it, as they did try and get me to take an interest when I first arrived at Kincraig Castle. I found the shocks took away the desire to look at anything and you need that if you're to take a good picture. All I could focus on was surviving one more day. That's what I'd say to myself: all you've got to do is get through the day and you'll be fine. That way I didn't see the future stretching out ahead of me. All there was, was one more day.

What were the shocks like? It was like God reached down from heaven and forced a thunderbolt into my brain.

It was the head doctor who carried out the shocks. We all called him God Almighty because he acted like he owned the place. He did in a way, I suppose. It was always him and a nurse that did it. They tried to make sure it was one of the nurses I liked, then I'd go along with it more readily. Otherwise I'd scream until my throat tasted of blood.

The first time, I was sitting in the day room minding my own business when the nurse came in and said, *Let's go*. The other patients turned away from me and tried to look busy. She walked me along a corridor I hadn't seen before and led me into a small room.

Put this on, she said.

It was a special gown, open at the back, but with no ties or anything, so I had to hold it closed behind myself to stop everyone seeing my undergarments.

Then she got hold of my hair, said *We can't have this mop, can we?* and she cut it. Red ringlets fell over the floor and I wanted to cry at the sight of it. I held my tears in even when they hardened into a great big lump at the top of my chest.

After that, we went through another door leading to an adjacent room. I kept my eyes open. I had no idea what was coming. I wanted to see. I was curious. The machine looked harmless enough standing by the bed and I wasn't afraid. The room was warm, warmer than the others. I'll get to have a lie down, I thought. I was always tired, so I was pleased at the prospect. I lay down on the bed and the nurse strapped me in, arms by my side, ankles locked. I started to worry when God Almighty fixed the metal plates to my temples with the strap across my forehead. It dug in and left a mark. The nurse put something in my mouth to stop me breaking my teeth. Then the current rushed through my brain and my eyes flashed bright white and blue and my ears drowned in the terrible sound and I thought my bones would snap in half and everything inside me would erupt through my shredded skin.

After that first time, I shut my eyes the second I walked into the room and the nurse had to guide me. I resisted more and more each time, digging my heels into the floor like I'd done the first night I arrived, so I suppose it was less guiding me into the room and more like brute force. In the end, two porters had to help the nurse strap me down. I had the shocks so many times I did end up breaking one or two of my teeth. I had the shocks more than the others. God Almighty said it was because I was worse than them. *You're the worst of the lot*, he said.

After I went to court it got a lot worse, when they decided that I had done what they'd accused me of doing. They shocked me three times a week, more sometimes.

Having the shocks makes you forget who you are for a while. I would walk around the corridors not realising what had happened to me, but then it would come back – why I was there, everything that had happened, what it was I'd done, what I'd done to you.

I suppose in that sense the shocks worked. For a few hours, days sometimes, I didn't know, the way I hadn't known back then when I was a child. And not knowing, really not knowing, had a peace to it that I enjoyed. But once I recovered and remembered, I would rage and rage, asking about you, and they would bind me up again and put me back in that windowless room until I calmed down. After that, they'd take me back in for another shock and it would all begin again.

I never want to go back to that place.

No, you're right, they don't do it to me here.

I understand that back then I was the worst a human being

could be. The shocks were my punishment. If I hadn't been the worst sort of person, if I hadn't done something so bad, then they wouldn't have done such a terrible thing to me.

Would they?

Tryggr, Falun, Orkney Islands
January 1956

It was January and Jeanie had been gone for five months. I walked out of the cool dimness of the Kirk's interior into the grey light of midday. It should have been the brightest part of the day, but the mists had rolled in making it dingy. I was pleased to see Mrs McLeod waiting by the gate. In her violet, floor length velvet coat she stood out like a jewel in the darkness. She greeted everyone who passed her in turn, friendly as always, but with that slight wry smile that told me she was glad she hadn't been incarcerated inside for the last hour, as the rest of us had been. I asked her once why she didn't come on Sundays as all the other islanders did.

'I don't believe in a god, Freyja,' she said.

I was shocked at first that she could even think such a thing, never mind admit to it so openly, but once I'd recovered I was pleased that she had the courage to say it out loud. It gave me the strength to do so too.

'I don't believe in God either,' I said.

Up until that moment, I hadn't realised I'd felt like that, but once I'd said it, admitted it to myself, I realised it was true. I couldn't believe in a Being that had allowed Jeanie to leave me so alone. A true God, the kind of God they told us about at school, wouldn't, surely, allow such a thing? On that basis, I decided He simply couldn't exist. I wondered if Father felt that way too and that was why he'd stopped coming with us to the weekly service, when all four of us had always gone together. Before.

'Good morning, Morag,' Mrs McLeod said, taking Mother's hand in both of her own. 'I wonder if I could borrow Freyja for the rest of the day. I need some help with a commission I've received.' In the preceding months, with her persistent encouragement, I'd spent many hours with Mrs McLeod taking and developing photographs and my interest in photography had grown.

They walked along the gravel path, arm-in-arm, chatting about the project Mrs McLeod was working on. I tried to walk as close to them as was possible so I could overhear their conversation. They spoke very softly, and Mother had her head bowed so it was difficult to make out their words. I sensed that Mother was reluctant to allow me to go, as Mrs McLeod patted her forearm as if to reassure her. This was something I wouldn't have noticed once, but spending so much time with Mrs McLeod, observing the way she watched and reacted to the people around her, had taught me to be more attuned to body language, as she called it.

'If you watch carefully enough, Freyja, you'll see that people will tell you everything they're trying to say before they speak. If you capture that in your photographs, they will not only be good interesting photographs, but they'll tell a story too.'

I didn't understand everything Mrs McLeod said, but one thing I did know was that she was continually trying to make me look and see, but at what and to what purpose I had no idea.

'You think it will help?' This was Mother speaking.

She looked back at me. Her eyes had grown larger at the same time as her face had shrunk, collapsing in on to the bones so her skull was visible. Her look scared me and I tried as often as I could not to stare directly at her.

'Yes Morag.'

We walked on in silence to the road. Mother took hold of my hand, clinging on so tight the tips of my fingers throbbed in time with the beating of my heart.

'Mrs McLeod has asked if you would help her this afternoon with an art project. Would you like that?'

I saw the flicker in her eye, the one that said *say no, say you're too busy*, but the thought of another Sunday sitting inside, Mother upstairs in her room, a monotony of prayers repeating themselves over and over, whilst Father sat in his armchair waiting and waiting, was too much.

'Yes, I'd like that,' I said.

Mrs McLeod grinned at me. 'That's great Freyja. We'll have some lunch and then set to work. Let's go and fetch your camera first though. We'll need that.'

The three of us set off home to collect the camera whilst Mrs McLeod explained to me that she had been asked to paint a child's eye view of Falun for a project in Edinburgh and she needed my help to enable her to see the island in that way. We would go out together and take the photos, and at her house later, we'd develop them in her dark room. The prospect of this excited me more even than the taking of the photographs and once we collected the camera from home, we sped off to Lochinsay.

After a light lunch of bread and cheese, we stepped outside. The wind was fierce and tore at our clothes, trying to rip them from our backs. The clouds raced across the sky, causing spears of light to shower on to the Atlantic as though arrows were being shot. We didn't take the Sky Path initially, but instead headed southwards to where the cliffs rose to their highest point on the island in huge multi-layered stacks of variations on black, white and grey called The Great Stacks. We hardly spoke, as the wind whipped our words away as soon as they were out of our mouths. I'd asked Mrs McLeod exactly what it was she wanted me to capture, but all she said was, 'Take what you see. I want to see Falun the way you see it. What's important to you and what's not. Don't think about it, just take whatever you want, in the way you want to present Falun to me.'

The Great Stacks were beautiful and full of chattering birds in the way the cliffs at Skopinsay had been. I snapped them close up so I could make out each individual bird, and from further away so they became a clustered mass of white. The images reminded me of my trip to Skopinsay with Joe. I'd hardly seen him since the accident last autumn, mainly because he'd been in hospital for many weeks with his leg, but once he'd returned home, the easiness we'd once had between us had vanished. I saw he didn't trust me, he didn't say so, not outright, but when I'd pressed him about visiting him again (his house was one of the few places I was allowed to go to unaccompanied and I wasn't keen to lose that small freedom) he said 'Jeanie wouldn't have been so careless,' before turning his head to the wall and not looking back.

I put the camera down. I didn't want to take these photographs. Mrs McLeod must have noticed my reticence as she indicated that we should head back northwards towards Tor

Ness Head.

'It's where you know best, Freyja. The results will be more interesting.'

We walked close together along the narrow Sky Path. Mrs McLeod took my arm through hers. 'Are you missing school?' she said.

I looked up at her surprised. We hadn't been discussing my schooling, or lack of it. I didn't know what to say. Of course I missed school. I missed the walk along the brae early in the morning; the anonymity of being in a class of other children rather than the spotlight existence I endured at home where there was nowhere to hide, no time to daydream out of the window for even a moment; my lack of friends now that even Joe didn't want much to do with me; no one to answer for me when I didn't know the answer. Not knowing the answer was something that happened less regularly. I couldn't bear the humiliation of being caught out in my ignorance and the corresponding look of disappointment on Mother's face, that had I been more than I was, I would have known. If I'd been Jeanie. So I made sure I did know the answers, swotting at night when I should have been asleep. I was better educated as a result, there was no doubt, but the days were long and my blood boiled and burned with agitation at the lack of an escape route.

What did Mrs McLeod want me to say? She was always honest with me, so I decided I'd be honest too.

'Yes,' I said. 'I am.'

Mrs McLeod paused for a moment before speaking. 'There's an opportunity for you, if you'd like. A boarding school, in the countryside on the outskirts of Inverness. It's a good school, for girls. I think you may like it there.'

'Is it where Jeanie was going?' I couldn't bear that. I couldn't bear to take her place there as well as here.

'No, Freyja. It's one I think would suit you more. I know the headmistress there, from years ago. When I was living in Ontario.'

'What about Mother?' I thought about how she'd been earlier, how distressed she'd been at the thought of me leaving her behind for that afternoon. How would she stand for me to leave her for a whole term? 'Aren't I too young? Jeanie wasn't going to go until she was eleven.'

'No, you're not too young. Many girls, with army fathers board from a younger age. Don't you worry about your Mother. She'll be fine here with me, if you agree that is. I'll speak to her on your behalf, tell her it's in your interests. You're a clever girl, Freyja. You need to make the most of your talents.'

I smiled up at her as she took my hand. I was glad she was my friend. Out of everyone I knew, she was my only real friend. She was the only one who, when she looked at me, saw me. Freyja MacAulay. And not the sister who was left behind.

We spent the next couple of hours photographing every inch of Tor Ness Head before heading back to Lochinsay with a film full of photographs. Mrs McLeod and I spent the remainder of the afternoon developing the photographs in the warm red light of her dark room, hanging the photos from lines by pegs until the room resembled wash day in our garden.

'As it's getting late, dear, I wonder if it would be better if you stayed the night. Shall I ask your Mother?'

I nodded eagerly. Unlike other children I knew who got to spend the night at their grandparents' homes or with their cousins, I'd never had the opportunity. Mother's parents were dead and she was an only child. Father's parents were too old and the only cousins I had, had moved away to Shetland and we never saw them, so spending the night at Lochinsay was more than I'd dared hope for. Mrs McLeod disappeared to call home and make the arrangements. I kept my fingers crossed, praying that Mother would say yes.

Mrs McLeod returned, holding a huge white canvas. 'That's sorted out. Now, what I'd like you to do is arrange a collage of the photographs you took today on this board. I want it to best represent how you see Falun. As you do it, I want you to remember that what you don't see in the photographs, what's not there, is as important, if not more important than what you've chosen to include. Later we'll look and see what you've done.'

Mrs McLeod put the wireless on to accompany us and as she painted, sketching out on the canvas images from our day, only briefly referring to the sketches she'd made in her notebook, I arranged and rearranged the photographs. I discarded the ones I'd taken of the Great Stacks and focused instead on the ones of Tor Ness Head. As I threw them on to the don't use pile, I recalled what Mrs McLeod had said about what not being there being as important, or even more important, that what was there and I knew she was right. I thought of Joe in his bed turning away from me; of Mother kneeling on her hard bedroom floor in front of that stark wooden cross; of Father sitting night after night in the armchair. All of them waiting, all of them knowing what I'd missed, what I'd not seen: that Jeanie not being here with us, was far more important than my still being here ever could be.

Tryggr, Falun, Orkney Islands
May 1964

I went to St Catherine's School for Girls in the Easter term of 1956. I was ten years old. Annie was right: it was good for me. I didn't realise at the time, but Annie paid for my education. Father's business floundered after Jeanie left; I don't think he had the heart for it in the way he once had and instead of spending hours at sea fishing, he trawled along the coastline looking for her. I became the daughter Annie never had, but had wanted so desperately. She became Annie eventually. She insisted on it and it felt more natural. Mother and Father didn't like it; they found it disrespectful and embarrassing, but between the two of us it was easy. Annie put me at the centre of her world. She made me feel loved and wanted. Being the centre of Mother and Father's attention, however, trapped me, leaving me suffocated and desperate to flee. Although I was nervous about leaving Falun and going to boarding school, I was excited too. I'd missed being surrounded by children my own age, missed having friends, but more than anything I missed the time before Jeanie left when I'd existed in a world where nothing bad had happened. Although time had passed, it hadn't healed the raw agony of us losing Jeanie. That continued to smoulder and burn in the midst of the three of us, veiling us in a sea of smoke so thick we could no longer see each other. I still looked for her out in the waves around Tor Ness Head, but it never was her I saw pushing up through the skin of the sea, or if it was, she preferred where she was and remained there.

St Catherine's School consisted of a big old house set in a remote woodland near Inverness. The dormitories were in a separate modern block and there were six girls in one dormitory. We had some privacy in the form of a curtain that we could draw around our beds when we wanted to, but mostly we didn't. For many of us girls, it was our first time away from home. Some of the girls found it hard being away from their families and cried themselves to sleep at night and I envied them their connections to their homes that they now missed. That's what Jeanie would have been like. She'd have found it a terrible wrench being ripped away from us and transplanted here in the middle of the woods, an unfamiliar landscape where shadows and light acted differently, making you see things that weren't there. I wished I missed home in the way the others did, but I found it a relief to be away from the oppressive gloom of Tryggr, to be free to walk in the woods with the smell of pine under my feet, to be somewhere where no one expected me to be like someone else, where no one was disappointed that I was the one left. I started cross-country running and soon I was on the school team, hurtling through the woods and across the open countryside leaving everything behind me.

As time passed, I preferred to stay at St Catherine's in the holidays rather than go home to Tryggr and so sometimes I stayed behind at school to assist the younger girls whose families were abroad, in the army for example, or in the diplomatic service. I'd tell them the stories of the selkies and the other myths and legends from my childhood that Jeanie had brought to life for me, but I never mentioned her, I pretended she'd never existed and I was an only child. I did it not so I wouldn't be asked questions about her, nor to save any embarrassment on their part, people never knew what to say if I did tell them, but I did it to spite Jeanie. I wanted to hurt her by rubbing her out of my life, the way she'd hurt me by walking out on me, not caring one jot how it would affect me, how I would survive without her.

Mother, Father and Annie were all avid correspondents whilst I was away. Mother and Father in particular. They wrote me long letters telling me about the life I'd left behind and I began to feel I knew more about them by being apart from them, than I'd ever have known if we'd remained as we were. Mother's latest letter described her new business venture. She'd bought the two rundown cottages along the track from Tryggr, about a mile away. Annie forced her into it, she said, along with her new friends in her women's support group.   That made me laugh as I imagined Annie doing just that. The twin spinster sisters who'd lived there had died within a couple of weeks of each other, their only relative a distant cousin in Edinburgh who had no interest in The Cottages.

'They had a quiet burial at the Kirk. Hardly anyone went. Sad really,' Mother wrote. That made me shudder. There's something about the dead lying side by side in that graveyard that I can't abide and I never went near the place. 'I don't remember if you ever went inside, Freyja but the kitchen was originally a small room at the end of a long corridor. Annie insisted, she did as you can imagine, your Father and I were against it, that we knock the wall out between the kitchen and the sitting room. She said it would be better, more sociable. I hate to admit it, but she's right. It is better. It's how the rooms are in Ontario apparently. I'm sure you'll be pleased, Freyja. When you come home and see it.'

I was pleased Annie had forced them into doing that. Mother and Father's letters became upbeat and jolly, providing me with a small glimmer of the way they'd once been, and Annie confirmed that they had started to live again, just a little, but enough.

When I did go back to Falun, I would, more often than not, go to Lochinsay and stay with Annie. I couldn't bear the isolation and loneliness at Tryggr, even with Mother and Father's better mood. I'd grown up, I'd seen new things, had new experiences, met people from all over the world. I'd seen that there was more beyond the tiny life I'd led on Falun, and yet at Tryggr nothing had really changed. Jeanie's absence bloomed as strongly as ever and showed no sign of wilting. Mother paced in the kitchen or prayed in her room and Father sat in his armchair all evening, all night mostly, waiting and waiting. If it hadn't been so overwhelmingly sad and oppressive, I would have laughed at the ridiculousness of it. But I didn't. I ran away. Like Jeanie. And I ran towards Annie who had the kind of exciting, wild life I now craved.

Any artists visiting Falun always found their way to Annie's house and it became a stimulating and exciting environment to be in. The people that came were often wild and carefree and Annie allowed them to indulge themselves as long as it contributed to *artistic freedom,* as she called it. I know Mother, in particular, was unhappy at my new lifestyle and she often called, either on the telephone or in person, to ask me to come back to Tryggr, but I hardly ever went.

One summer, I think it was my third or fourth one after going away, I met Joe in Skellinwall where I'd gone shopping.

'Don't you see what you're doing to them?' he said, meaning Mother and Father. 'It's embarrassing for them to have you living away from home when you're back here. They don't understand why you prefer to be with her.

He stood and waited for me to say something, but I didn't reply. I didn't know what to say, but at the back of my mind I knew there was some truth in what he said. I didn't recognise myself either. Although I loved Annie, and I was enjoying myself, I suspected that this wasn't me, that my artistry was partly an act to fit in.

'I don't know who you are anymore, Freyja,' Joe said as he turned and walked away.

I wanted to call after him, to make him come back so we could talk like we'd always done and he'd see that the old Freyja was still there, still inside me, but I couldn't do it and a part of me knew that I didn't know who I was either.

It was that same summer, I was fourteen, that Annie and I went on our first big trip. Annie had to go to London to meet the owner of the gallery where she was to show her work, and she said it would be good for me to broaden my knowledge of art by visiting the galleries in London. If I'd thought the woodlands surrounding St Catherine's were strange and exciting, they were nothing compared to the noise and chaos of London. Annie laughed at my expression as we stepped off the train at King's Cross Station. The air smelt smoky, but not in the way it did on Falun when we burned peats, but in a metallic, mouldy way that made me wrinkle my nose in distaste. I couldn't imagine the stench would ever leave my nostrils. And the noise! It overwhelmed me, there was so much of it hurtling towards me from all directions and at such different levels and tones I found them hard to distinguish the individual sounds. I loved it.

We stayed in a small hotel in Bloomsbury, near to where the gallery was. The room had heavy chairs with burgundy velvet seats and curly designs in the woodwork. They were the most glamorous things I'd ever seen. We ate in the hotel looking out on to Russell Square. The dining room was silent other than the clinking of cutlery against china and stiff waiters stood by us pouring our drinks into delicate glasses. After a while, we looked at each other and laughed at the ridiculousness of it. It wasn't us to be so staid and proper and after our meal we ran out of the room, holding our laughter in our stomachs until we were out in the noisy street and our voices could be drowned out by the beeping of car horns and the roar of engines.

We stayed in London for the whole week, visiting the British Museum, the National Gallery and Portrait Gallery and other smaller galleries exhibiting collections by only one or two artists. It was the Portrait Gallery I enjoyed the most, as the images were more akin to the photographs I still loved to take – that snapshot of someone's soul at one particular moment fascinated me. During the days we spent together, I realised that I loved Annie more than I loved Mother, maybe even as much as I loved Jeanie and the pain this realisation caused me twisted my insides making me nauseous. How could I think like that? How could I betray them both, with Annie? But even as I questioned myself, I knew the answers: Annie loved me back. She made me happy, excited, alive and saw in me a potential I couldn't see in myself.

One day, after we'd visited the Portrait Gallery, Annie decided she would paint my portrait every summer. I could watch myself grow up that way, she said. She started one evening in our room, making me sit on one of those elegant chairs and stare out of the window on to Russell Square. To begin with I couldn't sit still and not laugh. 'I'll paint you with your mouth open then,' she said. And she did. My head flung back, hair hanging in a thick tangled rope behind me and my cheeks red with laughing. I pretended not to, but I enjoyed the attention she lavished on me. It was the way she looked at me, as if she saw into the heart of me and who I was. No one had ever looked at me in that way before. Once we were home and she showed me the finished painting, it surprised me. She saw a different version of me, and it was one I didn't fully understand and not for the first time I began to worry about who

I was and where the old Freyja had gone. It was at Tryggr that I felt that the most. There I had no place, no corner to squeeze into, no place where I could fit.

By the summer of 1964 I was excited. Not only had I turned eighteen and was about to finish school forever and go to art college in the autumn, but Annie and I were set to go on our big adventure to Canada. She was having her first major exhibition in her home country for years and had asked me to accompany her. I couldn't wait. But a week before we were due to break up for the summer, one of the younger girls came to find me out on the tennis courts, saying that I had to go immediately to see our headmistress, Mrs Joyce. I served one last time and set off back into the main school building. I wasn't worried as I wasn't one of the naughtier girls, despite my wild reputation on Falun and during my whole schooling had rarely been in trouble. St Catherine's had shown me that there was an easier way to be and in the calm environment of the woodland setting and with no expectations of me as to who I was supposed to be, I had finally learned to leave everything behind and relax.

I knocked on Mrs Joyce's study door and walked in. The school nurse and my head of house, Mrs Ashcombe, were both there. Uh-oh, something's up, I thought. Their faces wore an expression that I'd seen before, a mixture of sympathy and pity, that flickered briefly then punched me in the stomach with its reminder of the days after Jeanie left.

'Come in and sit down, Freyja. I'm sorry to have to tell you some sad news. Our friend, Annie McLeod, she's passed away. A car crashed into her when she was shopping in Skellinwall. The driver had a heart attack at the wheel. She died instantly. I'm sorry, she's gone.'

I didn't understand Mrs Joyce's words immediately, my mind didn't at any rate, but my body did. My muscles contracted inwards, crushing my internal organs until I could barely breathe. With those sharp words, I knew I'd been robbed of my most precious thing. Mrs Joyce carried on explaining how my best friend had died, how it was part of the cycle of life to be born, to die, that it happened to everyone. It may well happen to everyone, but it didn't happen to me. I couldn't breathe. My lungs didn't work. They'd been ripped apart. No one could ever have experienced pain like it. Mrs Ashcombe grabbed the back of my head and pushed it, violently, in between my legs, commanding me to breathe.

'How can I breathe when she's dead?' I wailed.

Shouting caused a rush of air to expand my lungs so far, I thought, surely the bones will break. Between them, Mrs Ashcombe and the school nurse carried me screaming and wailing to the sanatorium and laid me on the stiff bed the school kept in there, then they wrapped me in an scratchy brown blanket until finally, my sobs still causing that broken, silent breathing I remembered Mother using after Jeanie left, I managed to fall asleep.

I left St Catherine's soon after that never to return. It was the end of my school career anyway, but to leave under the shadow of dark grief earlier than my classmates and miss out on all the end of year revelry felt doubly devastating. When the ferry docked at Falun harbour, I searched the sea of faces for the familiar sight of Annie who always came to greet me on my return, without even realising what I was doing. I vomited over the handrail. She'd never be there for me again.

As I watched the evening bustle on the quayside, the fishermen repairing nets, the shops shutting up for the evening, friends standing outside of the pub drinking, Betty Tidy from the haberdashery standing gossiping in her doorway, I struggled to comprehend the normality of the scene. The world of Falun carrying on as usual, but without Annie in it, didn't make sense to me. I couldn't understand how everyone could continue their day to day life. How could they not be weighed down by the burden of loss I was dragging behind me?

I walked home to Tryggr, although it no longer felt like my home, but there was no way I could face Lochinsay. My bags had been sent on ahead, but I wanted to reconnect with the island so I walked as slowly as I could. I couldn't bear to go straight to Tryggr, couldn't bear to see looks of pity on Mother's and Father's faces, so I carried on walking along the cliff path until I reached the lichen covered rock Jeanie and I thought looked like a mermaid where I turned inland, walking towards the long grasses where the corncrakes nested. I wanted to be where I'd been with Jeanie, I wanted to tell her the news and talk to her about it. Once I reached the tall grasses, I lay down looking up at the sky, waiting to hear the birds' familiar rasping call. I didn't have to wait for long. I loved that sound. It carried me away, away from Falun and the vacuum Jeanie and now Annie had left behind, to Africa where the birds headed once they left here. I flew on the bird's back across Scotland, over Hadrian's wall, down to London, where I crossed the Channel and headed home to Africa. For a moment I was free. I sat up. Something moved in the grasses. 'Jeanie?' I said. I sat there waiting for her to reply until the gloaming fell, but there was no response.

As I approached Tryggr the lights were already on downstairs. I greeted Mother and Father in turn and then headed upstairs. I couldn't bear to hear their words of consolation, couldn't bear to have to relive over and over again the news that Annie had gone. The bedroom I'd shared with Jeanie hadn't changed much. Our two beds stood where they'd always been with the chest of drawers between them. The blue glass dishes had gone, as had the rag rug on the floor, but the view out of the window over the garden and towards the lighthouse remained as it always had, the blinking eye sending out its searching beam into the half light of the summer night. Whilst I watched it, I had the feeling I often had: that something else occupied the same space as me, that if I turned my head fast enough I'd catch sight of it. All the time I spent looking for this something else, everything around me moved away from me and felt out of place and wrong.

A few days later, I led the funeral procession to the Kirk. It wasn't something either of us wanted, a religious send off. Annie had been vociferous about her lack of belief in any god, as had I, but there wasn't an alternative way to lay her to rest. Even if there had been, I'm not sure I had the energy to fight the general opinion that if Annie had thought about it properly, she'd have realised a proper Christian burial was the best and only way to achieve everlasting peace. What about my peace? I wondered if I'd ever find any again.

A sizeable crowd gathered at the Kirk waiting for us. I wasn't surprised. Annie may have been Falun's wild eccentric, but people liked her for it, admired her too, I think. At the Kirk's gate, my knees buckled and I didn't think I would be able to move forwards, not one inch. It was Joe who came to my rescue. He took hold of my arm, under the elbow like I'd seen him do with the island's older residents and led me inside.

'It's all right, Freyja,' he said.

As I entered the Kirk, the smell of incense and lilies hit me and I faltered again. This time it was Father who supported me. Images flashed through my mind: me as a child too small to reach the floor, legs swinging; Jeanie; chocolate; bells; lilies everywhere; the flash of the lighthouse and a cold stone floor against my face.

'You can do it, peedie one,' Father said.

And I did. I got through it. I sat in the front row and stared at the East wall of the small chapel without seeing. Annie's coffin sat in the aisle. *Don't look at it*, I told myself over and over. Reverend Thomas spoke, but I heard nothing until the silence. I looked up. He beckoned me. Yes, it's your turn to speak. I stood up and walked to the lectern at the front. I had imagined I would cry at this point, that I wouldn't be able to speak the words about her I had planned, but I was beyond crying. The numbness had begun. It started in my fingers and in the soles of my feet, then it spread, creeping silently under my skin until it reached my heart, squeezing it so hard I wondered if it would cease to beat.

Outside, we made our way to the newly dug grave. I saw Father speaking with Betty Tidy and her daughter, Mary. His expression changed from sadness to anger in a flash, blowing red on his cheeks before he turned his back on them and walked towards me, taking my hand and leading me to the grave side.

'What was that about?' I said.

'Small minded imbeciles,' he said.

I wanted to ask him more, but Bill MacKenzie joined us. I could hardly bear to watch as they lowered her into the cold, black earth on thick strong straps that were grotesquely plain. I knew she'd hate them, hate how prosaic they were, how lacking in joy. I should have found something better, found a better way, burned her in *The Ragnhild*, anything. I reached my hand out to grab the faceless men lowering Annie away from me, to stop them, but Father pulled me back and held my hand tight.

'Keep it in, peedie one. Hold it tight inside you. Keep it in.'

So I did. I pushed it down as far as it would go and held my breath until I knew it would stay there and not burst out and race towards the cliff edge, hurling itself into the ocean spreading out below.

People were kind and they waited in the graveyard for me to leave first, to lead the way to Tryggr where the wake would be held. To pay their respects, they said. I wanted them to leave me alone with Annie so I could say everything to her I wanted, everything I'd held back from saying during the service, unwilling to share how much I'd loved her with these people who pretended to know her, but who knew nothing. I headed along the gravel path towards the gate, passing Betty Tidy and Mrs Nugent.

'She stood at that graveside with a stony look of heartlessness,' Betty said. 'That poor woman, duped she's been, by her. She's used poor Annie to get what she wanted and abandoned her own sweet mother in the process. She got the lot, so I hear. That huge house at Lochinsay and money too. Quite a lot if my source is to be believed and I think it is. A right old wormer that one. Should be ashamed of herself. Hello, dear. So sorry for your loss.'

How I didn't hit her I don't know. How I didn't reach out and circle my hands around that thick, spongy neck and squeeze until they met the hard bones of her spine is a miracle, but I walked away from the graveyard and carried on walking. I returned to Tryggr late that night when everyone had gone and the wake was over. I don't remember where I went, only that it was necessary, vital that I continued to place one foot in front of the other and carry on and on until I'd walked myself out. At Tryggr, Mother and Father left me alone. It was the first time I felt they understood what it was I needed and respected me enough to care.

Annie's death changed everything. Betty Tidy was right. I

inherited all her estate, which was considerable, including her large house at Lochinsay. Initially, I said I didn't want it and tried to give it to Mother and Father, saying that they needed it more than me as their only real income was from The Cottages, but they wouldn't have it. They said I could use it to make a better life for myself.

'Go and live, Freyja,' Mother said. 'That's what Annie would have wanted.'

So I did, and whilst at the same time as I became a woman of means and to all intents and purposes things had changed for me quite radically, one thing remained as it had always been: I felt I was once again alone in the world and all I wanted was to be free of everything and everyone I'd known, to cut loose from Falun and run.

LIGHT

Lochinsay, Falun, Orkney Islands
June 1964

When we pulled up outside Annie's house, I saw immediately that the house had lost its soul, that it had closed its eyes and fallen into a sleep it didn't wish to be woken from.

'Shall I?' said the solicitor, holding out the door key.

'No, I will,' I said.

Mr Phelps looked surprised, but he handed it to me. I could see that he thought this was too much for me, that I wouldn't cope with walking into the house where I'd spent so much time, without Annie being there. I was also aware that, like most of the Falun community, he was unsure about handing over this house and all Annie's estate to an eighteen-year-old girl. Annie had made no provision in the will for my inheritance to be supervised or controlled in any way, probably because she had not expected to die when she had, but Annie had trusted me to do the right thing, to be responsible and I wasn't about to let her down.

The lock was stiff and it took me a couple of attempts to turn the key. Annie never bothered to lock the house. *Who would come all the way out here to rob a poor artist?* she would always say to guests who questioned her faith in human nature. Of course, she was far from poor, but no one had known that and anyway none of us Falun inhabitants ever locked any doors. There was little point. But someone, Mr Phelps probably, had locked it now; the house had taken issue with the invasion and together with the salty air had attacked the mechanism.

Inside the air was stale and thick with the smell of turps and oil paints. For a moment I couldn't take another step into the emptiness, couldn't disturb that last remaining element of her – the smell of her paints – for I knew that once I walked in and pushed it aside it would be gone forever. Her last breaths still circulated in the stale air, but with the opening of the door, even that part of her was gone.

I wandered around the house, which remained exactly as it had been the day she'd last walked out. She'd expected to come back, hadn't expected that the washing up she'd left in the sink to finish later, wouldn't be done, that her clothes still flapping on the washing line would never be worn again. I didn't want to move out of the relative safety of the main part of the house into her studio, but I knew I had to. I had to face the absence of her head on before it overwhelmed me.

Her last unfinished painting stood on the largest of her easels. The paint, still wet, glistened in the light. It would take weeks, months even, to dry as Annie painted with thick globules of paint so that her paintings had form and texture which leapt out at you from the canvas. This last painting was of Skellinwall harbour. Her boat rocked softly in the foreground. The ground beneath me felt far away. I realised that the boat too was now mine. How could I take her out without Annie's reassuring hand on the tiller?

I walked around her paint splattered stool, careful not to tread in the shadow of her leaning against it as she painted, towards the back of the studio where the series of paintings she'd painted from my collages still leaned against the wall. I couldn't negotiate the space, and I knocked over a line of turps bottles, sending them crashing to the floor. Mr Phelps came running in after me.

'I'm fine,' I said, but I wasn't.

My hands, my feet, my entire body felt wrong, out of proportion and I wasn't sure I knew how to bring myself back together again, how to rearrange myself back into the shape I'd once been. I no longer knew how to walk even.

I stood in front of the series of paintings not understanding why they were still there. I thought they'd been commissioned years ago for an arts project somewhere as a way of portraying Falun to schoolchildren who had no opportunity to travel and visit our remote island in the far outreaches of the country. I leafed through each of them. They were all there, all six of them. Annie had asked me to rearrange my collage many times, but I don't think she ever made me see what it was she had been driving at and eventually, after I'd gone to St Catherine's, she let it go. I looked at them afresh and although I noticed something strange about them, I couldn't articulate it.

A movement out of the corner of my eye disturbed my

thoughts: a man walking along the cliff edge. A man with shocking white hair tied back in a ponytail. His hair was so long at first I mistook him for a woman, but his height, build and gait suggested prime masculinity. He was very striking and I stared at his odd way of striding, trying to ascertain why he was walking in such an exaggerated manner. When I returned to look at Annie's paintings, I had forgotten what it was about them that had unsettled me.

Mr Phelps called me into the kitchen and as we sat at the old oak table where Annie and I had always eaten, he went through each of the documents he'd brought with him: one for each part of my inheritance. I signed where I needed to and various piles formed between the two of us, together with a list of instructions for me to follow.

'My condolences, Miss MacAulay. I'm sorry for your loss and that you have so much here to deal with. If I can be of further assistance, please don't hesitate to call me.'

After a suitable pause and moment of reflection he asked if he could drive me home. I had come to think of Lochinsay as my home, but I realised he meant Tryggr.

'No, thank you, Mr Phelps. I think I'll stay here a while. Bring in the washing, clear up, that sort of thing.'

'If I can be -.'

'No, thank you, I'm fine by myself.'

Mr Phelps tried to hide his obvious relief and I almost changed my mind and asked him to stay, but I preferred to be alone with the ghosts of the house and I was glad in the end to watch him drive away.

Outside, I walked around to the back of the house where I stood on the cliff edge, the great Atlantic rollers crashing into the rocks beneath me and looked northwards towards Tor Ness lighthouse. Something flickered in my mind, but it disappeared before I could grab hold of it. Back in the garden I gathered in the salt stiff washing and folded it into the wicker basket Annie always used. I would keep some of her more eccentric items. She'd worn them with joy and I would wear them and keep that aspect of her alive. Once I'd folded all the washing, I picked up the heavy basket and as I walked back towards the house I caught sight of the strange man again as he made his way along the Sky Path back towards Tor Ness Head. This time I saw the reason for his odd gait. He was sliding on what looked like skis with wheels, pulling himself across the rough ground with long poles.

Inside the house, I dumped the washing basket in the boot room and wandered into the studio. I shifted through the canvasses in the very back of the room, looking between them. I wasn't sure what I was looking for and I stopped and scanned the rest of the room. Then I saw her large sketchbooks piled up on the shelves above me. I pulled them down and found them: the collages I'd made all those years ago. Some of the photographs had come unstuck and they floated to the floor along with the dust that lifted from the disturbance. The photographs were faded and curled at the edges. I gathered them together and placed them carefully into one of the large envelopes Mr Phelps had left for me. It was clear to me how I would spend the summer before going to art college in the autumn. I'd retake each of the photographs and arrange them again. I hoped that by doing that I'd see it – what Annie had wanted me to see. It would be my legacy to her. It would keep her alive and I wouldn't be so alone.

During the years I'd been away at boarding school, Mother's new holiday letting business had become successful. The Cottages looked lovely. I particularly liked the fact that in place of usual door knockers they'd used iron cleats from one of Father's old dinghies from when we were children. Jeanie and I had loved that dinghy, playing with it in the surf, rushing in on the water, playing shipwrecks. Joe had joined in our games, playing the part of the native on the beach, hauling us to safety. In another version, I'd been the siren sitting on the rocks, luring Jeanie and Joe into danger. For me that had been the better of the two games.

One of the sisters had played the piano and Mother argued to keep it, although Father disagreed. Mother won and the piano remained in Number Two. Mother focused on letting The

Cottages to wildlife enthusiasts and it became a good business for her and for me too. When I did return home in the holidays, although I spent most of my time at Lochinsay, Annie encouraged me to run errands for Mother and our visitors and soon I began to earn a little money which I saved for my college fund. I enjoyed meeting the guests too, as like Annie they gave me a window into another world, a world far away from Falun and the ghosts that haunted me there, a world I was increasingly ready to rush into and join.

A couple of days after meeting Mr Phelps at Lochinsay, I was on the beach with the sun beginning to fall into the horizon. The remains of the Midsummer fire had finally been washed away, but the lanterns still lay at the base of the cliffs. I had a flash of memory of Jeanie and I placing the last lanterns we'd ever placed together nine years before. How excited I'd been that night at staying up late to watch the never-ending day. So many years had passed since her disappearance and other than the three of us – Mother, Father and I - no one remembered Jeanie any longer, not in the way we did, not enough to make it hurt. For a long while afterwards I asked everyone I knew each time we met if they'd seen her or had any clue as to her whereabouts, but they gave me strange looks, then shifted their gaze away from me and changed the subject and after a while I had stopped asking them. What had driven her to walk out of the door and never come back remained s mystery I had no answer to.

To the left of me, the lighthouse beam cut through the gloaming sending tunnels of opaque light up into the high clouds that had blown in. It was late and I needed to complete my chores for the day. Reluctantly, I left the peaceful quiet of the beach and I began to walk quickly along the road towards The Cottages. My job was to ensure our holiday guests had everything they needed; enough peats, milk, bread, eggs, butter and cheese. Our guests often commented that one of the reasons they stayed at The Cottages time and time again was due to the fact that their basic needs were catered for and they didn't have to trek into Skellinwall every time they needed things. Mother often gave them sausages and bacon too which everyone said were the best they'd ever tasted. It was only then that I saw

Mother smile, as though the act of providing for someone was the only thing that could make her happy. On the way to The Cottages I went home and put some cheese, bread, eggs and butter into a string bag to take with me. I decided I'd take my bicycle so that I could come back sooner. I had a few books I needed to finish before the library van arrived from Kirkwall. Soon I'd be at art college and I could look at as many books as I wanted without having to wait a month for the van to come.

Both cottages were occupied. Number One was let to two Danish women in their early twenties, who spent their time walking the coastline laughing and chatting, their long blonde hair blowing in the wind. They were sophisticated and incredibly glamorous and I yearned to have the freedom they had to travel abroad. That could have been Annie and me touring Canada as we'd planned. How I had longed to go with her, to stand by her side at the opening of her exhibition and taste my first glass of champagne. I steered my bicycle on to the grass verge and allowed it to fall on to the grass, the back wheel still spinning. I leaned forward, trying to pull enough air into my tight lungs, but no matter how hard I sucked the air in, it wasn't enough. I collapsed on to the ground and put my head between my bent knees. Why did you leave me, Annie? The tears finally came, thick and fast, and with them came the fury that I'd tried so hard to suppress; the anger I felt that she'd let me down and left me alone.

I sat on the verge until the damp had soaked through into my clothes and the tears had finally stopped. What a mess I must look. I rubbed my face and climbed back on to my bike and hoped I wouldn't meet any of our guests that evening. I hadn't yet met the man who was staying in Number Two. We hadn't seen him arrive on his due date a few days earlier; Mother had left the key in the pot on the windowsill so he could open up himself. Smoke had poured from the chimney the previous night, so we assumed he was there and wanted time alone. Although it was unusual for guests to not announce themselves and say hello, it wasn't unheard of. This man, who was according to Mother from the west of Norway, had booked the Cottage for the whole three months of summer. He'd have enough time to be alone during that time and I didn't understand why he'd kept himself so wrapped in his solitude. No one knew what he planned to do for three months. How anyone could choose to come and spend the summer here, when the whole world was available to them, was a mystery to me.

As I turned the corner of the track leading to The Cottages I saw with dismay that the downstairs lights were on in both of them. I rubbed my face again in the hope that would make me look more presentable. Dark grey smoke puffed out of Number Two's chimney. I leaned my bike up against the side wall and knocked on the door of Number One. No one answered, so I hung their bag of provisions on the hook Father had fastened to the wall and moved along to Number two. I could hear music playing inside; a single instrument playing a mournful tune that ceased the moment I knocked. I heard a muffled voice shout out what I thought was *wait a moment* accompanied by rustling and shifting, followed by silence.

'Hei.'

Standing in the open doorway was the man I'd seen out at Lochinsay. He had shoulder length hair, the blondest I'd ever seen and he filled the entire space. The Vikings had arrived. He leaned against the door frame with his right arm extended up along the woodwork and bent over at the elbow, so his fingertips rested on top of his head. In his left hand, he held a violin. That must have been what I'd heard, I thought. The angle pulled his t-shirt tight across his chest and I could see that he was fit, muscular. And he was younger than I had anticipated: mid-thirties probably. The strange skis he'd been using earlier were propped up against the wall in the hallway.

'Hei, Magnus Olafson,' he said, holding out his hand to me.

Hand him the bag, introduce yourself and walk away, Freyja. He stared at me with eyes so dark brown I couldn't make out the pupils. He really stared at me. Say something, you peedie idiot. But I couldn't either speak or look away, so instead I simply stood and stared back. His look made something stir inside me that I didn't understand. We remained like that for several moments until finally, I held the string bag of groceries out for him to take.

'What are those?' I said, pointing to the skis. Why did you ask him that? Of all the things. You haven't even introduced yourself.

'Land skis, to practise cross country skiing for the winter.'

I nodded and he took the bag from me. The back of his hand brushed against mine with the lightest of touches and I paused, my wrist against his, feeling the warmth of his skin. He left his hand there for a moment, his gaze still penetrating mine, then he took the bag, turned away and closed the door, leaving me alone with my hand burning. I remained on the doorstep for a moment trying to understand what had happened, but I couldn't explain it.

I headed back along the track edged with vibrant sea pinks and anemones that mimicked the reds and pinks of the evening sky looming above me. The light made everything sharper and more intense and I saw how beautiful Falun could be. As I walked, it was like I was balancing on a tightrope over one of the geos that plummeted into the sea and the only way to survive was to keep going forwards, to not look down or back, or I would fall into the raging ocean and drown.

After I met Magnus, I spent more time at Tryggr, hoping my proximity to The Cottages would lead to us meeting again. Mother liked me being there and a little colour began to creep back into her cheeks. Father though, barely acknowledged my return and like me, he spent hours away from home, but where he disappeared to all that time we didn't know. On his return, he would sit back in the armchair facing the door and remain there until it was time for him to go out again. I saw Magnus a few times out on his skis, marching up and down the cliff paths, and sometimes along the brae that led to the island school and into Skellinwall, but I couldn't find a good enough reason to approach him and I wasn't brave enough to speak to him without one. The wild weather arrived, bruising the sky and stabbing the landscape with its fierce biting winds. I didn't leave the house, not even to go to The Cottages, but I watched for him out of my bedroom window, desperate to catch a glimpse of him as I looked towards the lighthouse and the cliffs. That would have been enough. Every minute that passed without me seeing him my stomach churned, leaving me restless and unable to eat.

'You'll not go out into that wildness. We've work enough to keep us busy here,' Mother said when she saw me pulling on my coat after I'd been home for a few days.

I knew it was fear making her protective, her fear that should I venture out, the wind, or some other malevolent force, would pick me up and carry me away from her as Jeanie, and now Annie, had been. I gave in and took off my coat. I'd stay with her for now. Part of me wished she'd remained detached from us, as she'd been in the early months after Jeanie's disappearance, sitting in her chair unapproachable and distant, not noticing if I was there or not. Although she had improved, Mother still existed on the edge of panic and until she pulled back from it, I realised, she'd keep me there with her as a way of anchoring her to solid ground and stopping her falling into the abyss. I yearned to break free from her, to run out and push my way through the rain-soaked air and stand on the edge of Tor Ness Cliffs, with my toes reaching out into the emptiness and my arms outstretched and wait for the wind to pick me up and carry me away, but I didn't, of course.

Mother had harvested trugs full of tomatoes and marrows from the glasshouse before the weather turned and the vegetables were piled in huge mounds on the kitchen table ready for us to turn into chutneys and pickles for the long winter ahead. Mother handed me the knife and I began to chop the tomatoes into small chunks and soon the air around us was sharp and sweet with sugar, vinegar and spices.

'Have you spoken to Mr Olafson yet? Found out what he's doing here?' I said picking up a marrow and slicing it in half before scooping out the fluffy centre pitted with white oval seeds. I liked the sound of his name in my mouth and thinking of him made me smile. I remembered the way the cotton fabric of his t-shirt had outlined the taut muscles of his shoulders and abdomen and the way his dark eyes had seen right into me. I started to chop the marrow into small pieces. Annie would have understood. She'd have let me talk about him as much as I wanted. The knife slid out of my hand and clattered on to the floor. My throat thickened. My eyes bulged until finally they released a stream of tears.

'You keep away from him, do you hear me?'

The sharpness of Mother's tone surprised me and I stopped crying. She slammed her fist on to the chopping board and wiped her hands on the cloth. Her cheeks burned with red blotches as fury seeped out of her and glistened on her skin and I saw her whole body judder as she tried, and failed, to control her anger.

'Freyja? Listen to me. He's no good.'

Mother filled the kettle and slammed it hard on to the range, fixing the old black whistle to the spout. She kept her fist locked around the handle for a few moments and remained like that, with her back to me, as she took a couple of deep breaths. What was it she was afraid of? How did she know he was no good if she hadn't spoken to him?

'Why's he no good? What's he done?'

I hadn't meant to be insolent; I was genuinely curious as to why she'd taken against him when, despite his abruptness and the fact he'd barely acknowledged me, he held a fascination for me that I couldn't let go. I knew Betty Tidy and some of the other women, the usual gossipers, in the village had taken against him as I'd overheard them chatting in the bakers. They'd called him a rude brute, aloof and unfriendly for not having the courtesy to pass the time of day with them. This made me warm to him even more, as I had no wish to spend my time in idle chatter with them any more than he did. My attraction towards him had been as fast and furious as a gannet diving for a herring.

The slap, when it came, was hard and it left behind a tight ringing in my ears. We stood facing each other, Mother's hand still raised as though ready to strike again, and I flinched away from her. I hated her for it and she must have known it. She mumbled sorry under her breath, looked at her hand and lowered it to her side, gripping it with the other until her knuckles bleached. She wouldn't look at me, even though I stared directly at her, and instead she stared out of the window.

When she spoke, her voice vibrated as her lower lip wobbled. 'You have to think of your reputation, Freyja. You don't want to end up like Melanie Houghton.'

The whistle from the kettle pierced the atmosphere between us. Mother turned and removed it from the heat and closed the lid on the hotplate and walked away from me.

'I don't understand,' I yelled after her. 'What's Melanie done? And what's that got to do with Mr Olafson?'

She didn't answer me and next thing I heard she was upstairs, pacing the floorboards in her bedroom. I knew what she'd do next. She'd kneel down before the wooden cross hung like a warning in the centre of the east wall of her bedroom, and beg God for answers as to why he'd deprived her of her one perfect daughter and left the inferior one behind.

There would be no coffee and idle chatter now, no fifteen minutes listening to the weather and shipping forecast on the wireless as we sat at the kitchen table and rested a while, helping ourselves to a couple of spoonfuls of condensed milk straight from the tin. That was a love we both shared. It was the one tiny ritual we had between the two of us that Jeanie had not been part of and despite everything that had happened, and because it was the only thing we had that wasn't tainted with any memories of Jeanie, we had managed to hold on to it. I took the tin can out of the fridge, but my heart wasn't in it and I put it back without having any. I knew Mother would be in her bedroom for hours trying to reaffirm her faith in a god that had betrayed her.

I looked out of the window and saw a figure hunched forwards as he fought against the wind. The air filled his coat and he looked like a tortoise. Magnus Olafson. I didn't hesitate. I would show her that I was old enough to make my own decisions about who I saw and what I did. Annie would have wanted me to take control of my own life and not be constrained by what Mother wanted me to do. That was why she'd sent me away to that school, wasn't it? So I could learn to have my own mind and decide things for myself. It's what Father had always taught us. Before. I pulled on my raincoat and ran across the garden to the dry stone wall where it intersected the footpath on its way towards the moor. I wondered if Mother would look out of her window to see where I'd gone, but I kept marching forwards. I didn't look back.

When he saw me on the path, he smiled, as though he'd known all along that I'd be there waiting for him.

'Can I walk with you?' I said.

'Yes. That would be nice.'

His voice had the Scandinavian lilt I liked. He held out his hand to help me over the wall and once I was over and walking along beside him, I didn't want him to let go, but he did.

We walked along the edge of Tor Ness Cliffs until we reached the point furthermost west. We stood in silence, staring out at the evening sun, still high in the summer sky, our shadows burned on to the ground behind us. Neither of us spoke. Above, the gulls and the gannets screeched and yelled. For a moment I couldn't seem to catch my breath; the remnants of Mother's anger still resonated inside me. In front of us the lighthouse erupted from the foaming sea, the rocks on which it stood obscured by the high tide. The water at its base had turned a bright blue as the waves fizzed and crashed.

'This view makes you sad, yes?' he said.

I couldn't speak, so I nodded. We waited for a while until the sweep of the lighthouse beam started its revolutions for the night.

'Why have you come to Falun?' I said at last.

'I have come to write.'

'Books?' I said.

'No,' he laughed. 'Classical music. I have come here to write my fifth symphony. I used to come to these islands as a boy, with my parents, so I thought I would return and see if they inspire me now as much as they did then. When I last came, I started to write something. It was juvenile, not developed in any way, but there is something in it that has haunted me and the theme of it has started to come through in my most recent works. I want to see if I can find what it is I captured, see if I can make it come to life. You understand?'

'I think so,' I said.

'Shush now and listen with me,' he said.

We stood there the two of us, as still as the seamarks looking out over the ocean. His eyes were closed.

'Hear that roar and hiss of the sea beneath us, that is the bass line, the cellos and the double basses. They run underneath the whole sound. They are the solid rock on which the rest sits. There, that rumble against the rocks? Do you hear it, Freyja? Listen. Listen. That is the timpani. Then the wind as it whistles through the grasses? That is the woodwind. The oboe and the clarinet. Then above everything, the violins come soaring in. They are the birds coming in to roost for the night and there is a change in key and tempo here, Freyja, can you feel it? From G major to E minor, so satisfying, don't you think?'

He kept his eyes closed as he spoke. I'd not understood anything he'd said, but I knew the passion behind it, the joy he found in the sounds he heard. I recognised that as like the joy I had in framing an image, seeing the shot spread out in front of me clear as anything.

'Will you help me, Freyja?' he said. He turned to me. 'Show me your island. Show me the places that no one else sees. What it is that makes it special. What it is that makes it yours.'

He took my face in his hands. I nodded, cupping my cheeks into his palms. He bent his knees so he could look into my eyes. We remained like that, searching inside each other, for a long time. I didn't dare look away. In his eyes I saw something, pain, longing. I couldn't describe it, but for a brief moment I thought he might cry. He released me, kissed the top of my head, rested his cheek on my hair, then headed up the hill towards the seamark, the only witness to the moment I felt crushed by my feelings for a man I barely knew.

Ceredigion Mental Asylum, West Wales
June 1983 1.30pm

Shall we go for a walk outside?

We're allowed to go out after lunch, only as far as the tea-room on the hill. After that, only the men are allowed to walk.

They're not permitted on the top half. We're not allowed to mix except at the tea-room where we can be supervised. We can go and have tea and a Welsh cake. It's a nice afternoon. We have to take advantage of there being no rain.

Here's the path to the tea-room. We need to go this way. Don't the trees make you laugh, the way they're bent over like that?

It's the wind that does it. It makes them look like they're running away.

I'd like to be able to do that.

I'm glad you've brought me these photographs. It's nice to have an idea of what the years have been like for you.

This is a lovely picture. What a beautiful house sitting like that next to the lake. Such magnificent mountains too.

I never knew it looked like that. It's not like back home, that's for sure.

And that's you sitting in the doorway? Very nice.

I like this one the best. You look so happy.

I know what you're saying, that pictures can lie. I know all too well how photographs can hide the truth from you.

When I look closely, I can see it. Magnus has got that look in his eye, the one I remember from the last time we were together.

If you hadn't said that, that this was the moment you knew he could no longer carry on and you had to do something, I might have missed it. But you're right. It is there.

You must have wondered if he would survive.

Tryggr, Falun, Orkney Islands
July 1964

Billy Jansson hurtled along our track faster than usual, his bicycle tyres skidding on the loose stones by our gate as he came to a sudden halt. His bag, heavy with the day's post, swung ahead of him, carried forward by its own momentum and almost pulling him off the bike. Mother and I were standing outside shaking crumbs at the chickens from our aprons and we both had to sidestep Billy so we weren't injured.

'Billy Jansson, what in the name of all that's holy are you doing coming at us like that? Look what you've gone and done.'

Mother pointed to the squawking mayhem at our feet. The chickens flapped in a frenzy sending pillows of dust up into the air.

'Sorry, Mrs MacAulay.'

'What's with all the hurry today?' Mother said, herding the chickens towards the back of the house.

Billy rested his bicycle against the gate and took a bundle of letters out of his bag. He looked pleased with himself, his huge smile stretching his mouth.

'Melanie Houghton's said she'll marry me, Mrs MacAulay. We've planned to finish early today so we can catch the afternoon ferry to the Mainland. I'm going to buy her a ring.'

Billy stretched upwards and broadened outwards as he made his way through his speech and he went from being a boy to being a man in that moment.

'Well, I suppose that's great news, isn't it, Freyja?' Mother said.

She tried hard to hide it, and I'm certain no one else would have noticed, but I did. I saw that small flinch that began as a flicker in her left eye and made its way across her cheek like a subterranean worm until it grabbed hold of her neck and shook her head with a violent pulse. I knew what she was thinking about: Jeanie. Jeanie had been in the same school year as Billy and Melanie. That could have been Jeanie escaping on the afternoon ferry, her arms resting on the railings as the wind blew through her long hair, looking forward to a bright future with her sweetheart by her side. Instead it was Melanie Houghton who would marry. I tried to distract Billy from Mother's distress.

'What've you got there?' I said looking at the unusually large bundle of letters Billy had in his fist.

Mother stood motionless, her apron flying in the wind, staring into the distance. She hadn't heard what I said.

'These are for The Cottages, for Number Two. I was wondering, Freyja, would you mind?'

He held out the bundle which consisted of five thick, blue airmail letters. I looked at Mother, but she was still dazed, encased in a world of 'what if?' I took the bundle from Billy's hand. They were all from Norway. The handwriting, small and precise, was unmistakably female. The smile that had formed on my face at the prospect of having a good reason to go and see Magnus remained, but underneath it my skin felt taut and strained as I tried to hide the desolation that gripped me. Of course he would have girls writing to him, I reasoned. A man like him. He wouldn't be interested in a small island nobody like me. I slipped the letters into my pocket, saying I would take them. I prayed that Mother hadn't noticed and she wouldn't, therefore, stop me taking them to *that man*, as she referred to him when she thought I wasn't listening. She tried to hide from me the fact that she despised him, not wishing to appear rude about a guest which was a great sin in her eyes, but I knew all the same.

'Don't stand there looking stupid, Freyja. Here are the eggs, now off you go. You too Billy or you'll miss that ferry,' Mother said. She had brought herself back together enough to take over once again, but her eyes still glistened and when she thought we weren't looking, she stared at the ground and wiped her eyes.

Mother shooed Billy out of the yard and turned to go into the house. As I walked towards The Cottages, I remembered I'd forgotten my camera, so I darted back into the house. Mother and Father were in the sitting room and I could hear them discussing Billy's engagement.

I was about to leave when I heard Father say, 'I expect the Houghtons are none too pleased about it, a clever girl like her, who had a good future ahead of her. It's shameful.'

'Now, now, Wallace. At least he's doing the right thing by her.'

'You call that the right thing? Making the girl marry him and spend the rest of her life with a boy like that, one who can't tie two ends of a rope together? It's not right. Not on this occasion it's not. I'll be back for tea later.'

I didn't want them to know that I'd been listening to their conversation, so I grabbed my camera from my hook by the front door. I wondered how Mother and Father could see his actions so differently. Not wishing to think too much of matters I didn't really care about, I ran as fast as I could towards The Cottages, being careful not to break the eggs or the camera, towards the man who made me skittish and shaky every time he entered my thoughts.

As I approached Number Two, I could hear Magnus's violin piercing the air. He opened the door, took the eggs from me, thanked me and asked me to tell Mother how much he appreciated her efforts. I handed him the bundle of letters and his expression changed from smiling to cold and closed. He pushed the letters into his back pocket.

'Thank you, Freyja. Please excuse me. I must work.'

He closed the door, leaving me standing on the doorstep. The tears pushed against my eyes as I realised I'd been right – someone like him wouldn't have the time for a girl like me. I walked away, digging my fingernails into my palms to stop the tears falling.

I couldn't go back home and face Mother. I headed southwards around Tor Ness Head towards Lochinsay. At the mermaid rock, I turned inland towards the interior and the long grasses before pausing and looking back. Something about the vista in front of me reminded me of a similar image, one I'd seen Annie paint that summer she gave me the camera. I sat there for a long time staring at the view, until eventually the lighthouse's beam began its sweep through the simmer dim. I took the camera out of its case and adjusted the focus. I paused waiting to catch the funnel of light in the centre of the frame. It would be a good photograph. I remembered once I'd taken the picture that it was similar to one of the photographs I'd put into my collages for Annie. Similar, but different. What the differences were stayed on the outskirts of my vision, coming and going with the revolving light, and whatever it was I was trying to see didn't remain in view long enough for me to be able to grasp it. As I carried on walking along the path, the long grasses whipped against my legs leaving striations on my skin, but I didn't care. I pushed my hands into my pockets and felt for the red ribbon that was always there. I ran my fingers along what had once been the smooth silky side but was now worn and frayed at the edges and after a while the action soothed me as it always did. I followed the contours of the land as it dipped into the hollow where the corncrakes nested. The birds began to make their buzz, buzz, buzz calling, sensing an intruder in their territory and I was back in time, back in the game: lying down in the grass I turned to Jeanie, *we're the only ones left, Jeanie, the only humans left on Falun.* We were the last survivors of the Copolips; all that stood between Falun and The Threat. My heart thumped at the knowledge that we were each other's last hope.

Above me, the clouds had blown in and as they raced across the sky, I was racing with them. I gripped handfuls of grass to hold myself on the ground and stop the sensation that I was falling and the towering tors collapsing on to me. Why had Jeanie and I yearned so much to be alone on Falun? Playing Copolisp had been my favourite game. Now that I was completely alone, instead of giving me that uplifting sense of freedom, being alone, being abandoned by everyone I loved, was the worst feeling in the world.

I stood up as the first splashes of rain fell from the darkening sky.

'Where are you, Jeanie?' I yelled into the white night.

The rain fell heavily, splattering on to the grasses and the birds hiding within and there was no sound other than that. Nobody answered me, nobody had heard. Jeanie remained as always, silent.

For a few days, I managed to time my provisions drops at The Cottages for when I had seen Magnus leave. I suspected if it had been one of the beautiful Danish girls who had knocked on the door instead of me, he wouldn't have been so quick to turn them away. He had fallen into a consistent rhythm, walking along the cliff tops at the same time each day – when we were finishing breakfast, at teatime and again at about ten o'clock in the evening. So as soon as I saw him in the mornings, I would grab the bags Mother had prepared, rush along the track to The Cottages and leave them on the hooks. I couldn't face him after he'd been so abrupt when I'd given him the letters. After three days of avoiding him, he missed his early morning walk so I didn't take the bag. I could see the smoke rising out of the chimney. He had stayed in. If I stayed at Tryggr, Mother would make me go, so I took my coat and a sandwich and yelled that I was going to Lochinsay. I made it out of the house before she could reply.

I spent the day on the Lochinsay cliffs re-taking the photographs of The Great Stacks and Tor Ness Head in the distance, followed by hours in Annie's dark room developing them. I still thought of it as Annie's dark room, Annie's house, never as mine. It had taken me a while to be able to enter the dark room and I'd stood outside the closed door for minutes at a time before leaving and saying, *Next time, I'll do it next time*, until I finally found the courage to open it and step inside. It was in that room more than any other in the house that Annie's ghost still lingered. If I closed my eyes, I could imagine her long fingers working quickly and efficiently transferring each photograph from tray to tray. I'd always admired her long fingers which were so full of grace compared to my clumsy stubby ones.

'My mother wanted me to be a pianist. She said it was a shame to waste them, but I had no ear for music,' Annie had said when I'd remarked on them. 'I knew they'd be better at painting.'

I left the photographs from that day's work hanging on the lines; I planned to pick them up the next day. It would give me another excuse to visit Lochinsay and escape Tryggr. Mr

Phelps, the solicitor, had sent me many letters asking what I wanted to do with the house, but I couldn't decide. I walked back into the kitchen at Tryggr and saw the grocery bags still on the kitchen table. Mother pointed at them.

'You've spent the entire day out taking photographs, now you can be useful here, my girl and take these as you should have done this morning,' she said.

As I hurried along the track leading to The Cottages, I saw that the lights were on in Number Two. My stomach churned. Although I wanted to see him, I was terrified of being rejected. At the door, I stood for a moment to compose myself, smoothing my flyaway hair and pricking my cheeks to liven up my face. I licked my finger and ran it along both eyebrows. I took a breath and rapped the iron cleat.

As the sound of metal on wood rang out in the air, I heard a smattering of female laughter from inside, followed by Magnus's deep voice, though what he said I couldn't decipher. I wanted to take back the knock and run. I knew whose laughter that was: Birgitta and Solvej, the two Danish girls. I made to leave, but the door opened and I had no choice but to stay.

'Freyja, how lovely to see you. Come in. We are having coffee and cake,' Magnus said.

His arm circled around me without touching me, guiding me into the cosy sitting room. The peat glowed in the fireplace and together with the warm sugary smell of baking the cottage felt more cosy than I'd ever known it. Birgitta and Solvej sat at the table drinking coffee, a pile of buns laid out in front of them.

'Hei, Freyja. Come and share the cinnamon buns we've made for Magnus.'

Birgitta pulled a chair out for me. It was the one furthest away from where Magnus was. Magnus came up behind me and rapped his palms on the back of the chair.

'Yes, yes, come and eat with us,' he said.

Magnus disappeared into the kitchen, returning with a mug of coffee. Then he picked up his mug from the opposite side of the table before sitting in the chair next to mine. The buttery, cinnamon smell wafted towards me, reminding me that I hadn't eaten all day, but although I was ravenous there was no way I could eat with my stomach turning over and over. Magnus sat stretched out next to me, his legs parallel to mine under the table, his arm resting on the back of my chair so that I could feel the tiny blonde hairs on his skin pricking the back of my neck. I felt myself pulled inside out by my desire to touch him and didn't notice that Solvej had asked me a question.

'A good Norse name, Freyja. Are your parents Scandinavian?' she said again.

'No they're Orcadian. Apparently, Freyja is the goddess of love. We share our surname,' I said turning to Magnus, 'Olafson, is the Norse origin of MacAulay.'

'Ha ha! We are related,' Magnus said.

I knew he was looking at me, dipping his head towards me, but I couldn't look at him. Instead, I focused on rolling the edge of the thin cloth table mat in front of me into a tight spiral whilst I listened to Magnus, Birgitta and Solvej discussing their respective days' activities. Birgitta clasped her mug in between both her hands and leaned forward across the table towards Magnus, tipping her head to one side as if to hear him better. As I watched her watching him, I could see how attractive she found him, and how she was taking care to present herself in what she obviously considered her best light. Had he noticed? I'd seen the girls at school look like that at some of the more handsome boys when they came from other schools for dances. Those boys definitely noticed.

'Better get back to work,' Magnus said, standing up and pulling his chair back.

I saw both Birgitta and Solvej hesitate, unsure how to react to Magnus's sudden desire to be alone.

'Yes, of course. Thank you for the coffee. We'll be leaving you now. Will you be joining us tomorrow morning, Magnus? We're leaving at nine,' Birgitta said. She tossed her head to one side, scooping her long shiny hair into a bunch on one side like a pelt she had flung over one shoulder.

The room became very still. Birgitta's hand, which had rested gently on Magnus's arm, dropped away. Solvej stood with her hand on the door latch, ready to open it. I held my breath. Magnus looked at the floor, then made a movement so small, so delicate, it was almost, but not quite, imperceptible. I don't know if Solvej or Birgitta noticed, but I did. The slight shifting of his body weight from left to right, from them to me and at the same time he placed his arm on the back of my chair, blocking my pathway to the door. And I thought, does he want me to stay? What if he does? What will I say, do?

'I am going to stay here tomorrow and work some more on the slow movement. I will see you again soon I expect,' he said. 'Would you stay for a moment, Freyja. There is something I wanted to ask you.'

I said I could, although all I wanted to do was run out of the door with Birgitta and Solvej. And yet. He'd chosen me over them. Don't go red. Act like it's nothing. It probably is nothing. I should leave as soon as he's said what he wants. Yes. Listen, reply, go. He'd chosen me.

'Good luck with it, Magnus. We'll look forward to hearing it one day,' Solvej said. She turned to me and added, 'I have just remembered, Freyja, that your namesake is also the goddess of death and war.'

He closed the door behind them and rested his back on it for a moment. I sat back down. My legs wouldn't hold me.

'Help yourself to more buns, Freyja. I cannot eat all these.'

I took one and pulled it apart, but I couldn't put even one small piece into my mouth, my stomach was turning over so much.

Magnus came and sat down next to me, pushing the plate out of the way. 'Would you help me tomorrow, Freyja? Help me find the sound of here, of this place, the sound that you most associate with your home.'

'I can show you the corncrakes. They make a crazy sound,' I said quickly, far too quickly.

The panic of being alone with him, of not knowing what to say, how to be in his presence made me speak without thinking and the words rushed out of me before I'd even realised I was saying them and almost immediately I regretted it. But even though I knew I should shut up, shouldn't say anything else, still I carried on.

'No one knows where they nest, except me. The sound they make is the sound of Tor Ness Head. I could take you there.'

He leaned towards me, placed his mouth next to my ear so his hot breath curled inside the seashell shape like a hermit crab finding a new home.

'Yes please.'

I left The Cottages and headed back to the cliffs above Tor Ness Cove to watch the waves crashing into the lighthouse, pulling my breath back into my lungs as a way of trying to calm the shaking that had enveloped me the minute I'd left Magnus's presence. I paced up and down on the edge of the cliffs sending tiny clumps of rubble crashing on to the white sands beneath me, clenching and unclenching my fists as I walked, cursing myself for what I'd offered him. The corncrakes had been *our* secret, mine and Jeanie's, and since she'd gone it had been the one place where I could speak to her and feel at ease and free. That feeling of release enabled me to carry on, waiting for the day that the feeling would be permanent. Magnus would trample on that, would take that away from me and it was my fault, I had given it to him and I didn't understand why.

I stopped, faced the lighthouse and screamed as loudly as I could, hearing the sound bounce across the bulging rollers of the Atlantic. I carried on screaming until my throat could no longer make a sound and a rusty metallic taste filled my mouth. Enough. The feeling of panic receded as the tension holding my body stiff released its grip. I recalled the way Magnus had shifted towards me and away from the Danish girls; how in that tiny moment we were a unit that excluded them, excluded everyone else. Until then, I'd been the child left behind; the one everyone was stuck with once the true object of devotion had disappeared. No one had chosen me before. That's why I'd offered him the most precious thing I had: because when he looked at me, he didn't see what I wasn't, what had vanished, he saw what was in front of him. He saw me.

We had to postpone our trip, as for the next few days the wild weather tore at Falun as though trying to eradicate the island. When I had returned to Falun, I'd thought initially I'd move into Lochinsay. It was where I'd spent most of my time, but the emptiness inside the house now that Annie was gone was too much for me and to my surprise I found it easier to remain at Tryggr. I told myself that Magnus's proximity had nothing to do with my decision. It wasn't him I was there for; it was the comfort of being with Mother and Father again. I was glad no one knew me well enough to challenge the lies I told myself. During those turbulent days, I stayed indoors and looked through the photographs I'd taken, sticking them on to my bedroom wall in a way that pleased me, trying to recreate the collage I'd made for Annie. I'd hidden the old one out of sight so I wouldn't be tempted to refer to it. I wanted to see how the two differed once I'd completed the new one, to see if what I'd missed before would reveal itself once I compared the two. However I arranged the new images, something about the overall effect bothered me, as though I hadn't captured Falun in the way I wanted to. Whatever it was, it wasn't yet ready to reveal itself to me and so I abandoned it, hoping it would become clearer the more pictures I took and the longer I worked on it.

For once I was grateful for the foul Orkney weather as it prevented Magnus from asking me to take him to the corncrakes. Part of me wanted to take him there, to show him the place that was most central to me, but the other part of me rebelled against it and as a result I lived in a constant flux of fear over what to do. So instead I planned to take him somewhere else, to Tor Ness Cove to hear the seals calling each other on the rocks under the lighthouse, or to see the puffins on The Great Stacks at Lochinsay where the rollers sucked and hissed at the caves at the base of the cliffs, anywhere that wasn't to the corncrakes. I'd managed to keep away from The Cottages and him, but now I had to go as the Danes were leaving and Mother wanted me to go and say goodbye and clean their cottage, even though no guests were due to arrive for a while.

I turned back to the collage. The image shimmered as a ray of light through a gap in the clouds flooded my room. I took off one of the photographs, one showing part of the lighthouse, and shifted it to the right a little, towards the centre, my hand hovering over the exact spot I thought it should move to when

Mother called me from downstairs to come with her. I hesitated, the photograph still in my hand, unsure where to place it now that the moment of clarity, had passed. I put it back where it had been and went downstairs, annoyed that Mother had disturbed me at that moment and the thought that had teetered on the edge of my consciousness was lost. Downstairs, Father was listening to the shipping forecast and drinking tea. He paced up and down, then he stiffened as he waited to see whether he'd have to spend yet another day out of the water. I avoided him as much as I could when the weather was bad; he wasn't good on the land, always preferring to be out on the sea where he knew how to negotiate the landscape and read the signs. At home he was lost, trapped inside a dark silence neither of us could enter.

'Would you take this with you please, Freyja?' Mother said as she handed me the basket of clean linen and towels for Number One.

Even though we had no guests booked for some weeks, Mother still liked The Cottages to be ready and that summer it was my job to clean them. Although since Annie had died visitors had been few and far between, Mother always insisted The Cottages were ready. Mother cleaned and tidied them when they were empty over and over, only returning home late at night when the news came on the wireless and then she would often stand at the front window to listen swaying in her tiredness, looking out at the empty track, always ready, always waiting for someone that never came.

As I neared The Cottages, I could hear raised voices speaking in a language I couldn't understand. I turned the corner and saw Solvej march out of Number Two. If she saw me, she didn't acknowledge it. Instead she muttered to herself and shook with obvious anger. Once inside her own cottage she slammed the door behind her. I paused outside, not knowing whether to knock on the door or turn around and go home.

I was cross. The basket of linen was heavy and I had no wish to take it back home only to have to bring it back later, although I was too embarrassed to wait outside when it was obvious that something was wrong. Magnus's door opened and Birgitta marched out, followed swiftly by Magnus who was imploring her not to leave. They stopped when they saw me.

'Freyja, hei,' Magnus said. He walked towards me and relieved me of the heavy basket, placing it on the stone wall at the front of the building.

Birgitta looked at Magnus and said something I didn't understand, but from the way he flinched as she spoke it was meant to hurt him and it did.

'Goodbye, Freyja. It has been very nice to stay in your cottage. Please say to your Mother that Solvej and I are grateful for her hospitality,' Birgitta said.

Her voice was stiff and strained and not the laughing easy voice she usually had. She turned back to Magnus as though she had something more to say, but changed her mind and walked into Number Two and closed the door.

Magnus and I stood outside until he broke the silence. 'Can I offer you coffee?'

'I'll come back later, when they've left,' I said.

He opened the door, holding it in position and standing to one side. 'Come and wait inside while the girls pack their things. There is no need for you to come back later. I was about to make coffee and it would be good to have someone to share it with and you can tell me about those birds.'

I paused on the doorstep, my stomach kicking my ribs, wanting to go in, but afraid of him, afraid of the way he looked at me, his eyes deep inside me, more afraid of him turning away, afraid most of all of how I felt. I picked up the linen basket and went inside.

I didn't tell Mother about my plans to take Magnus out the following day. I said I intended to spend the day taking photographs in preparation for my college course in the autumn. The lies came easily, but they left a sour taste in my mouth. The next morning, I put together a packed lunch for the two of us: boiled eggs, some bread and ham and a couple of slices of cake. I decided to treat us and put two small bottles of lemonade into my bag too. Under my arm I carried our old tatty picnic rug which hadn't had an airing yet that summer and it held a musty mildew scent that lingered on my clothes. As I headed back towards The Cottages, the mizzle increased into a more persistent rain, but it looked as though it would clear quickly as the winds were strong and we'd have a good day.

At The Cottages, Magnus was sitting on the wall outside waiting for me. I had been right about the weather. The sky above had cleared and the rain had all but worn itself out. He had a tape recorder in a brown leather case looped over his shoulder and a small backpack on the other. He jumped off the wall and fell into step next to me. 'Is it far?' he said.

'I thought we'd go to Tor Ness Cove,' I said. 'The seals on the rocks around the lighthouse are a famous sight here, they make a marvellous sound too, a bark like a dog, and there are the puffins at Lochinsay, on The Great Stacks, they make a sound like no other bird, you have to hear that, it's a classic Orkney sound, Shetland too I suppose, if I think about it and there's also the guillemots, fulmars and razorbills, all of those sounds remind me of here.' I spoke quickly, one word tumbling into the next without a space in between. I didn't want to leave a space for him to say – what about the corncrakes?

'Sounds good. Let's go!' We walked side-by-side along the track towards the footpath. 'Didn't you mention another bird too? One that is hard to find?'

I managed to hold back the 'no' that wanted to erupt out of me and instead I mumbled, 'Maybe later, if there's time.'

The pathway was narrow and I was able to hide my discomfort by walking ahead of him, watching my step even though I'd walked the path many times and could have managed with my eyes closed. We climbed through the gap in the stone wall and headed towards the point of Tor Ness Head and the lighthouse. At the seamark I made to turn right towards the steps that led to Tor Ness Cove. I'd show him the lanterns that were still at the base of the cliffs – a little piece of Falun tradition I'd thought he'd enjoy.

Magnus stood by the seamark and didn't follow me. He looked back and forth, then stepped forwards past the seamark towards the edge of the cliff on the most western part of Falun, staring at the skerries and the lighthouse stretching out in front of him. Beneath us the incessant chatter of the birds rose up in a wave of raucousness.

'I have been here before, as a boy. I remember now. That lighthouse.' He turned towards me. 'Isn't there another beach that way? Yes, I remember now. A small cove, quite hidden away and difficult to get to. My parents always loved coves that no one else went to. Can we go there, Freyja? Freyja, are you all right?'

I couldn't answer, couldn't move any muscles in my body which had assumed a hunched over, crouching posture, paralysing my limbs which wouldn't obey any instructions I gave them to move. Magnus rushed to my side, gripped hold of my arm and lowered me to the ground. I couldn't breathe – there was no room left for air in my chest, so consumed was it by my massive thumping heart. Dark spots disturbed my vision, clumping together until I could see nothing at all, but through everything, through the crashing of the waves against the skerries, the screeching calls of the gulls overhead and the wind tearing across the moor, I could hear one thing: Jeanie's voice singing, *Oh my darling Clementine.*

I must have passed out, but how long I lay there I'm not certain. The next thing I saw was Magnus's face inches from my own. We sat there by the seamark for a long time. Magnus took off his coat and draped it across my shoulders to try and stop the shaking that had taken hold of me. He didn't speak, didn't question me as many people would have done. Instead, he allowed the easy relaxed silence between us to calm me. After a while, he took out a pipe from his jacket pocket and stuffed the bowl full of tobacco from a pouch. No one I knew smoked a pipe. It was something only old men did. I liked the smell of it – a rich vanilla scent, sweet and dark. I found it comforting and relaxing. We sat side-by-side on the cliffs, the ocean spread out in front of us, and I told him about Jeanie, about how much I loved her, how she'd been at the centre of my world, and how, despite knowing how much I adored her and couldn't imagine a life without her in it, still she'd left me, left all of us and how nothing had been the same since. And then I told him about Annie and how she'd left me too. Except with her it was different. She hadn't had a choice. He remained silent as I spoke, not interrupting me once, puffing on his pipe. He was a good listener.

'Leaving someone is not the worst thing you can do to them, is it?' he said.

I started so violently at his comment that I shook his coat off me.

'But of course it is. It's the very worst thing in the world.'

I took him to the corncrakes in the end. How could I not? After Jeanie had disappeared it was the place I'd run to and after the incident at the seamark it was where I wanted to be. I wanted to lay down next to the female bird sitting on her nest, listen to her chatter and imagine it was Jeanie speaking to me, telling me that she'd always be there, in that spot waiting for me whenever I needed her.

Magnus and I sat in the flattened grass, listening to the birds and the ebb and flow of the landscape settling around us. I watched Magnus as he listened, recorded and scribbled on his lined manuscript paper. He 'disappeared'; all his energy and focus turned inwards towards that part of him where the music pulsed with its own rhythm. I could tell there was no way to reach him until he came out of it again. He was totally unaware of his surroundings, even me sitting next to him; and I was able to see into a part of him of which even he wasn't aware and to me, a naïve island girl with no experience of the world, it was an enormous privilege. After a while the rain returned, followed by a darkening sky and out on the hilder the first flashes of the coming storm turned the sea into lead. Magnus gathered the papers on which he'd made his indecipherable marks. It was time to leave.

When we reached The Cottages, he hesitated a moment and I expected him to say goodbye, to dismiss me and what I'd given of myself, and I felt foolish and exposed, regretful of what I'd paid in exchange for a moment with him. But he took my hand and drew me into a soft embrace.

'Let me play something for you, to thank you for what you have shared with me today,' he said.

I followed him into the house, but before I crossed the

threshold, I turned to look at the Tor looming behind me. For a moment I saw Jeanie watching me leaving her behind, and the sorrow I felt at the distance I'd placed between us became a black absence that bloomed inside me, spreading out like an ink blot. When I looked again, to say a final goodbye, all I could see was the fog swirling in the wind, and Jeanie was gone.

The Cottage was chilly when we entered and the dampness made me shiver. Magnus threw a couple of peats into the fireplace and soon the room filled with the earthy smell of burning. I knelt beside him to feel the warmth from the fire, close enough for me to be able to smell the salty sea spray trapped in his hair. He warmed his hands against the fire.

'Coffee?' he said.

I smiled and nodded but didn't speak. I didn't feel I needed to anymore, unlike with other people, where I would want to rush to fill the silences that crept in. With Magnus the silences were companionable and easy, full of something other than embarrassment and lack of anything to say; they were a space to listen and reflect, to experience closeness, and although I didn't recognise it at first, desire.

Magnus stood up and moved into the kitchen and soon I heard the kettle popping as the water began to heat up on the hot plate. As Magnus clattered in the kitchen, preparing the cups for the coffee, I leafed through the pages of manuscript paper sprawled over the wooden table Father had made to fit into the alcove looking out over the garden towards the cliffs. There were pages and pages of Magnus's handwritten scores, many with thick harsh lines through them where he had obviously changed his mind and scrapped what he'd written, in what appeared to be a fit of rage. He wrote with a soft, dark pencil and I could picture his hand making the marks on the paper as his pencil skimmed the surface in his hurry to record his thoughts quickly as possible. I picked out one sheet which had more notes written at the bottom on the lines marked I, VI, II, V, Vcl and C-Bit than any of the others. I presumed this was the string section, that the V stood for violin, but I wasn't certain. Above, in the middle of the page, the lines for those instruments were blank and Magnus had filled it with a doodle of a pipe puffing out clouds of smoke. It took me a moment to see that, hidden in the clouds, were the letters that spelled out my name. My stomach turned over and I felt myself grow a little taller. I looked up and watched him in the kitchen, his broad back towards me. He thought about me when I wasn't there. He dreamed about me. Me. I looked away from him and back at the doodle. I didn't want him to catch me staring at him, not with the grin I knew I had stretching across my face.

I heard Magnus's footsteps behind me and I turned, having replaced the pages as they'd been. He placed two cups of coffee on the dining table. 'I wonder Freyja, before I play for you, whether you would mind helping me with something,' he said.

A blast of chilly air seeped into the room as he opened the door to the hallway. He was uncertain, shy even about asking me. I couldn't imagine what it was he wanted from me.

'Yes, of course.'

'One moment,' he said.

I heard his feet thud up the staircase and walk to the larger of the two bedrooms at the front of the house. I wasn't sure whether to sit at the table or on the sofa or to remain standing. For a moment I simply stood there, feeling out of place and ridiculous. As I heard him thud back down the stairs, I pulled out one of the dining chairs and sat down. It was more formal than the sofa and more appropriate. I picked up the coffee mug and warmed my hands on it. Magnus walked back into the room. In one hand he held an old battered case which I assumed contained his violin, or fiddle as he called it. In the other, he held a collection of bows.

'I like to play through the music for the strings once I have written it and each symphony requires a different sound and a different bow to make that sound. I wonder, Freyja, as you are so attuned to the local sounds, whether you would help me choose the bow that best replicates those sounds.'

How could I possible know? How could I, who had never even heard a violin played before, possibly help a man like him choose between bows?

'I...can...try,' I said.

'Good, yes,' he said.

He placed the violin case sideways on, on both arms of the wooden rocking chair by the front window and opened it. The violin was wrapped in a thick ivory silk sleeve which he placed with reverence back into the case.

'My mother's wedding dress,' he said.

I must have shown my shock that he could have cut up her dress for such a purpose as he added smiling, 'It was her idea. She said, *What other use is there for it?* Who am I to disagree?'

He handed the violin to me and I was surprised at how light it was. The wood was dark and dense.

'Is it old?' I said.

'Yes. Eighteenth century. See here and here, the use marks? This dent here, and here a piece has been chipped off – overzealous bowing at some point. It gives it character, don't you think? It makes a punchy, powerful sound for such a small thing. It has had some good players use it in the past, I think. Their sound still resonates in the wood, like it has a memory of those notes that it will not let go.'

His voice was soft and his face ecstatic as he admired his instrument. He looked at it as though it was the first time he'd ever seen it and I wondered how he could love it so much. He picked up the first of the bows. 'This one is a French bow, made by a man called Sartory. This is a very reliable bow in many respects and I use it a lot. See what you make of the sound.'

He took a moment to place the violin under his chin and loosen his arms before starting to play. The sound filled the room, reaching upwards and upwards before fanning out across the ceiling. I recognised the short tune immediately, but couldn't name it. I'd heard it in one of my school music lessons.

'You like it?'

'Yes.'

'The sound is good and the bow itself easy to manage, but is it right?'

He didn't wait for me to answer and I was grateful, as I had no idea what to say. The sound was to me perfect, incredible, like nothing I'd ever heard before.

'Here is the next one. This too by a Frenchman, all the best ones are. This bow was made by Hippolyte Camille-Lamy, in the 1920s. See what you think.'

This time he played a softer, slower tune, and the bow floated above the strings as though dancing a ballet. I felt the curl of excitement inside – I could hear a difference. This one was better. It sounded like a summer wave reaching the shore and gliding up the white sand, holding on to the land for as long as it was able.

'You hear it, Freyja. I can see you do. This one has a more velvety sound. You like it more?'

'Yes, I do.'

'There is one more bow.' He put the second bow back down on the table and picked up the last one. 'This bow was made by François Tourte and is the oldest of them all, made in the late seventeen hundreds, before the turn of the century. Tourte is considered the father of the modern bow. This is the heaviest of the three, but the tip and the frog - this part at the end is the frog – are perfectly balanced. And the strings, see they are flat like a ribbon. This had not been done before Tourte and the strings used to tangle. This is a masterpiece of design. The great violinist, Norbert Brainin, said that these Tourte bows are the best and that playing with anything else is like playing with a walking stick. See what you think.'

I waited for him to begin. He took his time to find his composure, adjusting both his chin and his fingers as they slid up and down the neck of the fiddle. I wanted to cry as the sound he made cut through me. This was music that I'd never heard before and I knew with a certainty that surprised me that this was the music he'd found out on the cliffs at Tor Ness Head as we'd stood watching the sun cut through the clouds, reaching down and grazing the top of the waves.

'That's the one,' I said before I could stop myself. He'd only that moment lifted the bow from the strings. 'That's the one.'

'It is, Freyja, isn't it? You are my mistress of the bows. Well, that is decided. The Tourte is the one I will use here. Now as a thank you for helping me and for taking me to see the corncrakes, let me play something for you.'

I thought I'd close my eyes and let the music wash over me, but it didn't happen like that. I couldn't stop watching him. The way he disappeared into the music fascinated me. No wonder he looked at the violin with such love. It was part of him; in a way it was him. The music throbbed and quivered in the space between us like it was alive and I wanted to reach out and touch it. I thought of the way our arms had brushed against each other as we'd walked along the cliff tops, how my skin had bristled at his touch, and I knew that something between us had changed. My heart beat so strongly that I felt the pulse of it at my fingertips which yearned to reach out towards him, to become entangled in his long white hair.

When he'd finished playing, he gave a little bow and I clapped, stood up and kissed him on the cheek as lightly as a moth's wing brushing against his skin. Under my lips his cool skin trembled, enough for me to know. To know that with my touch I had raised up within me a power he'd find impossible to resist.

When I left him that night I knew I'd discovered the most delicious secret in the world and I planned to hold it curled up inside me, to keep it safe, and to never, ever let it go.

The next day I woke early to a clear blue light shining through the curtains and the sounds of the birds outside mingling with my dreams, which had been full of the echoes of Magnus's music. I heard the back door close downstairs and I knew that Father would have taken advantage of the break in the weather to go out to sea. I turned over and pulled the covers tight around me. I felt warm and comfortable and for the first time since I'd returned to Falun, my first thoughts on waking weren't about Jeanie and her still empty bed looming next to mine, nor tinged with the heavy sadness that hung like a dead weight from my shoulders following Annie's death. My first thoughts that morning were of Magnus and the longing I felt for him in every part of me.

I'd left my most recent attempt at a collage of Tor Ness Head stuck to the wall on the far side of my room where I could lie in bed and look at it. The latest arrangement of photographs centred on the way the light fell on the curves in the cliffs, sending long purple shadows on to the barren flat moors. I lay there staring at it. I was wrong. The collage wasn't finished; it wasn't right. It didn't say to me *Falun* in the way that Magnus's tiny fragment of music had done the day before. Until I had captured the essence of what Falun, and Tor Ness Head in particular, meant to me, the way Magnus had turned its essence into those ethereal notes, I wouldn't achieve what I wanted and whatever it was Annie had wanted me to see.

I leaped out of bed and pulled on some clothes. I'd go out straight away, before breakfast even, and head towards Lochinsay along the Sky Path; from that vantage point I would have the clearest view of Tor Ness Head. That was the place I needed to be. Despite the sun, I could see from the white-tipped waves and the flattening grasses that a right gussel was blowing. I hoped Father would be fine out on the water. With gusts like that squalls come out of nowhere, turning the sea into mountains. I pulled a thick jumper from my drawer and put it on.

I made a flask of tea and put a slab of fruit cake into my bag, picked up my camera and headed out. The sun simmered above the hilder and it sent long fresh lines of light across the island, catching wisps of early morning mist in its rays. I paused for a moment on top of the dry stone wall at the end of our garden and observed the silence and the stillness of Tor Ness Head stretching out in front of me, punctuated only by the sweeping light from the lighthouse. As I watched the light swooping past, I started to take the camera out of the case, ready to capture the beam if I could. It would be interesting to see if I could discern the minimal disturbance the beam made to the dawn light, but I paused for too long as I waited for the perfect moment of clarity. The optic ceased and the moment had passed.

The tide was high and beneath me the rollers thundered against the cliffs, filling the air with salty spray as they crashed and hissed against the rocks. I headed southwards towards Lochinsay and as I rounded the bend, I could see Annie's house standing alone on its promontory. I thought about Mr Phelps's advice that I should sell the house, and soon, before the winter weather began its assault and no one would be there to protect it from the elements and nor would anyone be likely to visit to view it once the darkness fell. Both Mother and Father agreed. Father said that I could bank the money and buy a more suitable place that would be easier to manage. I knew they were right, all of them. Why would I want a large house like Lochinsay with its many empty rooms echoing with unfulfilled dreams? Especially when I was about to head off to college and wouldn't be living in it. Annie wouldn't have wanted me to be tied to it. She'd given me all she had so I could be free to do what I wanted. That's what Mr Phelps had told me she'd said when he'd questioned her decision to leave everything to me, a child. I'd been offended that he'd thought her decision negligent in some way, wrong even, as though I wasn't worthy of being given something like that. Now though, I felt comforted by the knowledge that she'd been determined in her actions, had thought it through and had her reasons. Annie had always been keen that women and girls should be independent and I could imagine her saying that to him. I would sell it, I decided. I'd tell Mr Phelps to do whatever he needed to do.

As I walked, the sky began to darken and the air became thick and drivvy and I was glad I'd had the sense to wrap up warm. I rounded the bend and saw Magnus sitting on the mermaid rock, smoking his pipe, staring out to sea. When he saw me, he jumped up and took his pipe out of his mouth.

'Hei Freyja. Good morning. You are, how do you say it? An *early bird* too?'

'Yes, an early bird. It's such a fine day, or it was. That's the thing about Orkney. The wild weather is always waiting to assault us again.'

'And what is this wind today?'

'It was a gussel, but now the clouds are rolling in, it's picked up and I think we'll have a skolder before too long.'

Magnus loved learning the many names we had for each of the weather elements. I watched his mouth moving as he practised saying them. He tried to swallow the sounds of them deep inside himself where they would be digested and come out later as something else, a bar of his music, or even one solitary note. It would be there though. I knew that much.

Magnus laughed as he repeated it. 'It is a good word, skolder.

118

Sounds good with my accent, don't you think?'

I nodded. It did. Better even.

'Come and sit with me whilst I finish my pipe.'

Magnus sat on the side of the stone and patted the space next to him. I sat down, conscious of the heat radiating from him, and leaned into him resting my head on his shoulder. He put his arm around me, resting his head on top of mine. Soon we were both enveloped in the sweet vanilla scent of his pipe smoke. I poured tea into the cup on the top of the flask and we shared it between us. I offered him some cake, but it wasn't something he was particularly fond of, he said. I put it away. I couldn't eat it either.

'Look! Over there,' I said. 'There's Father's boat, *The Maid of Falun*.' I pointed to the vessel chugging its way along the coastline. 'And there, jumping in the surf? Do you see there's a pod of porpoises?'

We sat and watched the pod as they danced like a collection of black commas cutting through the waves until they disappeared.

'Do you go out on the water with him?'

'I used to when I was much younger. I would be the one at the back, gutting the fish and throwing the titbits to the birds following us. Not now though. He doesn't like me to go with him anymore.'

I looked down at a bunch of sea pinks that had found a sheltered spot to flourish next to the stone. I picked one of the flowers and one-by-one I pulled the petals off until all I held was the stalk which I threw to the ground.

'There aren't any birds today,' he said. 'No guts to catch. You should be there with him.'

'He's not fishing. That's why there aren't any,' I said.

Magnus turned to me surprised. 'No?'

'No. He's looking for her. He does that more than fishing. Since she left. He takes *The Maid of Falun* and sails round and round the island. He searches by day, when he can, and at night he waits in his chair.'

Magnus took a lighter out of his pocket and cupped the bowl of the pipe in his hands as he relit the tobacco, sucking and puffing to aid the burning as the wind tried its best to extinguish the flame.

'But I do not understand. Where is he looking after so long?'

'He's looking for the selkies. Waiting for them to come and find him. They won't though. They won't give her up to him. Not now.'

Magnus held my gaze for a moment as if he was searching inside me for something. Whatever it was I don't think he found it, as after a few moments he patted my hand and turned back to stare out at the hilder. We sat on the stone watching *The Maid of Falun* until she disappeared around the headland. My hand burned where he'd touched me. I placed my left hand over the spot as if I could keep his touch and stop its warmth fading away. I watched Magnus's profile as he listened to the sea. I especially liked that view of him, us sitting side-by-side, me watching, him listening, finding a common purpose in our different experiences of the world. I didn't want to leave him and would easily have given up on my plans to take another roll of film to instead spend the rest of the day showing him more of Falun, but when I turned to suggest this I saw that he'd shut off from me, withdrawn as I'd seen him do before, and the feelings of closeness between us vanished. I became gripped by an intense panic that he would leave me too and I shuddered. He must have felt it as he stood up, pulling me into a long embrace, then held my face in his hands and softly kissed me, then buried his face in my neck.

'I have to go, Freyja. I am sorry. Work beckons.'

I wanted to say don't go, don't leave me, but I didn't. He picked up his bag and began to walk back to Tor Ness Head, leaving me standing by the rock. I would have cried if he hadn't turned around.

'Freyja, come to the Cottage later, when you have finished your photographs. Come and see what you have inspired me to write. Say you will.'

I knew then what the feelings churning inside me meant; feelings that had left me nauseous and unable to eat. Since I'd met Magnus, I'd alternated between being possessed by a never-ending joy that made me smile and skip, and a dark emptiness so deep and cavernous I couldn't make my way out of its tight grip. As I watched Magnus standing there, I recalled the way he'd listened to me earlier, really listened, unlike Joe who could no longer bear to be near me, or even Mother and Father who wouldn't speak Jeanie's name, yet acted as though she would walk back through the door at any moment and be able to carry on her life as though she'd never left. My need to be near him, to touch him and inhale the scent of him, to be unable to bear moments apart from him, were proof that for the first time I was utterly and completely in love.

I sat for a while on the mermaid rock, hugging his invitation tight to my chest, fizzing with the anticipation of seeing him later. I imagined his hand in mine, his arms around me, what it would feel like to be pressed against his chest, to have his mouth explore mine, to taste him. All the things we'd discussed endlessly at school, but had seemed unobtainable, until now. Was he thinking the same? I spent the rest of the day taking the two rolls of film I'd brought with me and developing them in the dark room at Lochinsay. I left them hanging on the pegs before making my way back along the Sky Path to Tor Ness Head and The Cottages.

The door to Number Two was open when I arrived and I could hear Magnus playing the same tune I'd always heard him playing whenever I came to The Cottages. I didn't know what it was, but it had a deep melancholy that tugged at something deep inside me and made me tearful. I waited until he stopped playing and knocked on the open door. Magnus's voice bellowed to come in. I walked into the sitting room where he stood, rubbing his fiddle and bow with a yellow cloth to clean off the rosin dust. I knew that because I'd asked him what he was doing before. He cleaned it in a very deliberate manner, starting under the strings of the fiddle near the bridge and working his way carefully up along the fingerboard. He covered the fiddle with the yellow cloth and the sleeve made from the remnants of the wedding dress, then put it and the bow back in the case and closed it. He was very meticulous about the way he handled his fiddle. Everything always happened in the same order. I liked that about him.

The room smelled strongly of wet bonfires and I knew that he'd recently had a pipe. The tobacco was different though, not the vanilla one I preferred. He leaned on the wall to stretch out his hands. He was always stretching and pulling on his fingers, even when he hadn't been playing.

'What was that piece you were playing?' I said.

'You like it? Elgar.'

'It's beautiful. Sad though, I think.'

'It is called Sospiri or 'sighs'. One of my obsessions I am afraid. It is sad, full of longing.' Magnus paused, stared at me, his mouth softening, then smiling as he took a stray sprig of my wiry hair and tried unsuccessfully to tuck it behind my ear. Then he unpacked his violin again, reversing the steps he'd just taken to put it away and began to play part of the tune. 'You hear there in the way it rises and falls, the descending seventh?'

I shook my head.

He played it again, singing with the notes, until yes, I could hear it.

'Elgar in miniature. All the traits in his symphonies and concertos are there in that one piece. It is perfect, I think. Simple on the surface, but hard to get it right. I have been trying to play it for a long time now. One day it will be right.'

He played the piece through again. This time he watched me as he played, standing so close my skin chilled and contracted along the length of my spine.

'It is better now I am playing it with the bow you chose for me. It makes it come alive. A good choice. Now come and look at this.'

He pulled a chair in front of the desk and we both sat down squashed together on the seat. Bundling together the pile of papers on the desk, he shuffled them around and laid them out flat in a sequence. He ran his finger over the score and hummed the tune.

'See, this is the main theme of the work, played here by the horn, this stretches over the first four bars and it is this theme that is repeated, with many variations throughout the work, ending with the closing sequence that is at the heart of this piece.'

Magnus hummed the tune, one arm holding me on the chair, one circling in the air. His eyes were closed.

'That is the seed, the tiny rivulet that starts up in the hills behind us, above the corncrake's nest, and it grows throughout, becoming bigger and bigger, until, boom, eventually it joins the sea in a tumultuous crescendo, here, see?' He opened his eyes and pointed at the score. 'And underneath it all, the bassoons and the double basses are playing the same as the horns from earlier except three times as slow.'

Magnus's fingers trailed along the lines on the score, smudging them a little in his excitement.

'But over the top, the violins are playing the actual theme, da da daa, but the bassists are foreshadowing what is to come so when we reach the finale we've already been primed to it, so it is like the whole work has grown organically out of what has come before. Clever, yes? Without this, without the structure, it is just disorganised notes, nothing.'

He stood up suddenly and moved to the piano and started to play, his hands flowing over the keys.

'And here, this is the part that came today, when we saw the porpoises cutting through the water, making a path through those tunnels of sunlight falling on to the waves. This forms the second theme of the whole piece.'

The music was bold and terrifying and full of drama and what I loved most of all was that underneath, hidden amongst the soaring melodies, there was an unmistakable sense of menace. And although I tried, I couldn't understand everything he said, couldn't see the patterns in the music in the way he saw them, but I could understand his passion, his ferocity, and what he was trying to express. The music erupted out of him fully formed and there was nothing he could do to contain it. I laughed, not at him, but at the sheer joy of seeing his devotion to something so ethereal, something that existed only for the briefest of moments then disappeared.

'You think I am mad? You are right.' He laughed. His laugh was deep and loud and as he roared his head flew back and his hair fell in a long white pelt along his spine. He stood up from the piano and walked towards me. Circling his arms around my waist, he spun me in a circle. 'But it is you that makes me so. This music I make is only made because of you. And because of you it will be the best work I ever make. Of that I am sure.' He kissed my forehead.

My stomach turned over. I wanted to believe him, but I couldn't be the one who made him feel like that, could I? With his music he offered me himself and there was nothing more I wanted. He cupped my face in his hands. The tips of his fingers were rough from pressing on the violin strings for years and smelled of smoke and pencil lead. I stiffened, scared suddenly of what he was offering me.

He stopped his caresses. 'I will make us coffee,' he said and we both stood up.

He stood in the doorway between the kitchen and the sitting room whilst the kettle boiled, watching me.

'What is it?' I said, unable to bear the scrutiny a moment longer.

But he smiled and returned to the kitchen.

'Please put on some music,' he shouted. 'There are some records by the player.'

I stood up and walked over to the sideboard on top of which sat the wooden record player. We didn't have one at home as Mother and Father preferred to listen to the wireless. They thought records and popular music were for other people, so I'd brought the records I'd collected at school and left them in The Cottages. There I could play them whenever The Cottages were empty. I'd pick one and put it on as loud as I dared until the music filled me with its beat. When I had a cottage of my own, I'd reclaim them. And when I left Falun in the autumn, I would go and see one of the bands play live. I wanted to be part of what was going on in the world. I wanted away from here and the records were one of the ways I allowed myself to hope. I sifted through the small collection Magnus had brought with him. They were all classical and I couldn't tell one from another, but Mozart at least I'd heard of, so I picked that: Symphony Number 23 in D Major. I slipped the record from its sleeve and placed it on the turntable. The music was jolly, and beautiful. Magnus came back into the sitting room with the coffee.

'A good choice, my bow mistress,' he said.

A few stray strands of hair had fallen in front of my eyes. Very gently Magnus brushed them aside and tucked them behind my ear. Then he stepped closer to me so I could feel the warmth of his body as he leaned his forehead against mine; his fingers circled my waist and I started to relax and lean into him, my body knowing what to do before my mind could grasp what was happening. His arms moved up along the curves of my body until they rested on my shoulders, his hands dangling behind my neck. He drew me into the space under his chin where it was warm and musty. My head softened until it rested against him. I smelled coffee and smoke on his breath and as his lips and tongue searched for mine, I could taste it too. For a split second I had a choice.

Later, as he bathed, I sat in the armchair by the window that looked out over Tor Ness lighthouse with my legs tucked underneath me, wrapped in one of his thick jumpers and a towel around my head. In the grate the fire blazed and the cottage had a warm cosy feel that Tryggr never had. Outside, the lighthouse beam cut through the simmer dim which had been dulled further by the thick rolling clouds banked up against the sky. Did I look different I wondered? Would anyone be able to see the change that had come over me? Two gulls swirled in upward spirals, caught in the harsh eddies blowing in from the sea, and as I watched them I wrapped myself in the memory of how he'd picked me up and carried me up the stairs and how through his t-shirt I'd been able to feel the oval shape of the muscles in his arms. He'd laid me on the bed, arranging the pillows to support my head.

'Yes?' he'd said.

I'd nodded, incapable of speech. Yes.

He'd peeled my clothes from me, starting with my thick boot socks, and alternating between something from him and something from me until we both lay naked and he'd stared at me and said I was beautiful and his hands explored every part of me until I trembled with a desire I hadn't realised could exist inside me. He lifted me on to his lap and I trailed my hands along the sharp lines of his collar bones, and ran them down the bumps in his spine as we'd faced each other until I reached his heaven and I'd held him there until he cried out as though tormented by an exquisite pain. He'd cupped my head in his hands as he trailed a map on my face. I looked into his eyes as he entered me and I felt myself known to him and in the same moment an image flashed in my mind too fast for me to grasp, but long enough for me to feel scared as I closed it down.

From my chair I heard his feet thudding back down the stairs towards me, and in that sound I heard the echo of another sort of thud, of waves crashing against the rocks and my feet, running, running, thumping against stone, screaming and crying as if my life depended on it.

Tryggr, Falun, Orkney Islands
August 1964

Mother and Father left to go on a shopping trip to Kirkwall. They would be away for a few days, so Magnus and I took advantage of the opportunity to spend both the days and the nights together. I couldn't bear to be apart from him for even a moment. We spent the day on the narrow stony beaches at the base of the cliffs at Lochinsay where streams flowed from the tors behind, breaking out of the rocks in small straight waterfalls that crashed on to the beaches beneath, the sound mingling with the cries of the birds on the cliffs above. We walked close together, touching constantly and barely minutes passed before he would stop, turn towards me, look into my eyes and kiss me. I hardly knew what to do with myself. No one had ever looked at me like that before – as if I was the only person remaining in the world – suddenly Copolips didn't seem such a lonely game after all.

We felt a desperation, Magnus and I, to completely consume each other, to extract every last second out of the moments we had together, for what we both knew, and what remained unsaid, was that our time was limited. Magnus would return to Norway and I would go to art college. I wondered if it were that which made us so besotted with each other, the knowledge that it would end. I thought not. No, this was real love. After all, he told me time and time again that he'd come back for me.

'I will go back, I will sort out everything that I need to and then, Freyja, and then I will come back for you.'

He never said what he needed to sort out and I never asked.

The following morning, I slid out from under the warm sheets where, next to me, Magnus still lay sleeping. He looked beautiful asleep, soft and relaxed. He lost that look of worry which pulled his eyebrows together, worry that the symphony wouldn't be good enough, that it wouldn't come together in the way he imagined. His translucent hair fanned out like a halo on the dark pillowcase. I reached out and brushed the straggling hairs away from his forehead, running his hair carefully through my fingers so it wouldn't snag and wake him. It felt soft and slippery like silk, unlike my own wiry red curls which fizzed around my head like coiled springs. I remembered the way his hair had slid over my stomach and breasts as he made his way up along my body, how I had arched towards his touch and his musky damp mouth as it connected with mine.

Outside all was still and quiet as dawn made its first footsteps towards us. I pulled on my clothes which were lying where they'd been discarded in erratic piles on the floor, still damp and salty from the beach. I took Magnus's thick Fair Isle black and white cardigan from the back of the chair slotted under the desk where he'd been working and slipped it over my shoulders, feeding my arms through the sleeves. It smelled of him and his pipe smoke. He'd bought it in Betty Tidy's haberdashery in Skellinwall and had christened it his Symphony Cardigan. He said he'd wear only that until he'd finished his symphony. The cardigan was far too big for me and I had to roll back the arms to free my fingers. I wrapped it around myself catching the scent of him in its fibres and allowed myself a moment's fantasy that it was his arms around me again, his touch that caressed my bare skin underneath, then I pulled on my boots and headed out to the village. I wanted to buy something for our breakfast.

I pushed my hands into the pocket of his cardigan and felt the perfectly round pebble I'd found for him on the beach at Lochinsay, when we'd laid ourselves out on the rocky beach and watched the gannets coming and going on the cliff face that loomed above us, the sound of the waterfalls crashing behind us. The stone was jet black with a line of white running around the centre of it like an equator.

'It is like us. Two halves come together to make a whole. That is how I feel when I am with you, Freyja. Perfectly round and whole.'

I told him that I did too and I believed it; I believed I'd stay that way too. But to me it also represented something of myself: one half the girl I'd been before I met him and the other the woman I was now. What I didn't know was that Magnus would break me; that the pebble that represented us would be split in half and shattered into so many pieces it would be turned into sand, as shifting and unstable as a dune.

I followed the brae that ran alongside the coastline; out to sea the hilder was thick with fog. The rocky seabed under the cliffs turned the sea porpoise grey with tiny crests of white like eyes flickering on the surface.

In the village, the door of the corner shop was open, held in place by Mrs McFarlane's sledgehammer: *One of the first things my husband ever gave me, that hammer. Should have taken it as a warning,* she'd said when I'd asked her about it. And you married him after that. Strange how love can skew your mind. As a result, the bell hanging above the door didn't announce my arrival. I heard voices in the back of the shop, but didn't pay them much attention as I concentrated on what to choose for breakfast. I realised that it was Betty Tidy from the haberdashers speaking to Mrs McFarlane.

'That girl's bringing shame on the family again, did you hear?' Betty said. 'Cavorting, no less, with that foreigner. On the beaches. Well, it's all to be expected, I suppose. Mixing with those artistic types like she did. That and coming into money like that, it does that to people.'

'It's Morag I feel for. To have lost the sweetest child ever and be left with that wild thing. It's beyond belief, isn't it dear? That's five shillings.'

I abandoned breakfast and ran back to Magnus. With him I was me. These people would never see me like that. I was glad I would be leaving Falun soon. I could leave Jeanie and her shadow behind.

Over the next weeks we spent as much time together as we could. I moved out of Tryggr and into Lochinsay to have more freedom to be with him. I told Mother and Father that the house needed to be lived in and feel alive or it wouldn't sell. They didn't like me leaving, but they accepted it. A few people came to view it, but not many and no one liked it or the location enough to want to buy it. Magnus taught me to land ski and I showed him the caves in the tors that echoed with memories of my childhood adventures; he taught me the basics of how to conduct – he conducted his own symphonies whenever he could, he said – and I took him out in Annie's boat and we sailed around Falun with dolphins and porpoises diving in our surf. I took roll after roll of photographs of him, his hair blowing in the wild Falun winds as he listened for the sounds he wanted to hear. And in the evenings, we sat on the cliffs and watched the sun skirt along the hilder. I sat leaning back into his chest with his arms around me and I knew I was happier than I'd ever been.

At night I watched him working with the oil lamp he insisted on having next to him that sent magnificent shadows across the table. Often these shadows would take on a demonic quality as he tore through page after page of paper. In the morning, when he bathed, I would look over the previous day's and night's work. Of course, I couldn't decipher the marks he'd made – they made no sense to me at all, even though he tried to translate them into something I could understand:

'See here, the strings must come in on the down beat or the sense of it will be lost and here, the timpani, the conductor must always watch out for the timpani, they are afraid they will miss their moment after so many bars rest.'

But despite my lack of understanding, I could still see the emotion behind his efforts, the agony he went through to pull the music from inside himself into something other people could use, could hear. Page after page had angry blots where he'd used the full force of his pencil to eradicate whatever misshapen notes offended him so; whole pages had thick lines through them that cut the music down to size - the anger he felt towards the mistakes he'd made visceral and visible. The smell of despair flowed off him and filled the whole room. He'd taken to calling the symphony his *schmerzen kind*, his pain child, such was the agony the composition caused him. At times I wondered if I could bear it, the agony of creation, but as time went on and we became more and more intimate I saw a change come over him, a small but perceptible relaxation, an easiness that spread over him and us, a tenderness that became, for me at least, intoxicating. I asked him outright to show me his music, something he'd started to hide from me the more he relaxed. I worried that he was ashamed of his lack of progress and the violent messy pages.

At first I didn't believe he was showing me his work, this draft was so neat and ordered, it was like it had been written by another person, but as I looked more closely I recognised the peculiarities of his handwriting, the loops and swirls where he'd linked the phrases, the arrows and annotations indicating where the priority was to be given, to which instrument. He liked to give detailed instructions to the conductor, fearful that unless he did so his music would be misrepresented and his efforts wasted. On these pages the revisions were minor, the occasional cross-hatching out of a single bar, but lightly done, no anger, no violence, simply calculated changes where he'd finally seen the way through. He looked pleased with himself when he showed me those pages. That day, when he told me that I was the reason, that I was his bow mistress and it was my influence that allowed the music to flow so easily out of him, I remember him sitting up in bed, leaning against the headboard, my head resting on his bare chest, and he was so beautiful and perfect to me I thought I was the luckiest girl in the world. Nothing stays the same though – especially not perfection.

Ceredigion Mental Asylum, West Wales
June 1983 2.15pm

It's nice here, isn't it? I love this tea-room when the sun's out like it is now. It's a good place to come and admire the cliffs. I like their blackness against the vibrant green of the grass on top and the grey-blue sea beyond.

Annie made me look at colour and light and that's a skill I've kept, like a part of her has remained behind within me.

The Welsh cakes are good, but they're the only ones I've ever eaten so I suppose they could be awful and I wouldn't know. Eat up, or if you don't want it, I'll have yours too.

Keep it in. That's what I remember everyone saying when I was young when there was any kind of trouble. *Keep it locked away.* Showing your emotions wasn't allowed, even when Jeanie disappeared and I didn't know what to do with my sadness. Mother made me feel that it was shameful to go about airing everything in public. *Button it up, Freyja, hold it in. Don't show us what's going on in your head. No one wants to know that, Freyja.*

That was at the heart of everything that happened to me. I understand that now, that no one, especially a child like I was, would behave normally when things go wrong when that's what they've been told their whole life. Mother and Father believed in it wholeheartedly. Showing emotion was wrong. They hid theirs and there was no way I could see past the masks they wore.

When I arrived at Kincraig Castle, they didn't allow that kind of silence. No they didn't. There they jabbed me in the arm, in the backside, in the leg, anywhere they could and told me to talk. *Spit it out, Freyja, tell us, tell us, tell us what you did. Speak. Speak, Freyja. Louder so I can hear. Speak. SPEAK.*

But I couldn't speak. Instead, I screamed like a wild creature as I scrabbled against the walls to get out. There were no words I knew to explain what I felt inside. I wanted to get it out of me, to find a way to understand what had happened and what I'd done, but I couldn't.

I screamed for Magnus to come. All night sometimes. I

promised myself, if Magnus comes, I'll calm down. If Magnus comes, he'll make everything all right and I'll be able to make sense of what's happening. But he didn't come. I begged them to call him, asked every day for at least the first year. When he didn't come, they dismissed my feelings for him as childish, said I'd made them up and it was all in my head.

Why would a man like him have feelings for you, Freyja? He hasn't given you a second thought, believe me. Anything you think was between you is a figment of your imagination, nothing more.

I put my hands over my ears, then pushed my head between my legs, squeezing my knees together so I couldn't hear the lies they were telling me. I told myself it wasn't true and convinced myself he would come for me. But he didn't. So I thought maybe they were right about Magnus, but then they said the same about Annie and I didn't know what to think.

Your relationship with Annie McLeod wasn't really as you've described it, Freyja. Was it? God Almighty said. *She didn't want you. She wanted a child and when she couldn't have one, she substituted you for all those ones missing. It could have been any child she took a liking too. There's nothing special about you.*

That's not true. You're lying, I said, but I was no longer certain.

I didn't have the words to explain how I felt and the jabs and the shocks weren't going to make them appear. They said I was difficult. I was difficult on purpose when I curled up in a ball on my bed and pushed my nails through the soft skin in the palms of my hands. I couldn't unwind myself. They didn't believe I had no way of expressing what had happened to us.

I tried to recall the way Magnus had spoken. Tried to imagine how he would have explained the emotions raging inside me. That's why I liked him. He was the first person I'd ever met who really knew how to express himself. He could make me understand not only what he was thinking, but how I saw the world too. He saw through me into my deepest thoughts and knew them. Even Annie hadn't been able to do that.

There's no changing it now though. Magnus never came.

What's past is past.

When I have my one-to-one therapy sessions, we sometimes talk about this. Here they tell me that they were wrong at Kincraig Castle. I try to believe them, that the friendship Annie and I had was real, just as my feelings for Magnus were real.

Surely they must have been, don't you think?

If they weren't, I'm not sure I can carry on.

Tryggr, Falun, Orkney Islands
September 1964

By the beginning of September, the lessening of our daylight hours became noticeable and I saw that familiar gloom etch its way into Magnus's face. Like many Northern inhabitants, the approach of the winter darkness caused a physical reaction in Magnus as he battled to retain the warmth of the light inside himself. Although I recognised the signs, Annie had suffered terribly from the lack of light, as did Father, it wasn't a feeling that I shared. To me the darkness provided a blanket and a comfort. That may be hard to understand, but the darkness obliterated the emptiness. In the small worlds we existed in, bathed only in pools of artificial light, I could shrink my world to that tiny illuminated part and with that shrinkage the absence that never left me, that stretched out to the hilder in the summer months, became less visible and I felt more secure and able to cope.

Alongside the approaching darkness came the dramatic storms that lashed our western coastline followed by sunny still days that were all the more precious for their rarity. And with those storms came flashes of anger from Mother and Father that I had ignored their warnings and was spending too much time with Magnus and was at risk of *ruining my reputation*.

'You should be planning for the future, not chasing around a man like that who can only be after one thing,' Mother raged at me. 'The whole island is talking about it.'

She'd seen the letter from Mr Phelps reminding me that I had yet to approve some documents. Until these had been finalised, he couldn't sell Lochinsay. It had been on my list of things to do, but since I'd been spending every spare minute I had with Magnus, a lot of things like that had fallen by the wayside and been left undone.

That the time I'd spent with Magnus was the islanders' favourite subject for gossip infuriated me. I couldn't bear it that we were so watched. It was one of the reasons I wanted so badly to leave. I shrugged her anger off, telling her that all I was doing was taking him to see the real Falun, not the one the tourists thought was the real thing, so that he could use that in his work. She wanted to believe me, so she did. I saw relief on her face that she'd done her duty and confronted me and I'd provided a plausible excuse and now she could retreat back into her world, on her chair by the range and not think about it anymore. As much as I was glad not to be questioned any further, my relief was tinged with anger that she cared so little she'd swallow my obvious lies so easily.

At Mother and Father's insistence, I spent the weekend with them to finalise all the documents for Lochinsay, which we managed to do with a minimum of fuss and I wondered how I'd not found the time to do it before. I offered once again to give them a part of my inheritance, saying I didn't need all that money, but they refused. They didn't hesitate to say no. After that I felt better about it.

The morning that my life changed forever arrived with a fork of lightening that hit the ground inside our garden, leaving a burned-out patch on the grass. The noise was so violent that I woke and sat up, fearing Tryggr was at risk of burning down. I must, however, have fallen back to sleep. I had planned to lie down for a moment only, to allow my racing heart to recover from the shock of the lightening and allow the nausea I'd experienced for the previous few days to subside. I pulled over me the quilt that Annie and I had sewn together during our last long winter together, but in that conscious sleepiness my mind jumped, flashing scenes and pictures at me: white sandy beaches, Jeanie and Joe jumping in the surf, numbers floating like boats on the crests of the waves, a crimson tide washing trouble up on to the beach, Mother screaming my name and me running and running, but going nowhere.

I should have been downstairs helping Mother prepare breakfast. She found me curled up like a hermit crab. She pulled off the quilt and the scratchy blankets, exposing me to the chill morning air.

'Who do you think you are lazing around in bed when there are chores to be done?' she said.

I pulled the covers back over myself and curled up again into a tight ball, the heavy sickness that sat on my stomach pinning me to the bed.

'If you don't get up right now, you'll have a bucket of cold water thrown over you,' she shouted from the stairs.

I dragged myself out of bed and pulled a thick cardigan over my night clothes. The darkness had faded outside to a grey-purple light and a thick mist had slithered off the sea silently sliding over the moors towards us. As I stood, the nausea over-whelmed me and I had to rush down the stairs two at a time, in my socked feet, to the bathroom where I vomited.

It was then that Mother began to show some concern. Once I returned to the kitchen, she sat me down in her chair by the range where a pot of stew sat simmering sending clouds of scented steam into the chimney above. She ran her hands over me, pushing my hair back and tilting my face towards her so it would catch the light and she could see more clearly. I was ill so rarely that when I was, it was a matter of concern. She searched my face, felt my brow as she checked me over. I longed to get up and remove myself from the kitchen as the cooking smell made my stomach turn itself inside out, trying to reject the meal before I'd even eaten it. I knew what her next question would be, it was always the same.

'Have you cut yourself? Anywhere? Freyja, tell me.'

Mother was obsessed with cuts of any kind. She used the strongest antiseptic she could buy on the tiniest of abrasions. She tried to soak Father in bottle after bottle each time he came home from fishing as his hands were always cut from handling the nets and ropes, but he wouldn't allow it now. He had for a long while, but eventually he'd lost patience with her madness and brushed her away with requests that he be left alone in peace. Although Father thought she obsessed over him, what he experienced was nothing compared to the way she treated me and with me she would never tolerate any dissent.

She inspected my hands, rolled up my sleeves and checked my arms. As if all illness resulted from injury. I pushed her off me with some irritation.

Mother spoke again, trying to bring me out of the fog of nausea that gripped me tight in its grasp.

'No, I haven't cut myself. I'm ill, is all.'

I caught a glimpse of myself in the mirror hanging by the kitchen door, the one Mother used to check her appearance before answering callers, and I saw the grey tinge around my mouth, the waxy sheen stretched over my face glistening with the web of perspiration woven over me. The nausea overwhelmed me again and I rushed away from her to vomit once more.

'I'm calling for the doctor,' she said.

I protested, but she didn't hear me, or didn't want to. He came quickly, within the hour. I imagine that he expected me to be near death by the tone of her voice when she'd called. He must have abandoned his usual morning surgery in Skellinwall to come. I felt bad, that he'd made so much effort for what I thought must be a tummy bug or a bad whelk amongst the ones Magnus and I had cooked on the beach.

By the time he did come, bursting like lightening into the hallway, Mother had worked herself into a state and was running between the open front door and peering up the track to see if she could see his car and fussing around me lying on the sofa, plumping up the cushions and tucking a blanket around me, so I felt hot and claustrophobic as well as nauseous.

Mother brought him into the sitting room and stood hovering next to me, stroking my forehead and trying to flatten my damp curls away from my face. Dr Curtis placed a thermometer under my tongue and took my pulse, then fitted a tight band around my upper arm and measured my blood pressure. He peered at me.

'I wonder, Morag, if you'd mind waiting outside whilst I examine Freyja?'

Mother didn't move and continued to run her hand across my forehead.

'Morag?' Dr Curtis repeated, gently but firmly.

'Yes? Yes, of course, whatever you wish, Doctor.'

Dr Curtis stood up and followed her out of the room, closing the door behind her. He asked me a series of questions, some of which I knew the answer to and others I had to reach into the crevices of my mind to answer. He asked if he could examine my stomach and carefully he lifted my top upwards and my pyjama bottoms slightly down and pressed gently in a circle all the way around my stomach. Afterwards, he pulled Father's stiff ladder-backed chair next to me and leaned forwards, his hands resting on his knees.

'Am I right in thinking that you have become... very good friends with your guest, Mr Olafson?'

'Yes,' I said. I supposed that we were *very good friends* although I hadn't thought about it in that way before, what to call ourselves.

When he didn't say anything I added, 'I've been helping him with his symphony. It's about Falun.'

Dr Curtis let out a long slow breath. 'And am I right in thinking you are hoping to go to an art college soon? In London?'

I nodded.

'I'm sorry, Freyja. You'll not be going, not this time.'

He patted my hand as though that touch, that connection, could possibly help temper the panic that balled in my stomach and tried to rush in a tidal wave up through my chest and out of my mouth.

'What do you mean? Why?' I pulled myself up so I could sit hugging my knees to my chest. The tears started to flow and the faster I wiped them away the thicker they fell. I had to go. I couldn't stay here.

He took my hand in his. 'Because Freyja, you're going to have a baby. In the spring I would guess.'

I didn't stop when Dr Curtis yelled; I didn't stop when Mother tore out of the house after me screaming at me that I'd catch my death in the rain. I ran and ran my exposed skin stinging with the storm's ferocity. At The Cottages I stopped. He was playing that same tune again – Sospiri. Its haunting melancholy took hold of me, but instead of running in to see Magnus, I kept going past The Cottages and out across the moors, past the seamark, until finally I found myself at the edge of Falun with the vast, raging ocean spread out in front of me. I stood on the lip of the cliffs, the wind buffering me, so I teetered precariously, tipping forwards. Tor Ness Cove lay empty beneath me.

'Jeanie,' I yelled. 'Help me.'

I scrambled as fast as I could in my slippers down the steps towards the beach, tripping and sliding in the rain. At the bottom of the steps I ran towards the skerries that hunched glistening in the foaming sea, topped at the end by the mighty lighthouse. I raced across the sand, kicking it up behind me so I could feel it hitting my hair. I clambered on to the rocks, slipping on the thick bunches of wet seaweed as I made my way out towards the lighthouse. It wasn't possible to reach it as the wild, frenzied tide covered the metal pathway between the rocks and the lighthouse. Eventually, I stopped running and I sat on the flat rock on the very edge. The waves boomed and hissed in front of me, covering me with their spray. Beneath me at that point, the sea was unnaturally deep where the cliffs continued down and down and the blue of the water smudged into darkness.

The rock was soaked and my thin night clothes were soon saturated. I knew I was damned and that it, this thing inside me that made me want to claw at my stomach until I managed to rip it out, would bring shame on me and on my parents. I had no idea how I could put it right; how I could rid myself of its monstrous occupation of me. In my mind, I could hear the music Magnus had been playing and I felt I understood what the composer had been trying to capture. Sighs – a long slow release of air, an expelling, a deflation that leaves you emptied of everything you need to exist. That's how I felt, emptied out, hollow, except for that one thing, that lump growing inside me.

The narrow, sharp point of a whale's snout pierced the skin of the black sea directly in front of me, its blow hole ejecting a fine salty spray that misted the sodden air. Its mouth gaped, so I could see the hair-like plates hanging down, closed on the fish that put up little resistance. As its body crashed back into the dark sea, the whale's eye met mine and in its inky blackness I saw myself and I knew I was more alone than I'd ever been. The water hissed and fizzed as the sea settled back over the hole the whale had made. Underneath the surface, I saw a flash of white as the whale turned its underside skyward before swimming away.

I clutched the tufts of seaweed that sprouted between the

rocks. Jeanie had sent the whale. It was a message from her. In the quivering silence left behind I sat as still as I could, willing it to come back. The sea slapped against the rocks and above me the kittiwakes cried their own name over and over. I gripped the seaweed harder and tried to keep each breath as shallow as possible, fearing that if I breathed too deeply the souls of the dead who inhabit the kittiwakes would fly into my open lungs and possess me in the way the thing inside me had. Again, the sea beneath me parted and the whale's snout broke through, but it was slower this time, gently probing as though it sensed my fear, not of it, but of what was to come. Its head bobbed above the undulating sea, tiny breakers hitting its far side. Beneath the surface I saw the distinctive white bands on each of its pectoral fins and I recognised it as a minke whale. For a moment I forgot everything and thought how Magnus would have loved to have seen it and how he would have translated the sudden breaching of the surface of the sea and the appearance of the creature into music. I watched the water as it dripped off the whale's head into its eye and followed the grooves of its mouth before it disappeared into the sea.

How easy it would be to let go and allow the creature to carry me away, to slip underneath into the sweet softness of the waves and be wherever it was Jeanie had gone. Tiny stones trapped in the tread of my slippers fell into the water with a quiet clatter and then there was silence. Even the rain's assault had ceased. The whale's unblinking eye remained on me, black and fathomless, as it answered the question I hadn't asked. I felt my feet slide further towards the edge, the trapped pebbles scratching white lines on the rocks. I was at the edge of the world with only the confluence of oceans ahead of me, mixing in a torment as each battled the other for supremacy. If I dropped into that wild, churning sea it would claim me as one of its own. My caul wouldn't protect me, the whale would make sure of that, and my future would disappear in the same way Jeanie's had.

The whale broke his gaze, closed his eye and disappeared beneath the sea's skin once again. I stood up, the better to see it, my foothold too precarious.

'Wait!' I yelled into the empty air.

The curve of its hump breeched the surface temporarily and it was gone.

'Freyja.' The voice was indistinct and faint, but I knew it was Mother.

I looked up at the cliffs and saw her clambering down the pathway towards me. I turned back to the sea to watch the whale break the surface one more time, but there was nothing except the sea, empty and desolate.

I'd never seen Mother move as quickly. I was surprised at how confidently and deftly she moved across the rocks, considering how rarely she left the kitchen at home. I made my way towards her. All I wanted was to be with her. Not Jeanie. Not Annie. Not Magnus even. No, I wanted my Mother and for the first time since Jeanie had left, I saw that she wanted me. She reached out and grabbed hold of me as soon as she was close enough, pulling me tight into her chest, panic and fear etching deep lines into her forehead and between her eyes. She cried and said *my peedie one* over and over. She hadn't called me that for years and I cried.

'Don't worry. We'll work it out,' she said. 'We will. I've spoken to that man. I've told him to go. We don't need him.'

I pulled back from her, not understanding.

'Who? Who have you told to go?'

'Mr Olafson, of course.'

'But why?'

It was only then that it occurred to me to wonder how the thing had got there – the baby. You may think I'm stupid, but us girls, we weren't told, about stuff like that. Most of the girls in this place, who had the same happen to them, they didn't know either. You don't imagine that can happen, do you? Well, it did. You had better believe it. I remembered what the doctor said, the questions he'd asked about my *very good friend, Magnus*.

Mother looked at me and I saw something. Shame. It wasn't directed at me. It wasn't the shame I'd brought on her by having a baby growing inside me and no husband. It was shame of herself, of the lack she'd shown towards me. And I understood her better than I ever had. But after that she woke up and came back into herself – the woman she'd been before Jeanie left. Like she'd been asleep all these years.

'It's him that's got you into this mess, Freyja.'

She drew me into her, so my head rested on her bosom which was still heaving a little from her dash towards me. Mother sobbed and sobbed and her tears ran down my hair and soaked my face. I knew she was right and I also knew that he'd left me too. Everyone I loved always did.

In every family there is an event that changes everything, that affects the people involved, changing their history either for the better or for the worse. I'd always thought that in our family it was the disappearance of Jeanie that changed everything, maybe because I was a child when it happened and when you are a child the world revolves around you, swirling in a tornado with you right at the centre, the person most affected, the most important. I thought her leaving affected me most of all. We were a pair, Jeanie and I, and we did everything, almost everything, together. But we were really four with Mother and Father. To me the loss of her felt like I'd been torn in half, but their hurt was worse than mine and far from simply being torn in half, her disappearance shredded them into so many pieces they didn't know who they were anymore.

I didn't realise there was another event, something that caused such a deep-rooted hurt and unbearable shame it was as though a giant geo appeared overnight right in the centre of the family, taking the ground from beneath everyone's feet so there was nowhere left to stand.

Back at Tryggr, Mother ran a hot bath for me and stripped me of my clothes. She put bubbles into the water, from the bottle she saved for special occasions that I always coveted, but had never been allowed to use. I was grateful for the bubbles as they covered my nakedness, which was probably her intention although we both pretended they were a treat and nothing more. I loved her then, a painful burst of love edged with a grey line of regret; she saw me and understood me in a way I'd never realised. All those wasted years of ignorance bunched up against my chest and crushed the air out of me.

Once I was out of the bath, she wrapped me in her own terry towelling bath robe which she'd warmed on the range, then she towel dried my hair and brushed it, working through the knots. I couldn't remember the last time she'd brushed my hair. Even when Jeanie still lived with us, we would sit in a line – Mother brushing Jeanie's straight glossy hair and Jeanie battling to brush the knots from mine. I always thought Mother had instigated that routine, but now as she caught my hair, snagging the comb on the knots and ripping hairs from my scalp, I remembered how I'd screamed at her not to touch me, and it had been Jeanie who'd suggested *the train*. Jeanie. The only person I'd allowed near me physically until now. Until Magnus.

'When my mother was your age, younger even, she fell pregnant. With me. I never met my father. I don't know his name, even now. I did manage to find out many years later that he was the local doctor's son, expected to follow in his father's footsteps, and couldn't be saddled with a local girl and her bastard child when he hadn't even started his first year at university. My mother wasn't from here. Her family came from Westray. They were good people, but they were poor and not good enough for my father's family. My father's family moved away once they were discovered. The whole family! They upped sticks and left so they could avoid being associated with my mother. Imagine how that must have been for her. The whole island without a doctor because she was pregnant. It was in the papers, splashed across the front page for everyone to read: *Local girl in surgery scandal*. After he went along with what his parents wanted and walked out on her, she didn't have a hope. She was sent to a home for fallen women. Her whole family left Westray soon after too. They couldn't bear the shame apparently. I don't know where they went, there aren't any records. Two families broken and scattered because of me. When I was born, the people who ran the home found me a nice respectable family – a married couple who couldn't have children of their own. They were smart and everyone looked up to them. Yes, Freyja, Grandpa and Granny. They were nice enough, good to me and raised me here, on Falun, as their own. I was lucky. I had a good life with them, better than I could have hoped. Being adopted by them made me go up in the world.'

'And your mother, your real mother?' I said.

Mother paused and stopped the rhythmic brushing she'd fallen into once the knots had been worked out. She left the comb lodged in my hair.

'I don't know. I never saw her again. She died not long after I was born.'

'How did she die?' I placed my hand over the small swelling that already made my belly dome upwards in a hard ball. My hand felt like ice against my warm skin.

'Puerperal fever. Something that can come on after childbirth. That's what it says on the death certificate.'

'You don't believe it?' I turned to look at Mother. She'd removed the comb from my hair, but her hand remained poised in the air. She shook her head.

'I spoke to one of the nurses who worked at the home. She said my mother had been desperate after I'd gone. She refused to sleep and tried to escape from the home night after night. She clawed at doors and windows until her fingers bled. They had to put her in a straitjacket eventually and pin her to the bed. She screamed and screamed, day and night. When she died she had no fingernails left. She wanted to find me, but she never did. Puerperal fever was put down on the death certificate, but what had done for her was her heart. She died of a broken heart.'

Mother grabbed hold of my shoulders suddenly. Her grip was fierce and it cut into my skin even through the thick towelling of the robe.

'I won't let that happen to you, Freyja. You'll not be sent away like my mother was.'

I remembered the conversation between her and Father about Melanie Houghton marrying Billy and I understood. Unlike Mother, Father would want me gone, away, where the shame of my situation wouldn't infect him.

'But Father?'

'Leave him to me. I'll talk to him, make him understand. Now listen. You've still got the house at Lochinsay, thank goodness. We'll move you there. You'll be secluded and isolated and you'll have time to think and plan and prepare in peace, away from prying eyes and village gossip. Bless Annie, God rest her soul. I'll find someone, a housekeeper, to stay with you and care for you until the baby comes. After that... we'll see.'

Mother paced up and down, counting points out on her fingers as she thought through each part of her newly formed plan. I thought about Billy and Melanie rushing off to the mainland to buy her a ring. Melanie would have a wedding and a dress and she'd stay here on Falun, the wife of the postman, raising her child, not running a hotel abroad somewhere hot as she'd planned. She'd have to give up her job as manager of the Skellinwall Hotel, as I'd have to give up my plans to go to art college. How would she stand it? How would I?

'And will Magnus come with me, to Lochinsay?' I had to see him. Tell him about the baby. He'd be pleased. He'd never spoken about children, but surely, like Billy, he'd be happy, wouldn't he?

Mother ceased pacing and came and stood behind me, taking the comb and starting to run it through my hair once again. She brushed with one hand and with the other she smoothed the curls, trying to make them lie flat.

'No, my dear peedie one, he'll not.'

I turned to face her, but she wouldn't meet my eye, and kept her head hanging down as she reached out and pulled me close to her so I could smell the scent of the bubble bath lingering on her chest.

'He's gone Freyja. You remember? I told you. As soon as I told him about the baby, he packed up and went back to Norway. He took the first ferry to Kirkwall this morning. I don't think he'll be back.'

At first, I didn't realise where the sound had come from. The scream hung in the air bouncing back and forth from one wall to the next, ringing in my ears. It carried on and on, a never-ending echo, until Mother grabbed me and hugged me close to her so I could smell her talc. She repeated over and over that it would be all right, I'd be all right, she was there for me.

Magnus had packed everything: the pages of his manuscript, his fiddle, his few clothes, whilst she was still there. Couldn't get away fast enough, that's what she said. She didn't look at me when she said this.

After the scream came the shaking. It started in my hands and worked its way along my arms until eventually even my head shook in a weird, twitchy way. I couldn't make it stop even when Mother grabbed hold of me again and tried to hold me still.

He'd told me he loved me and I'd believed him, said it back to him too. We'd gone down to Tor Ness Cove one evening. I'd laid some creels out earlier in the day and I'd been lucky enough to snare a couple of lobsters. Magnus lit a small fire from old driftwood he'd found in one of the caves. It had been there for a long time, probably since the days when Joe and I had collected it, and it roared and crackled as it burned and soon the canteen full of sea water was boiling. Magnus killed the lobsters first by pushing a knife into their brains. He didn't like throwing them into the water to boil to death. Wasn't humane, he said. The meat was sweet and tender and soon we were covered in the mess of eating them. He kissed me, despite the fact that I had lobster juice all over my face, and whispered that he loved me, that he couldn't be without me, that I was his inspiration, his peedie bow mistress. How could he say those things to me, touch me as he did, with such tenderness and care, hold me so I felt safe, if he didn't love me? He said I completed him, reconnected him with the world, made him make sense, and that being with me was everything. Was it possible to say those things and not mean them? No, I didn't think so. The man I knew, and loved, who played that tune, Sospiri, with such truthfulness and honesty, wasn't capable of saying anything simply to get what he wanted. So why had he left me, left our child? I wouldn't believe what Mother said. He wouldn't abandon me. There was a reason for his absence I didn't yet understand. He'd come back to me. I believed in him. I had to.

I became aware that Mother had taken hold of my arm and was trying to pull me upright and force me upstairs.

'You need to lie down a while is all and you'll feel better,' she said.

For a small woman she had remarkable strength and soon she

was half carrying, half pushing me up the stairs.

The last time I'd screamed like that it had been Father who had carried me up the stairs and tucked me into my bed. The house had been full of people speaking in hushed tones and Mother had sat still, cradling the panda. As Mother dragged me upwards, my vision blurred and my legs started to give way beneath me so I couldn't find the next step up the staircase and I collapsed in a heap lying face down, my nose pressing into the carpet. Before I stepped over into the darkness, Jeanie leaned over me and whispered in my ear, but later once I'd recovered and Mother had set a cup of tea by my bed, I had no recollection of what she'd said, only the fragile memory of Jeanie singing *Oh my darling Clementine* as she jumped and splashed in the surf.

Mother worked hard to make Lochinsay comfortable for me and by November I'd moved there permanently. She brought a woman over from the Scottish Highlands, who'd grown up on Falun, to look after me. Mother didn't want a local woman, one who would gossip about my condition with the villagers and so Mrs Hanson was the perfect choice. She knew the island enough for it to be easy for everyone, but once her time was over, she'd return to her husband and her life in the Highlands.

Once I moved permanently to Lochinsay, Father never visited me. Mother though came every day. Sometimes we'd chat about Granny and Grandpa and her childhood and how Falun had changed since she was young and other times we'd sit quietly together and play cards or sew. For the first time, I began to see her for who she was. I had Mother back and I liked it. She made excuses for Father's absence: he was busy with the trawler repairs; he had business with Bill over at Kirkwall. In the end I asked her outright.

'It's too hard for him, is all. Seeing you this way. You're his peedie one. He can't stand to see you all grown up. For him it's like it's over, your childhood, and he's missed it. One second it was there and now it's not. He's blaming himself. Says he should have been there for you. He's failed you, is what he thinks.'

The one person, other than Mother and Mrs Hanson, who was there for me during those long, dark months of my confinement, was Joe. I was surprised, more than that, knocked sideways wouldn't be putting it too strongly, when I answered the door one morning to find Joe standing there. He had a whole load of smokies with him and a loaf of his mother's homemade bread and, for old time's sake, a bottle of strawberry Cremola.

'I've come for lunch,' he said.

The uneasiness that had existed between us disappeared and we reverted into the roles we'd had as children: me telling him what to do and him going along with it. It was nice. Easy and relaxing. We worked well together in the kitchen laying the food out on plates for lunch. I lit the old oil lamp Annie had liked to sit in the centre of the table and soon the kitchen had that warm friendliness it had when I'd spent my holidays there. Joe had grown tall and muscular, manly: the lost, awkward boy he'd once been long gone. I felt his strength and kindness calm me as he divided the food between the two of us.

'How are you doing?' he said as he ripped the bread apart and smothered it in swathes of thick, yellow butter.

'Apart from this?' I said, hand on my enormous stomach.

Joe grinned. 'Apart from that.'

'Fine, I suppose. There's a lot to sort out here and I'm working on a collage. Something I'd started with Annie. Trying to keep busy.'

I tried hard to sound upbeat, but the reality was that I was bored to death, uncomfortable with constant heartburn and I could no longer sleep. I'd asked Mother to bring me all the photographs I'd taken of Falun over the summer and I had spent the majority of my days again putting together the collages, but they were never right and I despaired that they ever would be.

The days passed into weeks and then months and the sun sank lower and lower into the hilder until eventually it failed to raise its head at all and my days were spent in a grey darkness brightened by Joe, who came more and more regularly. The days he didn't come were the worst and I sank into a gloom out of which I found it harder and harder to climb. Mother tried to help me by bringing me sweets and cakes as treats, but it wasn't enough. As the baby grew inside me, instead of filling me up with something real and solid, it created an empty space, a vacuum that stretched out into every part of me. On the days I spent alone, that vacuum acted like a black hole, sucking every part of what had been me in on itself, until all that remained of me had disappeared, leaving nothing but an aching emptiness.

I waited too for any news of Magnus, but despite asking Mother everyday if he'd written, the answer was always the same.

'No, peedie one. Not today.'

I asked her to bring his address so I could write to him. I couldn't accept that he'd leave me, but she wouldn't give it to me. Said it was better this way and I was better off without him.

One day over lunch, I asked Joe the same question.

'Find it for me, Joe. I need to write to him. I need to know what he thinks about this,' I said, pointing at my huge stomach.

I didn't consider the lump as anything other than an inconvenience that had yet to be dealt with. The nauseous feeling I dragged around everywhere, I blamed on The Parasite as I'd taken to calling it, rather than on the longing that gnawed away inside me that could only be healed by the feel of Magnus's arms around me and the smell of his vanilla-sweet tobacco lingering in his hair.

But Joe shook his head too. 'I can't do that Freyja.'

'Why not?' I said, banging my fist on the table so the plates rattled. 'I thought you were my friend, Joe MacKenzie.'

I ran out of the kitchen and curled myself up on the sofa from where I could see the sea raging in the storm that lashed the island and had left Joe marooned at Lochinsay for hours. I wanted him to go, to leave me alone with my memories of Magnus, but even they upset me. It had been so long since I'd seen him that I struggled to bring his face into my mind, much as I had once struggled to resurrect Jeanie's image. If it hadn't been for the constant swelling of my stomach, I'd have doubted that he'd ever existed.

Joe found me lying on the sofa, sobbing. It was something that had started to happen a great deal: the crying. It was as though a layer of tears had wormed its way under my skin and the slightest dent or scratch, angry word or look, would cause a rupture and out the tears would flow.

'The only one who knows his address, is your mother, and she's not saying.'

Joe shuffled in the doorway like he had more to say, but didn't want to say it.

'What is it?'

'From what I've overheard, my mother and yours discussing it, it looks like he's not coming back. I'm sorry, Freyja.'

Joe sat next to my feet, perching on the edge of the sofa. 'Freyja, look at me,' he said very quietly.

I turned my head towards him, wiping my nose on my sleeve, something I would never have done in front of anyone else but Joe.

'There's something I wanted to ask you,' Joe said. He sat very still and composed. The boy he'd once been long vanished. 'I wonder if you'd agree to marry me Freyja.'

I laughed. I thought he was joking. He wasn't.

'Don't say anything. Hear what I've got to say first, please. You're in trouble. You need help. All I want out of life is to stay here on Falun and build boats. I'm not interested in girls. Not like that. That's why I was so annoyed about missing the rugby that time I broke my leg. Rugby was my cover and you messed it up! You must know that. Freyja?'

I realised that, of course, I did know and I always had. Other than having been sweet on Jeanie when we were small, Joe had never been like the other boys I'd known. He wasn't like the boys from school who'd leered at Jeanie and I in a way that made us uncomfortable and he certainly wasn't like the boys I'd met at school dances who wanted to kiss you within minutes of meeting you. Horrible disgusting kisses that excavated your mouth and left you wanting to vomit, rather than the kisses Magnus had given me that had made my stomach dance up into my chest. No, Joe had always been my friend and nothing more. We'd fished, dug peats and cried with laughter, dancing under the moon at Midsummer. I'd been relaxed with him, had sat between his legs with his arms around me to keep me warm on long, white nights on the beach. Joe was just Joe. Except now I saw that Joe wasn't Joe in the way that I wasn't Freyja. We hid behind our masks, the two of us.

'You could do whatever you wanted if you marry me. Go to art college if you like. The baby, I'll bring him or her up as my own. We can stay here on Falun. Be normal. We'll all be safe if you say yes. Say yes Freyja.'

How easy it would have been to say yes. Everyone would be happy, wouldn't they? Father could pretend it had been Joe's all along, as I knew he pretended he could be the one to bring Jeanie home. Mother wouldn't have to fight him for me to keep the baby. Over time everyone would forget the strange blond-haired man who'd invaded our shores and disturbed the equilibrium. With Mother and Mrs MacKenzie to help, I could find a way to go to college. I could even make friends with Billy and Melanie. We could have family days out together. Joe and I could hide behind a mask of respectability in the way Mother had. We could make an effort to be happy.

I thought of Annie then, how she hadn't ever hidden behind masks, how she'd always been herself. She'd made me feel unique, that I wasn't something to be improved upon, perfected in some way and that being myself was enough. It wasn't until I met Magnus that I understood Annie wasn't the only person in the world capable of making me feel like that. But Joe? Joe was my friend, but he didn't love me like that.

When I looked at him sitting on the edge of the sofa, handing us both a lifeline, I couldn't take it. Whatever had happened between Magnus and I, it had happened to us. I couldn't allow Joe to saddle himself with me and my bastard child, however much he thought it would help him too. I didn't want Joe. I wanted Magnus and I believed that he would come back for me. I would wait for him. So I said no.

Ceredigion Mental Asylum, West Wales
June 1983 7pm

I'm glad you're still here. I wasn't sure you would be. Now I've started I want to get to the end, but the worst is yet to come and I needed some time to think things through before carrying on. I haven't told this story all the way through in one go before and it's harder than I thought.

It's supper now. Ellie will bring us some sandwiches soon. I don't much like sandwiches, but that's all we get in the evenings, so you have to put up with it or go hungry.

Here's Ellie with our plates now. I'm sorry, it looks like it's ham today. They're the worst ones of all.

Of course, you knew that part of the story was coming. It wasn't a shock for you in the way it was for me when the doctor first told me what it was that made me feel sick the whole day long. You'll think I must have known; I must have suspected something.

I didn't, I couldn't have. Life was different on our isolated tiny island and we didn't know about things like that in the way people do today. I've seen it on the television in those soaps that are on. Youngsters know things now that we couldn't have even dreamed about. We were innocent and if I had to choose, I think I'd still choose my childhood of innocence, even though it left me with no concept of what having a baby meant.

I've talked about what happened with many people now over the years. With Mother and Father, the court, the people here and at Kincraig Castle, although not so much there. I didn't mind talking about it, I didn't like it, but I knew it had to be done, so I did. Talking about it with them was nothing compared to how I feel telling it to you.

You broke me, worse than Jeanie, worse than Magnus even, but you saved me too. Once I finish telling you everything, I hope you won't break me again.

You won't, will you?

Lochinsay, Falun, Orkney Islands
April 1965

By mid-April the rainbows arrived in abundance, lighting up the sky in waves of colour. I thought for a while that if the baby was a girl, I would call her Rainbow. When I suggested this to Joe, he wrinkled his nose and squashed his mouth together the way he did when I offered him a gingernut biscuit instead of a flapjack. Joe still visited me most days. I think he thought I'd change my mind and I nearly did on many occasions when I saw how hard he was trying to show me that we could be good together, but I didn't.

During the long hours I spent alone, I worked and re-worked my collages and I filled the entire wall of my bedroom with the countless photographs I'd taken. I chopped them up into pieces, some as tiny as mosaic tiles, some I enlarged to four or five times the usual size. The lighthouse moved further to the left along the wall as I rearranged the design, yet the seamark, that stood watching it, remained in the centre of the picture. The skies charted the progression of the light and the weather through the seasons with the darkest section above the lighthouse. I liked the contrast of the white of the lighthouse against the storm darkened skies, which I often shot in black and white to add more drama.

'You still working on that, Miss Freyja,' Mrs Hanson said.

She left the tea, cheese and crackers on a tray on top of the chest of drawers I'd brought from my room at Tryggr. Mrs Hanson advocated eating for two and brought me food at regular intervals throughout the day, staying to make sure I ate in front of her as I *had to keep my strength up*. As a consequence, I had gained three stone and could hardly reach the top sections of the collage, my stomach protruded so far forwards.

'How's the peedie one doing?' she said as she placed her hand on my stomach.

The Parasite obliged by giving her a forceful kick. I could hardly look at my naked stomach now. I didn't like the way I could see the arms and legs moving around inside me, pushing against my skin like it was preparing to punch its way out of me. It made me feel sick. I know that's not the thing to say, but it's how I felt.

Mrs Hanson stood back as far as she could to look at my collage. She stood observing it head on, which wasn't the best way to appreciate it. I always stood sideways on to it, which gave a better feeling of being immersed in the landscape of Tor Ness Head.

'It's finished, is it? Only I hear you muttering, *It's not right, it's not right*, the whole time you're up here rearranging it. Though I can hardly see any difference one day after another,' she said.

'It's almost done, I think,' I said.

Mrs Hanson rolled her eyes and tutted. I knew she thought I was crazy working on it constantly. She didn't see the point in it.

'You've a bairn coming to care for soon. That's what you should be planning for. Not wasting time on this.'

She watched me drink the tea and eat the cheese and crackers, then put everything back on the tray. Before she left the room, she turned and took another look at the collage.

'It maybe me, I'm not saying it isn't, but it is funny, Miss Freyja, how you've taken a picture of every angle of Tor Ness Head it's possible to take and stuck it on that wall. Seems like every blade of grass is up there, except, only the Lord knows how you've managed it the amount of time you've spent on it, but you've missed out the most beautiful spot. There's a big hole, right there, where St Ninian's Cove should be. You're daft, you are. Baby brained, that's what.'

She walked out shaking her head and laughing at my idiocy. I turned back to look at the image on the wall and the emptiness inside it that I'd never seen.

'That's where I last played with Jeanie,' I said.

I woke later, it was at some point during the night and I knew something had changed: a disturbance in the atmosphere of the house. My first thought was – the baby's coming – but there was no pain, no tightening of my abdomen. There had been a sound, I was sure. One I wasn't used to. Not the weather, or the sea, or Mrs Hanson busying herself in the kitchen. I listened again. Nothing.

I heaved myself out of bed, my full stomach hindering my movements. Acid rose up and burned the back of my throat and I sat on the edge of the bed for a moment waiting for the sensation to pass and for the prickling fear that chilled my skin to take precedence.

Outside, the sea roared and crashed against the rocks on which the house perched as though it wished to devour us. I switched on the light, but it didn't work: the electricity must have been cut off again. I fumbled in the drawer for the matches I always kept there, struck one against the side of the box and lit the stub of a candle stuck on to a saucer. The large shadows created by my grotesque physique made me shudder.

I strained to hear again the sound that had woken me, but all I could hear was the wind whipping the ocean into a frenzy and the banging of a loose outhouse door. I reached out to the end of the bed and found my old cardigan lying there. I pulled it around my shoulders, hugging it over my swollen abdomen, and lumbered to the closed door. I pressed my ear against the cool wood and listened. Nothing but silence. I stood there for a few minutes, the silence ringing in my ears until, there: a sound, a new sound.

I leaned back against the door, my legs shaking so I feared the baby's hold on my insides would be loosened. I wrapped the woollen cardigan around myself tighter still as the cold air pinched my skin, supporting the weight of the baby within the hammock of my hands. On the wall opposite, the shadows danced as the breeze licked through the gap around the rattling window frames. I knew who it was out there. Knew she'd come for me at last. Jeanie.

When was the last time I'd seen her? Had really it been nine years? I tried to remember the stories Jeanie had told me. I was sure that selkies could only contact humans for a short time before they had to return to the sea. They couldn't make contact again for seven years. She'd come to take from me the one thing I had that she didn't: my baby. I slid down the door, my legs no longer capable of keeping me upright.

The voices downstairs grew louder. There were at least two. Footsteps marched along the stone flagged hallway. I heard the front door open, then close, then silence. I felt the fear as a rush as it shot along my nerve endings, forcing me into action, and I scuttled into the darkest corner of my bedroom behind the wardrobe.

I'm not sure how long I sat huddled in the corner shivering, but eventually daylight seeped through the heavy curtains and I no longer needed the candle.

Then Mrs Hanson came in.

'There's someone here to see you,' she said.

I sat up too quickly and my head rushed upwards away from me. Would I recognise Jeanie after all these years? In my mind Jeanie had stayed the same. She was still that eleven-year-old school-girl about to head off on her big adventure to boarding school. She'd be twenty now. What would I say to her? All the years of her absence bunched up inside me.

'There, there, Miss Freyja. You'll be right as rain soon enough,' said Mrs Hanson. She put her arm around my waist to steady me.

She opened the wardrobe and pulled out one of my maternity dresses, red velvet with a dark blue sash under the bust. Mother had found it in a secondhand shop in Kirkwall. It was the one I looked best in, but hardly wore. I didn't need to look good shut away out here at Lochinsay.

'You'll want some proper clothes on. Here, wear this.'

I raised my eyebrows at her. Why?

'Just put it on.'

She turned her back as I removed my nightdress and pulled the dress over my head. Mrs Hanson took the hairbrush from the top of the dresser and ran it through my hair. I pushed her away. What was wrong with her?

Downstairs in the sitting room, a small, delicate woman stood in the centre of the room. She had long blonde hair dragged back into a rough ponytail. Her long black coat had droplets on the shoulders that caught the light and sparkled. It was still raining outside. I placed my palms flat over the front of my stomach. I had never seen this woman before, but I knew with a certainty that surprised me who she was and the despair that came over me at the realisation made me wish she had been Jeanie.

The woman turned towards me. She was beautiful, but I could see she didn't know it. She'd made no effort with her appearance, no make-up, hair scraped back, dowdy clothes. None of that mattered. I felt foolish in my best dress. As she appraised me, it wasn't anger I saw in her eyes, although it should have been. It was sadness, pity even. I knew then what love really was. It wasn't the joy and hope that everyone made you believe. It wasn't sunsets and flowers; music played in a candlelit room; it wasn't that overwhelming urge to press yourself into the other person and meld into them so that you became a whole entity together. Or rather, it was that, but it was also cruel and hurtful and demanded from you sacrifices that could be too painful to bear. Love can take you to hell. I thought of Mother kneeling before her god praying for something that could never happen, hoping her love would change everything. I thought of Father, sacrificing everything he had, his whole life, to a love that wouldn't die. I looked properly at the small delicate woman standing in front of me. She didn't have to say anything – I could see the horror that love had brought her, how it had punched her in the guts and carried on doing so even though she put up no resistance and stood there taking every blow. Love sickens us at the same time as it lifts us up to be the best we can be. Love demands and sometimes it demands too much.

She'd made no effort with her appearance that day because she didn't have to. She considered that the love she bore cloaked her enough and it did.

We stood for a moment staring at each other, taking in Magnus's past and his future and although I wanted to hate her, to put on to her all the anger and jealousy that clawed at my insides at what Magnus had visited upon us both, I couldn't. I couldn't hate her. All I felt was an overwhelming sorrow.

'This is Saga Olafson, Freyja,' Mrs Hanson said.

'Magnus's wife,' Saga said.

Mrs Hanson made tea and sat us on the sofas and got the fire going again so at least there was some semblance of hospitality, of warmth and friendliness even, though the ice that lay between Saga and I, sitting on different sofas opposite one another, may as well have been Antarctica.

'You are not the first,' Saga said.

She didn't move, didn't fiddle with her hands, her hair, her clothes. Her fingers sat still like they were made of wood and needed the attention of a puppeteer to bring them to life. They reminded me of Jeanie's wooden dancing doll, the one I coveted throughout our childhood. She always kept the strings spun into a single strand and wrapped in a tissue so that they didn't tangle and would always be ready for use. My doll's strings were a mass of knots, rendering the puppet unusable. Saga's controlled composure was comparable to the stiff unyielding face of Jeanie's doll, but the tone of her voice had changed and now had a sharp edge of menace that made me wary.

Saga took small delicate sips of her tea and placed the cup and saucer on the side table. Her stillness made me fidget and my skin burst into a round of itches, one leading to the other.

'Let me ask you something, Freyja. When he first played his violin for you, did he ask you to choose which bow sounded better? Even though you know nothing about music and couldn't possibly be in any way helpful to his decision?'

The cold from the stone floor shot upwards through my feet and wrapped itself in a band around my chest finding the spaces between my ribs and squeezing tightly until I became lightheaded.

I remembered the time he'd shown me the bows and I'd chosen the Tourte. I remember holding them, feeling the difference in their balance. I could tell, couldn't I? A flash of anger rippled through me at Saga's words. Despite my lack of musical knowledge, I had been sure at the time that I had been able to tell the difference and had made a definite choice, but now I doubted myself. Who was I to think that I knew one bow from another? I'd never even seen a bow before, never held one in my hands and considered its merits. I remembered how he'd played each of the pieces. Had he guided me to choosing one over the other? Had I been stupid, gullible? No, I was sure I hadn't. I had been guided perhaps, as any novice would be. He hadn't tricked me. I started to protest, to say that she knew nothing of our relationship, but she carried on speaking so I stopped.

'Yes, I remember the day he asked me to help him choose. It was in the early days, when I too was young and naïve like you, but unlike you I did at least understand what he was asking me. I had held bows all my life. As a violinist from two years old and later with the viola. I, at least, understood what he wanted, but since then, no, not so much. I think Amelie, a beautiful little French girl, remembered when he asked her the same thing, as did Greta, the Austrian and Sofia, the Italian. Lovely girls, all of them. Lovely like you are lovely. Young too, he always finds the young ones, the ones that fawn over him and can't believe that someone like him would even look at them. It makes an impression on you, doesn't it? A man like him standing alone and exposed so close to you, playing his fiddle just for you, making that beautiful sound, a sound so pure and light that it pulls the tears out of your eyes. I can picture it now. His face in profile, so handsome, a distinguished silhouette, his long white hair vibrating with the movement, with his passion. Yes, it was quite something for me too, I know how you felt.'

I put my teacup down. I couldn't take even one sip. I would be sick. That's how it had been. That was it exactly. But how could this woman know how I'd felt? She couldn't unless it was true. She wanted me to doubt him and now I was beginning to. Saga paused for a moment with her eyes closed. When she came back to me her eyes flashed and I saw another Saga, a dangerous woman, a woman with a blade of steel running straight through her; one who would fight for what she wanted.

'Where's Magnus?' I said. Where was he? Still in Norway? Had she come alone to confront me? The Magnus I knew, or thought I knew, wouldn't have left me to face her alone, but I didn't know him. Not at all. I thought of all the moments we'd shared together, the look on his face as we'd made love, and how he'd cried out my name, repeating over and over that he loved me. Had none of it been real? My stomach tightened and relaxed and I pushed myself forwards to the edge of the sofa.

'You thought you were the only girl in the world, the way he looked at you, focusing his eyes on you, didn't you? He doesn't turn away from your gaze. He can be mesmerising. When he wants to be.'

Her cheeks were flushed and her chest rose and fell more quickly than it had before. My stomach turned over and over and I wondered if I would vomit. Saga stood and walked over to me. She moved with such poise and grace, as though she were dancing to music only she could hear, and I was afraid of her. I'd heard the phrase rooted to the spot before; I'd thought it nonsense, a cliché, but that's how I felt – as though a thick icicle had shot from the stone floor and stabbed the sofa I sat on, pierced my stomach and carried on into my chest so I couldn't move.

'I was the first and I will be the last of his bow mistresses. That is what he calls all his women, did you know that? You are the fifth now. He has had one for each of his symphonies. I am at least a string player and he knows it. In the end it will be my opinion that counts. He needs a muse, someone to give him the passion, the desire to write. He likes to be carried away by his emotions and those first moments of love, when it feels as though it is controlling you, consuming you, twisting your guts so you cannot eat or sleep. He needs to feel that to find the place within himself where his genius lies. His favourite composer, Sibelius, had whiskey, a bottle a day by the end, God help him. I am sure other composers had their vices. Magnus has his girls. He would not have been able to write this one without you. You must have chosen well. Which bow did you decide on? No, let me guess. It was the Tourte, wasn't it? Yes, I am right. A good choice. It would have enabled him to reach into himself for the sound he wanted, to expel it and put it on the page. It has worked. The symphony is magnificent. His best. You look surprised, Freyja, that I know. I have read it. We met through music. Him on his fiddle, me on viola. We played quartets together in the early days. I have never been second fiddle, Freyja. I never will be. I am the one who has supported him all these years. I have given up my own chances for him. He knows that. He always comes back to me. He brought this symphony back to me first, as he always does, but it has gone too far this time. There has never been a child before.'

I saw the way she looked at me. She looked at me with relish, like a she-wolf about to devour her prey and within me something switched on, something rose up in a red-hot flame that galvanised me into action when I realised why she was here. She didn't care about telling me this about Magnus: no, it wasn't that. She hadn't even come to claim him back for herself, not if she was honest. She'd come for my child.

Outside, the wind dropped and the rattling of the window frame receded into stillness. The air curdled into something so thick I couldn't draw breath from it. Saga took a step towards me. I stepped back, my hands covering my stomach. You'll not have it; you'll not have my child.

'Get away from me,' I said. I carried on walking backwards towards the hallway and the door. Every part of my body screamed at me to run, run, as fast as you can, away from her. I kept my gaze fixed on her, watching, waiting, expecting that at any moment she would leap at me and rip my stomach open to snatch my baby. I'll not let you. I'll fight you with everything I have.

Saga reached out towards me. Her hand a claw that would tear me apart. Get away, leave me alone. Don't touch me. My arms battered the air in front of me, trying to keep her at a distance.

'Go away, go away. Leave us alone,' I screamed.

Mrs Hanson grabbed my arms and stood between Saga and me. 'I think it's better if you leave now, Mrs Olafson. We don't want to continue to upset Freyja in her condition, do we?' Then she guided me back into the sitting room, forcing me to sit down on the sofa and cajoled Saga towards the sitting room door. 'I think it's better if you go. This is a big shock for the girl, you understand.'

Saga protested, but Mrs Hanson wasn't having any of it, repeating, *No, I think it's for the best*, and forcing her out of the sitting room and into the hallway, leaving me alone.

With Saga gone, everything she'd said came flooding back. All those others. Was it true that I'd been one in a long line of girls? I remembered the way he'd looked at me, the love in his eyes, the way he'd embraced me and allowed himself to be cradled in my arms. He'd been so vulnerable, so open and unprotected. He'd exposed the heart of himself to me and I'd held his soul in my hands and nurtured it like the precious gift it was. Was it really possible to act in such a way simply to get what you wanted? I didn't believe it. I needed to clear my head, think. Hearing that Mrs Hanson had gone upstairs, I took my chance. I pulled one of the blankets off the sofa, wrapped it around myself and ran out of the door, through the garden and out to the cliffs.

As I ran, all I could think was where was the Magnus I knew in the stories she'd told me? It didn't make any sense. The rain, still heavy despite the drop in the wind, soaked into the blanket making it a heavy burden to run with. And what about Mother? Had she known about Saga all along? I thought back to that time on the skerries, when I'd see the whale. What had Mother said to me? She said she'd spoken to him and told him to go. She'd known, hadn't she? She'd known and hidden it from me.

What Magnus and I had was real. It wasn't possible to lie so convincingly. My heart told me this was true, that there was no other conclusion, but Saga's presence and Magnus's absence stood between my heart and my head and however I tried, I couldn't see around them. I reached The Great Stacks and stood on the cliff edge watching the roaring sea. Over there, beyond the hilder, lay Canada. I could have gone there, with Annie, touring art galleries, having a ball. I could have been at art college armed with my new knowledge. I could have been anything I wanted. Instead, I was about to give birth to a child already abandoned by its father. I stood there so long I started to shiver with cold. The blanket and my red velvet dress soaked through. The answers I sought couldn't be found here. I needed to go back. I needed to find Magnus. I wanted him to tell me the truth. I would only believe it if it came from him.

Back at the house Mother was there. Mrs Hanson had called her to come. I started to ask her what she knew, why she'd kept this from me, but Mrs Hanson wouldn't let me speak until she'd taken me upstairs, removed my wet clothes and dried my hair. Back downstairs, Mother made me sit in front of the sitting room fire and Mrs Hanson brought me a bowl of soup. They left me to eat and retreated into the kitchen. They spoke in whispers so I couldn't hear. I didn't need to. It was obvious what they were discussing. I could tell from the tone of Mrs Hanson's voice that she was annoyed she hadn't been told the facts. *If you'd told me, I would never have let her in*, was the only thing I heard.

Through the open curtains, I watched the lighthouse beam as it began its sweep across the bay, illuminating the black sea and the static clouds holding the moon on the edge of a precipice. Once I'd finished eating, I stood to take my bowl into the kitchen, but I was gripped by a sudden and overwhelming urge to cry. I couldn't move and held on to the marble mantelpiece; it felt clammy under my touch, but I couldn't let it go. If I did, I was afraid that I would collapse.

The pain, when it came, seized my insides, twisting them into spirals tighter and tighter so I couldn't move. I curled my bare toes into the rug beneath my feet, gripping and gripping so I could remain upright, and closed my eyes as tight as I could. I started to shake and then the tears came in great convulsions which horrified me they were so furious. The water I'd carried around with me for an eternity left me in a sudden shock, warm as it hit my body. I bent forwards and the moan that escaped surprised me it was so alien. I felt completely and utterly alone.

Mrs Hanson and Mother ran in from the kitchen and held me upright, guiding me out of the room.

'Oh my dear. Baby's coming. Let's get you upstairs and into bed. It'll be more comfortable. There, there, it'll be all right,' said Mrs Hanson.

The pains came quickly, like the waves that crashed and tore at the beaches and I had no time to recover in between. Mrs Hanson used a cold flannel to cool my forehead and allowed me to squeeze her hand with each wave of pain as the contractions tore me in half. Mother knelt at the end of the bed, waiting for the baby to appear. I closed my eyes in shame at having her see me like that. When the moment came, Mother told me to push with every ounce of strength that I had within me. I pushed and pushed with everything I possessed to expel the baby out of me and finally the slimy body slipped into Mother's hands.

Mother cut the cord, then wrapped the screaming baby in a towel. She cleaned its face and handed the bundle over to me.

'Congratulations, Freyja love. It's a girl,' she said.

I looked into the face of the child. Our child, mine and Magnus's. She was a tiny little elf with a mass of blonde hair: Magnus's hair. But the face was Jeanie's. I knew her name immediately: Jeanette. I ran my finger along the length of her cheek, watched her tiny mouth practise sucking and her eyes flicker as she became used to the light in the world and I thought: this is love.

A couple of days later, I saw him from my bedroom window - the flash of his white hair bright against the grey skies. He was striding towards Lochinsay, towards me. I moved away from the window, pressing my back into the wall, hoping that the coolness from the stone would calm me. I peeked again. Yes, I was right. He was coming to see me. He'd come back. He loved me after all. I pinched my cheeks to liven up my tired complexion. I stood poised, waiting for the knock on the door, but it never came. I turned back to the window and saw him again as he disappeared around the headland walking towards the Sky Path and Tor Ness Head. Why hadn't he come to see me, or his child? He must have known Saga would have told me everything. Why had he gone away? He didn't love me. Didn't want us, the baby and me. That was the only conclusion, wasn't it?

Since the baby had come, I hadn't slept. I watched her sleeping in the makeshift crib Father had placed next to my bed a few days before the birth. I hadn't seen him bring it. I'd been asleep and he'd crept in and placed it there on the floor. It was small and had been hammered together in a hurry. I knew if I lay down and closed my eyes sleep would possess me, but whenever I felt it pulling at me, I'd sit up and pace the room, looking out of the window. Watching. I rubbed my face with my hands, then thrust them into the water jug Mrs Hanson had left me to wash with, splashing the water on my face. I couldn't think straight. What did it mean that he was here, but had walked away? It wasn't good. Think of the lies, the deceit and the humiliation, how he'd used me, betrayed me. Think of how much he'd hurt me, leaving me like he did. Not sending one word to explain why. Focus on that, not my churning stomach, not the ache pulling me back towards him.

I looked back at the baby. She fitted here, as if the room had been waiting for her to come along and fill the space left by all the babies Annie had planned to have. She had her arms thrown over her head. She'd be fine for a while. I had to see him. I had to know. I pulled on a thick jumper, and ran downstairs and out into the garden, yelling to Mother and Mrs Hanson that I needed to take some air and I'd be back shortly. I didn't stop to hear their reply.

I didn't know what I was doing, what it was that I expected from him, but I knew that I had to go, I had to see him. Ahead, on the horizon, the black thunderheads gathered like mourners at a funeral, but the cliffs in front of me were bathed in the harsh white light of the pre-storm sky. On the very edge of the cliff I could see Magnus sitting, his legs dangling over the edge. I froze, unable to move towards him, then I smelled the sweet vanilla scent of his pipe tobacco. Out of all the tobaccos he smoked, that one was my favourite; it was the one that lingered in my hair, the one that reminded me most of the days when I couldn't bear to be parted from him, when time would move too slowly when we were apart and all too quickly in the time we found to be together. As I watched him, I sensed something was different about him. I walked slowly towards him, even though my heart told me to run, to forgive him, and beg him to leave Saga, to forget all the others who had come before me and to stay with me, with our child, to be a real family. It could still be possible.

It was then that I saw it: his stillness. The silence that held him in a grip had rendered him stiff and I saw that everything Saga had told me was true. I also saw that Magnus no longer heard the music. He turned around, suddenly aware of my presence behind him. He looked lost, vulnerable like a child, and I wanted him, I wanted to make it better, to draw him close to me and hold him in my arms, even though I knew there was no way I could. He stood up and faced me, but he made no effort to walk towards me. Instead, he waited for me to reach him. He leaned forward and kissed me lightly on the cheek, a kiss so chaste I could cry. I cupped his face in my hands, drawing it towards me and kissed the salty dampness of his forehead. He looked down and smiled, but it was a sad, sorrowful smile. We sat next to each other, side-by-side looking out over the sea. There was a distinct divide cutting the ocean in half. One side dark, the other light. We were on either side of that line. Would we have the courage to cross it?

We sat in silence for a while, watching the storm rolling towards us together with the rising tide that crashed against the rocks. Magnus relit his pipe and leaned in towards me, resting his head against mine.

'I came here to be with you,' he said. 'This is where I hear the music I wrote for you.'

'Not today, though,' I said.

Magnus shook his head. 'No, not today.'

The storm out to sea drew closer, sucking the last remaining rays of clear light into its centre. The wind grew stronger and I felt the chill from the damp grass creeping into me. Magnus reached out and took hold of my hand.

'Why did you leave me?' I said.

He didn't have a chance to answer. We saw her at the same time: Saga. Walking towards us along the Sky Path. Father was by her side. He stood up and helped me to my feet, let go of my hand and turned away from me, watching his wife.

'I'm sorry, Freyja. Forgive me,' he said. He walked towards them.

I stared at his profile, the way his long nose curved over and his forehead arched backwards. It was a profile I loved more than I'd ever loved anything or anyone before. Even Jeanie. But it was different now. He'd hidden a part of himself from me. He'd kept something back, something I'd had a right to know and although I wanted to pull him back towards me, to feel the curve of his body next to mine, I couldn't. I saw him for who he was and I wasn't sure I liked it. I could no longer trust him and because of that I couldn't forgive him for not being the person I believed he was before I really knew him.

The baby. I turned away and ran back to the house where I'd left the baby sleeping. As I ran, I realised I'd been so focused on seeing Magnus that I'd ignored the approaching danger. I shook my head, trying to focus on what it was I needed to do, but lack of sleep weighed me down and I couldn't think quickly enough. I was certain, though, of one thing: there could be only one reason why Father and Saga were heading towards Lochinsay. I remembered the look I'd seen in Saga's eyes. Magnus's distance, his apology. The baby. They were coming for my baby.

Back at the house, I ran in through the back door, along the hallway, up the stairs and along the corridor towards my bedroom. The baby's crib lay empty. Nevertheless, I pulled out the sheets and blankets throwing them to the floor, searching through thin air to find something I knew wasn't there. I ran downstairs and into the kitchen. Empty. Through the hallway and into the sitting room.

Mother and Mrs Hansen had the baby laid out on a mat cleaning her. They looked up at the same time.

'What is it, Freyja?' Mother said.

I pointed towards the cliffs.

'Father. Saga.'

Mother fastened the buttons on the baby's cardigan and wrapped her in a blanket and handed her to me, then guided me to the sofa where she pressured me into sitting down. She sat next to me, placing her hand lightly on my knee. She wouldn't meet my eye. Mrs Hansen nodded at Mother and left us alone.

I stood up, clutching the baby tight to my chest. 'No,' I said. 'No.'

I started to back out of the room. I'd take her, go anywhere. To the Mainland, to England even. I'd find a way.

'It's for the best, Freyja,' Mother said.

I thought she'd run towards me, try and stop me leaving, but she sat there picking at a thread that had come loose in one of the sofa cushions. I turned to leave, but I was too late. Father and Saga were already standing in the doorway. Mother had known all along that they were coming. She'd lied to me too. I thought she'd changed her attitude to me, I thought we had become closer, but I was wrong. I couldn't move. I didn't turn away from her. Instead I stood and faced her, even though the geo that had once opened up under her mother now opened up under me, and everything I'd believed and everything I had ever known disappeared into it until there was nothing left to stand on.

Father walked in. Saga at least had the sense to remain out of the room. Where was Magnus? Had he agreed to this? Of course he had. Through the fog of my mind I wondered whether this had been his plan all along; that this is what he'd wanted: to find a girl to have his child and then steal it away. The bow mistress story was a lie, a cover-up. This had always been their plan. I clutched the baby tighter to me, inhaling the biscuit smell of her head. She wouldn't be taken from me. I wouldn't let her. Father stood before me. He looked older, diminished since I'd last seen him. He nodded hello at me. He didn't look at the baby asleep in my arms; the child who was the spitting image of Jeanie and of him. He turned to Mother and whispered something to her that I couldn't hear. In my head, I heard Jeanie singing to me *Oh my darling Clementine,* a song I now sung to the baby. Her singing turned into the screams that haunted my sleep, until I realised it was the baby crying, and I pulled her into my breast and rocked her gently back to sleep. Mrs Hansen came back in with cups of tea on a tray which she placed on the coffee table in the centre of the room, then she left.

'Don't do this, Wallace,' Mother said.

The thud as Father's fist hit the doorframe made us all jump and the baby stirred, stiffened and started to cry again. I laid her head on my shoulder and jigged up and down on the spot to calm her.

'This is not your decision,' Father roared.

I had never heard him shout like that before, and seemingly nor had Mother as she looked as shocked as I felt. He indicated that we should both sit. Mother turned her back and carried on looking out of the window in an act of defiance I admired, but I sat. It felt as though the blood had drained from me, leaving in its wake rivers of ice that reached into every part of me, turning me blue and cold.

Father didn't sit, but stood towering over us.

'This is what's going to happen,' he said. 'The Olafsons will take the child back to Norway and raise it. He's not the simple man you think he is, Freyja. He's famous, in Norway and the rest of the world. People have heard of him, they play his music. He can give the child a good life. Saga hasn't been able to have a child of her own. This way you can go to art college as you've planned. No one need know. This arrangement is good for everyone.'

My tiredness lifted then, rose out of me and disappeared. I stood up and faced him clutching the baby tighter.

'Not for me. It's not good for me.'

'I'll not listen to any more from you. This is how it'll be. It's better for you. You'll be able to move on with your life. And the baby won't have to live with the shame. Like your Mother has.'

At this Mother moaned and bowed her head, but still she didn't intervene.

I thought about Joe, about what he'd offered me. When I'd refused him I hadn't been desperate. I was now.

'Joe'll marry me. He said he'll raise the baby as his own.'

That stopped him. Thank goodness. I'd said enough, but he roared back at me.

'You'll not take that boy down with you too. Is there nothing you'll not stoop to, to get what you want?'

I shrank away from his anger.

'If only... If only...' he said.

The effort to hold back what he wanted to say turned his face puce. Mother stepped towards him at last and placed her hand on his arm, but he flung it off, pulling at his hair with his hands.

'If only you were like Jeanie,' he yelled eventually, as I knew he would. His face was twisted, ugly and I could hardly stand to look at him. 'Jeanie would never have had her head turned by a man like Magnus Olafson. A man after one thing and one thing only, something that you were so obviously prepared to give him. And for what? A bastard bairn that will only ever bring shame on you, on me, on all of us? And then to try and push the burden of that on dim-witted Joe, a boy who doesn't know a good thing from a bad? Jeanie would never have done such a thing.'

Outside the storm crashed into the house, flinging clods of rain against the glass in great booming thuds. Would I ever be able to live up to Jeanie? I was a mother now. I had a child. I had a man who'd once loved me. I still believed that. He'd loved me for who I was. He'd seen I was worth something. Why was it that in spite of that, Father still felt me lacking next to the shadow of the beloved eleven-year-old Jeanie? I stepped towards him, into the shadow of his fury, my whole body shaking.

'Maybe she wouldn't have, but we'll never know, will we? Because Jeanie didn't stay long enough to bring shame on us. She got out of here as soon as she could. Where's she gone? Tell me so I can go and join her. I've waited long enough, haven't I? She took her opportunity and left us, left me. And although you can't forgive me for what I've done, I'll never forgive her for leaving me alone here with you. Look at what she did to us and yet you still put her above me. You've spent the last nine years keeping her side of our bedroom perfect for her, her coat still hangs on its peg. Her mug still hangs on its hook in the kitchen, her boots which you clean and polish every week are by the front door. When are you going to realise she's not coming back? She hates you, hates us. What did you do to her to make her leave?'

I hesitated only for a fraction of a second before picking up one of the cups from the tray and throwing it into the fireplace where it smashed into tiny pieces sending tea everywhere. The sound of china breaking echoed up the chimney until it petered out. Father took a step back from me, his knees buckling, scraping his heels against the tiles. His eyes widened and his mouth turned downwards. I've hurt him now. Good. It's what he needed to hear. What have you got to say to that, Father? I raised my chin upwards to meet his eyes. They shone, watery, desolate. I didn't understand. Fight back. Defend yourself. But Father fell to the floor and scrabbled around trying to put the pieces of the cup back together.

'Wallace,' Mother said, as she stepped towards him.

She placed her hand very carefully on top of his head and left it there until he stopped trying to press the fragments of the cup back into their original shape. Once he was still, she bent down and very carefully she threaded her arms underneath his and guided him to the sofa. She took one of the blankets off the armchair and wrapped it around his shoulders. He was shaking and his unseeing eyes glistened with tears.

'Father?' I said.

I didn't understand the look in Mother's eyes; the weariness weighing her down. Mother stroked Father's hair out of his eyes and showed him a tenderness I hadn't ever seen her show him or me. She turned away from him and stepped towards me, placed her hands on my shoulders and together we sat. I'm not sure I'd ever looked into Mother's eyes like I did then. I saw how green they were, how they caught the flickering light and how like my own they were. And in them I saw an unbearable sorrow and I was scared. The tightness in my throat burned each breath as I forced the air into my lungs and a distant ringing in my ears grew louder and louder. I wanted to clasp my hands over my ears and not hear what she had to say to me, but instead I pulled the baby tighter into my chest.

'Freyja, I thought you knew, peedie one. How could you not know? How could you think Jeanie had left us? After all these years?' She shook her head, her hands over her face rubbing her eyes.

'I don't understand,' I said. My left leg started to vibrate uncontrollably, sending a tap, tap, tapping on to the hard floor.

I remembered it all so clearly. The day Jeanie left us. The day she walked out of the door and never came back. She took off as though she were going to Skellinwall to buy something for us. Meat, I think. Sausages maybe? She walked out of the door, and the sun was shining. Summer. It was a beautiful day, one of those rare Orkney moments when the sun lights up the land and this is the most beautiful place on Earth. She paused by the gate, turned and looked up at me waving to her from our bedroom window, her long hair brushed and shining. She had the wicker basket with the rosebud lining over her arm and she was wearing the red gingham dress I'd always loved and wanted her to grow out of, so I could have it for myself. She smiled the biggest Jeanie smile I'd ever seen, and that was it, she was gone. She walked down the track, along the Brae and out of our lives and never came back. She'd swum away with the selkies. They still had her, didn't they?

And I'd never forgiven her for leaving me, for making me the child who wasn't her, the disappointment, the one who could never have *high hopes* attached to her. Jeanie had lied to me. She'd sat on the end of my bed, the atlas open between us, telling me about all the places we'd go to together, and she'd lied. She'd promised me freedom and adventure and instead she'd left me trapped and imprisoned with no way out.

Mother ran her finger along the cheek of my baby and then along my own, wiping away the tears that fell silently. My collage came into my mind and I saw what was missing. It had almost been right – gulls and cormorants making white flashes on the blue sky, the waves reaching upwards to their very brink, so that for one perfect moment the curve was like a sheet of glass that gave a clear view of the seabed beneath, before they crashed on to the white sand sending droplets of spray into the air. The seals lounging by the lighthouse, lines drawn in the sand and Jeanie singing *Oh my darling Clementine*.

'Freyja, love. Jeanie's dead. Jeanie died. You must know that. How could you not know? She's never coming back.'

DARKNESS

Lochinsay, Orkney Islands
April 1965

At that moment Magnus arrived. I sat aware of the kerfuffle going on around me – voices, talking, shouting, blame being dished out to Mother, Father, Magnus. Mrs Hanson trying to keep the peace, holding Father and Magnus apart – but these sounds were happening somewhere else, behind a window, under the sea, apart from me. The real maelstrom was inside me.

Jeanie's dead. She's not coming back. The words repeated over and over, twisting in my mind, stripping away every part of me I thought I understood. I stood silently, held the baby close to me and slipped out of the room. And then I ran.

I stumbled outside, poorly dressed for the weather and with no idea, no plan. I headed for the cliffs, running, running, not looking back, until I settled into a breathing pattern and found my stride as I'd learned at school during all those cross-country races. I don't know how I found the energy, but having the baby there next to me pushed me on. They wouldn't take my baby. My baby was all I had. As I ran, I thought about Jeanie and how I'd managed to miss it – the grief that had penetrated everything around me, how I'd mistaken it for hope. I thought about Mother and Father and how they'd stared into the black heart of the abyss, with its never-ending emptiness; they'd seen its darkness, its terror and its horror and I hadn't. I'd circumvented it and seen the light around the darkness. But now I too had stared into that black absence and I could never turn back.

Had I not known that Jeanie was dead? The question ran around and around in my mind. Images toppled over themselves in an attempt to become real, so fast and with so much fury I could hardly make sense of them, but I couldn't ignore them, not with them shouting *look at me, look at me.* And in each of those images I saw the hole in my collage – that great big aching space I'd worked so hard not to see. As I ran, visions of Annie at Lochinsay appeared before me: her opening the door to me the moment I arrived, before I had even knocked, so that I knew she'd been watching, waiting for me, her bright clothes dusty with the flour she'd been using to bake something for me; her handing me Ben's old camera, imploring me to see what I was so determined to turn away from; Annie holding me that night, covering me with a blanket; Father carrying me upstairs...

The images stopped. Don't go there.

I raced across the Sky Path, my hair saturated with salty dampness and I and the baby began to shiver with cold. The baby's face scrunched itself into deep wrinkles as she began to build up to a major cry. I hurried along the path as fast as I could, my feet slipping on the damp ground as I continued to head north, running towards the lighthouse.

Eventually, I spied its beam cutting a swathe of light in the dim sky and Tryggr standing proud on the moor. I was almost there. I picked up my pace, all the while speaking softly to my baby saying everything and anything that came into my head, trying to soothe her and keep myself calm at the same time. The name of our house struck me, Tryggr, from the Old Norse for true. It had been Mother's choice to name the house that. Previously it had been Tor Ness Farmhouse, but the house hadn't lived up to its new name and instead it had become a haven for lies and deceit. The path ended at the dry stone wall. I stood, staring up at the house. Part of me expected there to be some change, some difference to account for the catastrophic changes that had happened to me since I had been away, but of course there was nothing.

The baby was hungry. She turned stiff with rage that I wasn't doing something about it. Five minutes. That's all I needed. Five minutes to feed the baby, have a short rest and I'd run again. The kitchen smelled of baking bread as it always did and threading through that smell were all the other familiar smells of home: the salty scent of Father's sailing clothes drying over the range; the beeswax polish Mother used on the ancient dresser in the corner; the ever present stew and stock that simmered on the hot plate and the talcum powder scent Mother always gave off when she was hot and working in the kitchen. These were the smells of home and it was suddenly too overwhelming and I couldn't move, couldn't take one more step forwards.

I sat shivering in Mother's chair by the warm comfort of the range, adjusted my clothing and began to feed the baby who took to me greedily. The stinging release her sucking caused was too much and again the emotion overwhelmed me. I recalled the last words I remember Jeanie saying to me as though she was sitting in front of me.

'Don't cry, Freyja. Before you know it, it will be the holidays and I'll be back. It'll be like I've never been away.'

Was it after that she'd walked out, along the track never to return? I didn't know. I wasn't sure of anything. I didn't know what was true and what wasn't.

I thought it had been a week later that I had run upstairs to see if Jeanie wanted to go to Tor Ness Cove, our very favourite place to go in the world, but was it a week later or the same day? Or the night before? When was it? Had she even said that? I did know that when I had gone to find her upstairs, our bedroom was empty.

Jeanie's bed was unmade, I remembered, something that would make Mother angry if she'd seen it, but that day she had *a lot on* and wanted us out of her way and quiet and she obviously had so much to do she hadn't checked we'd finished our chores. I looked out of the small window that had the best view over the garden, the moorland beyond which terminated in Tor Ness Cliffs and the deep blue Atlantic beyond that. She wasn't there.

The room was cold, as though Mother had opened the window as she always did to let the fresh air in; she always hated stuffiness, even the slightest hint of it. But this was a different type of cold, not fresh and welcoming, but the kind that felt as though it was biting me, tearing at my skin trying to worm its way deep inside, into my bones where it would take root, hide and never be dispelled again. I ran back downstairs to see Jeanie coming out of the bathroom. At that time, we were one of the only families on the island that had an indoor bathroom. She didn't look herself and a tangy scent crept out of the room after her.

'Come to Tor Ness Cove with me,' I said jumping up and down and pulling on her sleeve.

'Not today, Freyja. I want to write a list of everything I need to pack so I don't forget anything.'

Did I notice anything unusual about her? Yes. She had an unusual colour; she'd vomited, but not said anything about it even though I could smell it. I didn't tell Mother, and instead I accepted her excuse and ran off to Tor Ness Cove by myself and thought no more about her.

When I got there, Joe was fishing.

'What are you doing?' Joe said, as he watched me running up and down the black stone steps which one of our ancestors years before had carved into the cliff face.

'Wearing myself out.'

I did that a lot as it was something I was told to do as a way of curbing my excessive energy. I sat next to Joe and watched his line and float bobbing in the gentle swell. I looked in the bucket he had wedged in between two rocks next to him; it was empty.

'No luck?'

'Not yet.'

Joe and I sat quietly for a while until I grew bored. I went to inspect the rock pools that formed in the dark crevices between the rocks, pushing aside the seaweed and revealing the whelks stuck to the edges. These I pulled off and put into Joe's bucket. This was an activity that Joe and I excelled at. During the holidays and at the weekends at low tide, Joe and I, and Jeanie too, would comb the rocks for whelks which we'd put into jute sacks and sell. We had to have at least a bushel, which was half a sack, and we nearly always managed that in one go, or if we didn't we'd put a few stones on top of the sack and leave it in a secret safe place in the rocks until the next day when we'd top it up. We'd sell these to a company in Kirkwall. We were good at making money. I stayed on the beach all that day with Joe until he'd caught a good load of fish and I had enough whelks.

That evening back at home, despite having worn myself out, I was still desperate to do something with Jeanie and couldn't understand why she lay on her bed staring at the ceiling. She must have been there all day. Mother wasn't back from doing whatever it was she had to do, and Father was with Bill

MacKenzie talking about commissioning a third trawler. I jumped up and down next to Jeanie something that usually annoyed her as she hated her bed clothes being creased and crumpled, but that evening she put up with it, making only the slightest of objections.

'Do you think you could put the chickens away for me tonight, Freyja?' she said. Her voice was small, far away and not like her usual voice at all. I wondered if part of her had already gone to Kirkwall, like fairies and things could do, leaving her body here on the bed, or if this was one of the things that happened to you when you grew up. Like getting bosoms, which I expected would one day appear overnight, fully formed. I kept checking Jeanie's chest for the miracle to happen, but as yet I had been disappointed.

'If you give me one of your mint humbugs,' I said.

Jeanie pointed to the paper bag on her shelf and nodded. I reached up and took one, popped it into my mouth and went out to deal with the chickens. We had quite a few chickens which we kept for their eggs and sometimes for the pot.

I took the basket and looked in all the usual places for eggs. I don't remember how many I found, but it would have been quite a few, and then I shooed the hens back into their house for the night and locked them in. Apart from at night when we locked them up, they roamed free. We clipped their wings periodically to stop them flying away and they spent their days pecking around the garden. I think we had about thirty hens at that time and a couple of roosters who'd crow in the morning and for much of the rest of the day too. Back in the house, Mother was in the kitchen.

'Where's Jeanette?' Mother said.

I hadn't heard her return from Skellinwall. She had a brown knitted bag with her which meant she'd been to the butchers.

'Lying on her bed. She gave me a mint humbug,' I said.

'Did she now.'

'For doing the hens.'

I didn't tell Mother about the glassy look Jeanie had in her eyes or the red sheen that slicked her usually pale face.

'Well, you tell her to wash and come and help me with the

dinner,' she said.

Did I tell Jeanie straight away or did I go outside first and watched the gulls circle over the cliffs, screeching out their calls as the gloaming came upon us? By the time I did eventually make it up to our room, Jeanie's eyes were rolling in her head and she had a bluish tinge around her lips staining her whole mouth a purplish colour, like she'd been eating berries.

I sat next to her for a while, watching the way her mouth grabbed at the air, trying to suck it in. She had a horrible sickly smell about her too that I didn't like. I wandered away from her to be rid of it and opened our bedroom window so that some fresh air could come in and clear it away. I stood by the window for a while, hanging my head out and taking great big gulps of the misty evening air. When Jeanie started to make a moaning sound, I turned back and I realised her face had doubled in size so that it looked like a moon.

'Help me, Freyja,' she said. 'I can't move my legs. Call Mother.'

I ran downstairs and shouted for Mother to help.

Mother was angry when she came up and saw Jeanie looking like that. She raged and raged at me. Blamed me for it all. If I'd done this or that or something else everything would have been different. That's what she said. Why hadn't I come to Skellinwall to find her? I didn't know the answers to her questions, so I kept quiet. I cowered in the corner of the bedroom, crouching down and pressing myself as far as I could go into the triangular space where the two walls met, hands over my ears to blot out the screaming. Hers, mine, Jeanie's. The doctor arrived running up the stairs two at a time, shouting at me too: run a cold bath, open all the windows, make everything as cold as possible, call for Bill, for others, help him carry Jeanie who was limp and lifeless her head lolling to the side, place her in the freezing cold bath. Quick, quick, hurry. The plan was to transfer her to the Mainland. Bill MacKenzie and some others arrived to help. The shipping forecast blared out into the night. The weather had taken a turn for the worse and no boat could manage the crossing, not in a squall like that, not with a child on the edge of darkness and light.

She died later that night. She'd cut her foot, most likely on the beach or in the sea the doctor said. She'd probably cut it a few days before when we'd gone to St Ninian's Cove to play on the bright white sand. The cut had turned bad and poisoned her blood. That's what she'd died of - septicaemia.

I didn't realise immediately what Jeanie's death would mean for me. I thought I'd lost my best friend and my room had a stark emptiness that never left it, and so I suppose I blocked it out, pretended it had never happened. I'd seen her leave and wave goodbye to me as I watched her from my bedroom window. I'd seen her walk down the track in her red gingham dress, her hair bouncing behind her, swishing to the side as she turned her head to give me one last wave, her huge smile stretching her face, her beautiful face, not the swollen septic one she went to her grave with. But I hadn't seen any of that. Regardless, I wave back and blow her a kiss as she carries on walking, until the image of her begins to distort, then evaporate and finally she is no longer there.

The baby finished feeding and her head lolled to one side. I refastened my clothes and hugged her to me, her head resting on my shoulder. I ran upstairs and took a sheet from the linen cupboard. I placed the baby on my bed and folded the sheet into a triangle, then wrapped the baby and me together in a sling. That way I could run more safely. I raced back down the stairs and into the kitchen. On the side of the kitchen sink Father's pocket knife lay drying. I took it. I might need it. I stuck it in my pocket and ran out into the night. I felt lightheaded after feeding the baby and I realised I hadn't eaten for some time, but regardless I pushed myself onwards, running towards the lighthouse.

The first time I fainted was at Jeanie's funeral. The cold stone floor came up towards me like I was magnetic, sucking the world into me in a reversed explosion. Mother had forced me to wear an awful black lace dress with a starchy collar that scratched against my childish skin. It had tight smocking around the chest that rendered it far too small for me and I struggled to breathe. As she tugged it over my head, all I could think was Jeanie would hate this dress, she'd never have wanted me to wear it. Jeanie and I hated girly clothes. We wanted to be comfortable and practical, not trussed up and ridiculous, and mostly we wore whatever we liked. My clothes were hardly ever new and they were patched and repaired, but that was how I liked them. The history of their previous owners was stitched into the fabric so that their stories became intertwined with my own.

The three of us: Mother, Father and me, walked to the Kirk behind the coffin. Annie met us at the end of the track. She wore a diaphanous purple dress that caused quite a stir. As we passed each of the houses on the way to the graveyard people joined us. Our silent procession grew steadily and by the time we were inside the building there wasn't an empty pew. Mother hadn't said much to me since Jeanie died, had hardly even looked at me. She made my food, tidied up the things I left around and gave the appearance of acting as she normally would, but the silence that penetrated everything and everyone around her was as impossible to breach as the ocean to Canada. She didn't cry. Instead she inhaled in staccato: three rapid intakes and then a pause, three rapid intakes and then a pause. She didn't stop doing that day or night. Her tears had simply run out, but the crying continued nevertheless. I hated the sound of it and the way it consumed her making her as invisible to me as I was to her. Father was silent and lost too, but in a different way. He made himself absent by taking the boat out and that was easier to deal with as I could pretend that nothing had changed, that he was simply out fishing more than usual, but would be back and would carry on where we'd left off. Except that didn't happen; he too wrapped himself in a mantle of silence as black and deep as the sea he turned to, one that no amount of light could penetrate.

No one asked me how I felt about Jeanie suddenly leaving me, except Annie who tried hard to make me speak about what had happened, even though I couldn't. I didn't understand why she spoke about Jeanie all the time. I was jealous of the attention she lavished on Jeanie, angry that so much of our precious time was wasted discussing her when Annie was my friend. I carried on in the same way as I always had. I fed the chickens, cleaned them out, collected the eggs and took them in my basket to everyone who wanted them. In my spare time I read and looked at my encyclopaedias and I waited for Jeanie to come back as she'd said she would. In doing so I achieved a level of something approaching happiness, or if not as strong as that, an easiness with my life that contrasted sharply with the weight of distress and anguish that everyone else carried heavily on their shoulders.

The church bench was hard and uncomfortable and the air thick with the sweet smell of incense wafting in great clouds of smoke. I started to swing my legs forwards and backwards, but I'd grown and it wasn't possible to swing them, not even if I sat with my back rigid against the back of the pew. Instead my feet crashed into the stone floor, scuffing my shoes. I remembered another time I'd been in the Kirk: Easter Sunday. I had swung my legs without any difficulty. Jeanie and I had sat next to each other, desperate to escape. I had been shocked but delighted to find that Jeanie had brought with her a chocolate rabbit she'd been given. It wasn't a large one, but we managed to split it between the two of us, nibbling at the edges a little at a time trying to make it last as long as possible. Jeanie placed her finger over her lips, *hush, don't tell*. I didn't of course. The chocolate melted on to my fingers and I licked it off, trying as hard as I could not to make a sucking sound.

As I sat on the unyielding pew, I tried as hard as I could not to look at the white coffin sitting in the centre of the aisle, but the more I tried to look elsewhere, the more it loomed in my vision and with the smell of the flowers sitting on top of the coffin mingling with the scent of the incense, I could both see and smell the rotting Jeanie huddled inside. The scratchy collar and smocking tightened around my throat and chest and the air in the Kirk thinned until there was none left for me. The priest's voice mumbled on and over me. He started to walk up and down the aisle swinging the brass canister with the burning incense inside. I would die if I didn't get any air. I pulled on Mother's sleeve, but she ignored me. The tears had once again started to stream over her cheeks and they fell and splashed on to my hand. A deep heat started in my feet, rushed up my legs and into my head so that I couldn't see for the fire that burned inside me.

When I opened my eyes, I thought, it's the dry stone wall at the end of our garden that had smacked into my face, but it was the Kirk's stone floor.

Outside in the wild windy air, Mother turned on me. She said I'd embarrassed myself, and her and ruined the service. How could I, she said. How could I ruin my own sister's funeral? Such shame I'd brought on the family. She stormed off down the road, but she stopped and headed back, coming to a halt right in front of where I was standing with all our friends and neighbours gathered behind me. Annie walked up to her, and tried to guide her away, calling to Father to help her, but Mother wasn't going to be stopped, her rage was too fresh and raw.

'You choose that moment to show some emotion. You choose that moment to make it all about you.'

She bent down to my height as she spoke, her black dress and overcoat rustling as she moved, her finger an inch from my nose as she waggled it up and down, her spit like mizzle on my cheeks. She made a decision, I saw it as it flickered across her face, a moment's pause before she decided to say what she said next, a moment's pause when she could have made another decision, a better decision, but she didn't. She chose to say it, she chose it to be hurtful, to hurt me, to make me suffer like she was suffering. She didn't have to.

'Our Jeanie would never have done that. Our Jeanie was the kindest most lovely girl in the world. But she's dead. And you're alive and by God I wish it were the other way around.'

In the distance, I could hear voices. They were coming for me. I couldn't let them stop me. I couldn't be with any of them. Nothing was as I thought it was. The past far from being something solid and reliable, stationary, had become a moveable uncertainty, something that was even now reaching its deadly fingers forwards towards me, grabbing hold of me and trying to drag me back into it, trying to drown me in its mystery. They'd all lied to me in different ways - Mother and

Father by their silence, Annie even by trying to make me come to my own conclusions when it would have been better to have just said it. But most of all Magnus had lied. The others had lied for my benefit in their own ways, but Magnus had lied for himself. All the promises he'd made me flashed through my mind. He'd told me I was the other half of his soul, that I completed him, that after all the years of searching he'd finally found me. That I was all he ever needed and that when he met me, the ground on which he'd always relied had shattered into a thousand pieces so he no longer knew how to go on if I wasn't there. Lies. It was all lies. All the time he'd had Saga in the background, waiting for him to bring her the baby she desired. She was the rock on which he'd stood. She was the one he relied on, the one he'd never leave. Me? I was nothing but the foam on top of the sea. I would eventually disappear and be forgotten like all the others; remembered only in a collection of notes on lined paper.

I kept on running. Up ahead, I could see the rotating beam from the lighthouse. I kept it in my vision once again. It was where I had to go. Suddenly I saw with a great clarity that that was where I had been heading ever since Jeanie left, since Jeanie *died*: towards the lighthouse. Everything I needed to understand I would find the answers to there. Over the pounding of my heart, I heard the distant cries of Father calling my name. No time to stop, keep moving. I thought my feet would take me to the cliffs at the top of Tor Ness Cove, but I was wrong. At the seamark, I found myself turning left and heading off on the narrower path that led to the adjoining cove, St Ninian's Cove, where I never went. The fear of taking that path nearly stopped me and I had to pause to retch and vomit. I looked behind me and I could see torches bobbing in the coming darkness. I didn't have long. The terror was almost too strong, but I knew I had to finally face what it was I'd been avoiding for so long. Although my legs felt heavy and lifeless and my head light and detached from the rest of me, I forced myself to put one leg in front of the other, to keep moving forwards. I stumbled many times and I almost fell to the ground, almost gave up and allowed them to catch me, but holding the baby close to me in the sling kept me focused, kept me going.

Up ahead in the mist I saw Jeanie.

'Wait for me, Jeanie,' I whispered. 'I'm coming, I'm on my way.'

She stood on the edge of the cliff, the mist swirling around her ankles as if she were floating. She was still wearing her red gingham dress. How cold she must be. Her finger beckoned me on, towards her, towards St Ninian's Cove. She smiled her beautiful wide smile. I'm almost there, Jeanie. Wait for me.

Finally, I stood on the westernmost point of Tor Ness Head. Below me, St Ninian's Cove stood bleak and sorrowful illuminated by the white light of the full moon. The moon shadows from the cliffs stretched out towards the sea, creating fingers of darkness. No one ever went there. The path down to the cove was difficult and out to sea the rocks made fishing impossible. Only seals and birds went there. Not since we were children had anyone set foot on that virgin white sand. We would go there when we wanted to be completely alone and play shipwrecks as it was a more authentic location, but even we were too lazy most of the time and preferred the ease and splendour of Tor Ness Cove. I looked around the cliff top for Jeanie, but she had merged into the mist and I could no longer see her.

'Jeanie,' I screamed over and over, throwing my voice out over the raging ocean. I couldn't lose her now. Not when I had waited so long for her to return to me.

'Here I am,' she said.

I spun around looking for her.

'Down here, Freyja. Don't you remember?' Her voice had an edge to it, a sharpness that I didn't like.

I walked to the edge of the cliff and peered down, holding the baby close to me so the hammock I'd made didn't swing out over the edge. There she was, down below me on the sand and I was amazed at how clearly I could hear her even though she was so far away, standing on the edge of the water where the moon shadows from the towering cliff stacks couldn't reach her. She turned to look up at me and her face was no longer the beautiful Jeanie's I remembered. Instead, it was rotten, putrid and all around me the air vibrated with the sickly, sweet smell I remembered from that day.

She didn't want to play hopscotch; she didn't want to go to St Ninian's Cove even. She tried to persuade me to go to Tor Ness Cove instead, but I wanted us to stay out as long as possible, to delay the inevitable, and so I insisted on making the extra effort to go to St Ninian's. I behaved like a spoiled child. I felt bad about it, knowing that if Mrs McLeod had heard all the things I said she'd be disappointed in me. She often told me off for trying to make others, particularly Jeanie and Joe, do whatever it was I wanted and not take their feelings into consideration; she said I had to learn to be more civilised and people other than her would like me as much as she did, but I wanted the day to be special, knowing that it was likely to be the last time the two of us would go to the beach before Jeanie left, and as a consequence everything that Mrs McLeod had told me lay forgotten in the depths of my mind.

I won as I knew I would; I persuaded her and we had a lovely day. We took a picnic and a ball and we played games and lay in the rare sun, swam with the seals and dived underneath the wild ocean to see what we could find on the sea bed. Once we'd dried off, Jeanie wanted to go back home and once again rearrange all her belongings, to make sure she had everything she needed ready. I couldn't understand it, couldn't understand why she was so keen to go to boarding school, to leave our life behind, to leave me behind.

'When it's your turn, you'll want to go too, Freyja. You will,' she emphasised when she saw me shaking my head. I could never imagine leaving our island, being away from everything and everyone I loved.

'One more game, then we'll go back,' I promised her.

'All right. One more game. You draw it up while I sit here,' she said.

I knew I'd regret it, making Jeanie play hopscotch on the perfect white sand by the jagged black rocks, but it didn't stop me. All I could think about was preventing her leaving me; that I had to find a way to do that, to get her to change her mind and not go to boarding school. If I could delay her departure a little while longer, she'd see that it would be more fun here with me, finding things washed up on the beach that we could sell and catching crabs and lobsters to cook on an open fire. If she stayed a little longer, I would see to it that we'd have so much fun she'd decide I'd been right after all and she'd stay for now; later when I was old enough we could go together and we wouldn't have to be apart.

The brown ale bottle had washed in on the tide that morning. I'd put it to one side hoping that I could take it to the shop in Skellinwall and get the deposit back on the glass. We did that a lot and made enough money to keep us in sweets. Jeanie was distracted, watching the barking seals, and singing *Oh my darling Clementine* to them as she always did, claiming that they liked it and were joining in with her. I picked up the bottle and smashed its neck against one of the rocks. The jagged shards that fell on to the sand glistened in the sun like pieces of amber. I took a stick, a long piece of driftwood that had also washed up and drew the hopscotch on the sand. I made the marks deep so they wouldn't disappear too easily as we jumped around the numbers. I took the broken bottle and I buried it in the sand with its jagged edges pointing up, but hidden. I planted it in the centre of number four. Jeanie always landed in the middle of the squares, she had a real knack for it that made her hard to beat.

Once I had finished, I called to Jeanie to come and play. We started the game and I played as badly as I could so that I didn't race ahead of her. Jeanie was a lovely girl who always put others first, but she had a competitive streak too and I knew she wouldn't hesitate to try and beat me, particularly as she was eager for the game to be over quickly so she could go home. When she threw the pebble on to number four she made the leap. She landed right on top of the bottle, as I'd planned and the glass went straight through her foot.

Jeanie and I stood staring at the shard piercing through her skin for a number of seconds in total silence. It was the shock. At first, she didn't seem to feel anything and I wondered if I'd done enough, if I'd hurt her enough to stop her leaving. Then the screams started. Hers and mine. That's all I can remember.

I didn't think it would kill her.

When I looked again Jeanie had gone. Had she gone for good? If that was true, I knew that I had made it so. The wild empty ocean glittered with the reflected light of the full moon on the rippling surface. The darkness of the sea spread out beneath me and its utter desolation reflected the darkness and loneliness inside me as the lighthouse beam circled round and around. I fell to my knees, unable to sustain the weight of myself and the baby in my arms. How could I continue to live when I had caused such horror in the world? When I had killed the person I loved the most? The wail that left me came from the very depths of the sea, from hell itself and it shocked me with its venom and intensity. My stomach contracted violently and I vomited on to the ground.

The baby started to cry as I leaned over her to empty my stomach. I looked down at the child's face and saw Jeanie's face staring back at me. I had to know for sure that she'd gone. If I'd seen her, maybe she wasn't dead? I could find her. I pulled myself upright and over by the edge of the moor I could see the bobbing lights coming towards me closer and closer. I scrambled, half upright, half on my hands and knees, the baby swinging beneath me, to the steps leading down on to St Ninian's Cove. I had to go down there, but every part of my body screamed at me not to go. The first step was the hardest and I cried out as my foot twisted, my toe caught in some tendril that tried to hold me back. Beneath me, the twisting path snaked its way down the cliff face. I slipped down the first step, but managed to right myself and stop myself falling. The baby started to whimper. Hush little one, hush now. The steps were damp from the sea spray and so overgrown with plants that the surface of the flagstones was slippery. My feet slid on one step after another. I fell, thudding down on to the rocks, scraping my calf. I could hear voices in the distance, shouting. I heaved myself upright. The baby's cries became louder.

'Hush now,' I said, sharper as my irritation with the sound grew.

How like your father you can be. So demanding on me,

wanting my attention on you always and on nothing else. I shifted the weight of her on to my shoulder and in the process the sheet I had wrapped her in started to unravel and fall so that it dragged on the wet ground. I left it like that as I slid down the remaining few steps until I was once again standing on the pure white sand of St Ninian's Cove. The sudden rush of cold air made the baby cry even more. Her cries cut into the night so I feared that the old gods would rise up from the sea and subdue her. I placed the sheet on the sand and lay the baby on top where I left her crying. I paced up and down the shoreline, the tide sucking sporadically at my feet as the waves came in and out. I pressed my hands against my ears to keep the sound away, but it was no good, her screams were so loud that they pierced the skin of my hands and wormed their way inside me. I could no longer stand it and I ran to the other side of the cove leaving the baby to cry.

The few clouds, lit from the light of the moon, raced with unnecessary violence across the sky as though the moon and the stars were being tossed and sunk on a wild sea. I looked back out towards the horizon where the occasional light from a fishing boat flashed. I ran up and down the shoreline, the water splashing around me screaming to the emptiness,

'Jeanie, where are you?'

I stepped further and further into the water until the waves were lapping against my stomach. The cold sucked the breath out of me.

On the top of the cliffs, I heard shouts. I looked up and could see the lights of the torches. They wouldn't have my baby. I would not let them have my baby. I forced myself out of the grip of the waves and back on to the sand. I remembered how much Jeanie had hurt me, telling me how excited she was to be leaving, how much fun it was going to be staying in the school dormitory. She'd had no thought as to how I would feel, left behind alone, and I had shown her what I could do if I had to. Yes, I'd shown her. I could do it again. I looked up and saw that they were using torches to scan the beach, to see if they could find me. I raced to the top of the beach, into the deep darkness where I knew they would never see me. If I was quick, I would have enough time. My sodden clothes impeded my progress, but I no longer felt the cold. I headed back to where my baby lay whimpering on the cold sand. Already she was worn out, tired by the cold and the crying. I looked up at the ocean. Jeanie floated above the waves. *Yes*, she said. *Come to me.*

He couldn't take my baby. He wouldn't love her as I loved her. I had loved him like no other woman in the world has loved before. And yet it hadn't been enough. He'd discarded me, thrown me away like I was nothing, like I was rubbish. I would break his heart as he had broken mine. The baby stopped crying.

'My baby, we'll go together,' I whispered into her ear. 'We'll go to Jeanie together.'

I picked her up and held her close to my cheek, inhaling her intoxicating baby smell one last time, then I placed her back on the cold sand. I picked up the sheet and bundled it into a pillow. On the cliffs, the bobbing torches were making their way down the steps. I could hear a number of voices all shouting my name, screaming it into the wind. I didn't have much time. God forgive me.

I placed the bundle over the baby's face. She was already exhausted and she didn't struggle as much as I feared. The tears fell down my face with such violence I couldn't see what it was I was doing, but I could feel. Her tiny legs kicked against me until finally they lay limp and lifeless on the cold sand.

I took Father's knife that I had in my pocket and plunged it into my wrists, hacking at my skin so white and so luminous under the light of the moon until the darkness fell in rivers on to the white sand.

Lightheaded and shivering, I staggered to the shoreline and felt the sweet, cold water grab hold of me. The tide had turned and the air was charged with the rush of it towards the land. It was seductive and quiet. I could no longer hear the shouts of those who ran towards me and on the skin of the sea the moonlight reflected its bright white light towards me along with the pulsing beam of the lighthouse.

Shouts pierced the silence. There were many voices, voices that I couldn't distinguish, screaming my name. The wind carried the desperate cries towards me as I turned and saw

Magnus bent over the body of our baby daughter.

I stepped further into the water, trailing my fingertips along the surface, feeling the tension and the sea's resistance to accepting me. There was not a man or a woman alive who couldn't feel anything but hatred towards me. I would slip underneath the waves and beg them to fill me up and take me into the silence. As I stepped over the underwater ledge, over the lip of the ocean floor, I believed for a moment that I would do it, I would manage to escape this island and everything that had happened, the devastation I had left behind.

In the dancing jewels of light, I saw Jeanie again. She had come for me at last with her beautiful face restored.

Jeanie, what did I do to you?

I watched Jeanie dancing in the waves, her long hair softening with the water that grabbed at her, pulling her under, and the mist that she had always had around her since the day she disappeared.The lighthouse's beam rinsed the sea's surface and Jeanie's image came and went as she moved closer towards me, cutting through the night.

'Take me with you, Jeanie,' I shouted.

The water held my neck in a vice and forced me to see the pain and destruction I had wrought on Jeanie. She held her hand out to me. I stepped forwards towards the bottomless abyss and expected my body to accept its fate and allow itself to pay for the life of my lovely girl with my own. A life for a life. Reasonable enough. I kept my eyes open. I wanted to see my own ending, be a witness.

My head fell through the skin and into the silence beneath. I held myself there, suspended in the water. I opened my mouth and waited for the water to rush inside me and accept me as part of its own. The sea, though, had other ideas. It wouldn't take me, it couldn't, not with the magical protection of my caul wrapped around me. I pushed back up through the sea's skin and looked back at the beach. They were all there: Father, Magnus, the police even. Mother running, running to the back of the beach towards the doctor. I fought to draw breath into my frozen lungs, pushing the air past the rock in my throat.

Magnus rushed towards me. He crashed into the waves,

grabbing me, pulling me, out of the water, on to the shoreline and up on to the beach where we collapsed on to the sand together. He held me like he'd held me before and he stroked my hair away from my face and held my head in his hands. I knew I hadn't been wrong after all: he loved me and I loved him. But Father came upon him like a mad man, fists flying, I'd never seen him in such a rage. He dragged him off me, although we clung on to each other as hard as we could. He had to pull us apart. I think the police helped him, although I'm not clear on that part because all I remember is screaming and screaming. As they dragged me away from him and the beach, Magnus yelled that he'd come back for me. But he never did.

After that, I don't remember anything except bright white lights bringing a deep impenetrable silence and then, darkness.

Ceredigion Mental Asylum, West Wales
June 1983 10pm

I'm sorry, it wasn't a very nice story in the end, was it? I suspect you feel differently about me now you know what it was I did, how much I hurt everyone around me, including you.

'Do not say that, Freyja. I am fine. There is a lot you do not know. I can tell you, if you would like.'

Yes, you can, I'd like that. I'd like to know about everything that's been kept from me, but first I want to say that there are many excuses I could make for how it ended, but in the end it comes down to me and me alone and I want you to know that. That's what my therapist here has taught me to understand. That I'm responsible for my actions, all of them, although he does say that I'm not as responsible for Jeanie's death as I think. I don't believe that though. I knew what I was doing, I knew I would hurt her badly, burying that bottle in the sand. I wanted to hurt her. I didn't know it would kill her, but wanting to hurt her badly, that still makes me culpable. That's the word they use, in the courts, in here, culpable. It means I knew what I was doing, that I had intention behind my actions. It's funny, but they think I'm culpable for what I told them I did to the baby, but not for what happened to Jeanie. In my mind it's the other way around. I knew Jeanie would suffer and I wanted her to, for leaving me, for wanting to leave me. It was a betrayal of us. That's what I thought. In my mind she'd chosen to leave me. I didn't see she had no choice. It didn't occur to me. When I found out Jeanie was leaving me, it was like I'd been torn in half and I wanted to do everything I could to put myself back together.

But the baby? I've told them I've accepted I was culpable to keep everyone happy, so they leave me alone. If I hadn't gone along with it, they'd have kept on and on and I couldn't have stood it. I wanted silence. It's easier to say *yes, I agree*, in the end, but I don't agree. I wasn't in my right mind after the birth, before that even, although all the doctors disagreed and said I knew exactly what I was doing. That the fault sat squarely on my shoulders.

I sat through that trial remember, so I know what was said.

You can't say now that it wasn't like that, it was. People didn't think the way they do now. No one thought to ask me how I felt when Saga showed up and shattered the land under my feet, when Magnus chose her over me. They didn't experience the grief I felt, didn't understand it at all, how it formed inside me like a raging scream that couldn't find a way out and how that scream terrorised every inch of me. They didn't understand that at all.

Do you know what they called me? A wanton seductress. I was eighteen, only just eighteen. He was thirty-five! How could I have been more powerful than him? They acted as though I'd possessed his mind and tormented him with my sexual power and made him helpless. They didn't understand me. I screamed at them in the court to call him, to make him come and say it wasn't like that, I wasn't the person they were making me out to be. Expert after expert stood on that stand and said what happened had happened because of me. Magnus never came. He didn't come and defend me. I told them that I loved him, is all, but my love turned into loss and then it turned into a devilish fury I couldn't control.

They didn't ask me either how I felt when Mother told me Jeanie was dead. They didn't believe I hadn't known – they didn't think it was possible to blot it out of your mind. But you can, you know. Your mind can play tricks on you. But when it came back to me, when I realised what I'd done and that Jeanie wasn't coming back for me and that Magnus didn't want me either, that he'd rather go back to Norway, even after he'd promised me everything, all I could see ahead of me was devastation, a life of emptiness and darkness trapping me in a cage. I didn't care what would happen to me. I wanted to die, I think I did, but I couldn't do it.

Once I'd managed to pull myself out of the water, the cold took hold of me and I began to shake violently. My sodden clothes clung to me dragging me into the sand. I couldn't have moved without Magnus pulling me up the beach. In the water the cuts I'd made to my wrists stopped bleeding, but once I was back in the air the pumping started again and the pain tore at me with greater vehemence. When they realised what I'd done to myself, they shone torches at me, in my face, my eyes, all over me, then everyone started grabbing at me, pulling me in different directions. I couldn't think straight. Magnus tried to hold on to me and Father and the policeman pulled at us both, ripping us apart. I kept screaming, *my baby, my baby* as I tried to release myself from their grasp and race up towards the cliffs. But I couldn't do it. I didn't have the strength. The torch light in my eyes blinded me. Everyone screamed for the doctor to come quick. I couldn't see what they'd done with my baby. I screamed, *where is she? Where is she?* For days afterwards I yelled this over and over. It was the only thing I was capable of saying. I asked everyone I met, but no one ever answered me. They looked away like I wasn't there. At Kincraig Castle and all through the trial I kept on asking. I asked and asked every day, *where is my baby? What have you done with her?* I kept on and on until I moved here. It was Ellie, the nurse you met earlier, who finally answered me. *Freyja, hush now*, she said. *You've got to let this go. Your baby's gone. She's never coming back.*

Magnus will never forgive me for what I did to our baby; how could anyone forgive that? That's why he hasn't come, I know that. Although I've always hoped he would.

Of course I wanted him to leave Saga for me, but that alone wouldn't have been enough, for him to leave Saga because he wanted a different life, because she wasn't right for him. I wanted him to want me so much he had no choice but to choose me over her. That was asking too much, I know that now. I didn't hate her when I met her. I liked her. I could see in her parts that were like me. I suppose he was looking for an ideal woman in a way, one who encapsulated everything she had, but a little better. I thought that person was me. That I could give him everything he wanted, but I was a child. How could I understand what a man like that wanted? I tried to, but I failed.

'Freyja, can I take your hand? Is that okay, if I hold it like that? I need to tell you something, but I don't want you to be alarmed.

'Magnus is here... Don't cry, don't worry. You do not have to see him if you do not want to.

'He has been looking for you since that day on the beach, but no one told him anything. He asked, but everyone shut him out. He has been looking for you for eighteen years. He did not give up on you. He blamed himself, said he should have stood up to Saga and your parents, should never have agreed that they would take the baby back to Norway with them. *If I had been braver everything would have been different*, that is what he said, but he lost his music and without it he didn't know how to be. He was a coward. He has not forgiven himself. Even now. That is why he has never finished his sixth symphony. He cannot bear to. *It will be like I have moved on from her, and I have not.* That is what he said.

'Saga married someone else a few years ago. She could not bear to be the one Magnus did not want. In the end, however, it was Saga who took control of Magnus's depression. She made him move to our house on Hardangerfjord. The one in the photograph. It was more peaceful, she said and it would rejuvenate him. She told Magnus he was wasting his life, so she arranged a festival to celebrate his work as she thought it would help him recover his music. That's when the recording was made, the one I've given you. It looked for a while like that had worked, but once he played the Fifth, he remembered how he had let you down and he withdrew in on himself once more. Once we returned to Norway, Magnus could not move or speak. I begged Saga to do something to save him. Eventually, we went to Orkney, to Falun, a few weeks ago. We found Wallace and Morag. They no longer live at Tryggr as it is too remote for them. They have moved to a small house in Skellinwall. Saga made Wallace tell us where you were. She stood in their tiny house looking huge and powerful against them and said she would not leave until they told her. She was frightening, even to me. When Magnus broke down, when he completely fell apart in front of her, that changed something in the way she thought about what had happened to all of us. I think she finally realised what it must have been like for you.

'She said to Wallace, *Imagine what it must have done to her for her own parents to take her child away.*

'She said it had been Wallace's plan from the moment he found out about your pregnancy. He could not live with the shame of it.

'He said *People will say she's got bad blood from her grandmother.*

'Morag though, she always thought it was wrong. She fought Wallace and they argued over it so much it nearly destroyed them. She knew what it felt like to be taken away from your mother, but once Magnus told her he was married, she knew she did not have much of a hope. That is the only reason she let him go back to Norway. He said he would sort it out, but he could not, not once Saga found out. She was desperate. She wanted a baby.

'There is one question more I wanted to ask you... before Magnus joins us. If you do not mind... You do not have to answer, maybe you cannot. Magnus told me he thought you were trying to drown yourself, that is why he jumped in to pull you out, and that is what you have said too, but he realised that he had not needed to save you, that you were already fighting to get out of the sea. Why, Freyja?'

Don't you know?

When I came back up to the surface and Magnus shouted at me from the beach. I saw Mother on the sand. She was on her knees, bending over the baby. I saw her stand up and start running, back towards the steep steps to where the doctor was, running and screaming, the bundle clutched tightly in her arms. And I heard it. Crying.

For all these years, I thought I'd been mistaken, that I hadn't heard that crying after all. But I was right. I don't know how Mother did it, but she brought you back to life. And now you're here. That's why I couldn't die. I wanted to carry on breathing for you.

Acknowledgements

Many people have helped me write this book and to all of you I am very grateful. The Northern Lighthouse Board for their help with optic on and off times. To all the tutors I've had along the way: Louise Doughty, Patrick Gale, Romesh Gunesekera, Hugh Martin, Ross Raisin, Barrie Sherwood, Richard Skinner and Francis Spufford. Each of you provided enormous encouragement and helped me understand my errors and mistakes. For those that remain, I'm sorry. All my class at The Faber Academy, particularly: Tamsin Barrett, David Burnand, Adrienne Chinn, Stacey Duguid, Carolyn Gillis, James Graham, Maria Iglesias, Colette McBeth, Lori Miller, Emma Parsons and Melissa Reiner. I hope I've started in the right place. My fellow MA students at Goldsmiths: Eliza Creese, Sam Dixon, Olivia Dunnett, Laura Hammond, Ben Patten, Declan Pleydell-Pearse, Phil Robinson, Kate Venables and Daphne Walker, thanks for your editing advice. To my wonderful writing students at ACRES, in particular Carol Clark, Cathy Lovell, Diana Martineau, Angela Moore, Flic Paterson, Marina Pirotta, Fiona Thornely and Virginia Sheldrake who have taught me more than I ever taught them. You made me live up to my own expectations. To Clare Preece for reading drafts of other books that led to this one. To Sarah Camburn who has been asked to read more than is fair, particularly in the early days. My three children Charlie, Alexandra and Alice who have had to put up with their mother writing her book for their entire lives. This one is finally in print. Most thanks of all to Joseph Wolfe. I couldn't have done it without you.

ABOUT THE AUTHOR

Julie Didcock-Williams lives in rural East Sussex where the landscape inspires her work.

juliedidcockwilliams@gmail.com

Printed in Great Britain
by Amazon